AL
DARCY COATES

The Haunting of Ashburn House

The Haunting of Blackwood House

The House Next Door

Craven Manor

The Haunting of Rookward House

The Carrow Haunt

Hunted

The Folcroft Ghosts

The Haunting of Gillespie House

Dead Lake

Parasite

Quarter to Midnight

Small Horrors

The Haunting of Leigh Harker

From Below

Gallows Hill

Dead of Winter

House of Shadows

House of Shadows

House of Secrets

Black Winter

Voices in the Snow

Secrets in the Dark

Whispers in the Mist

Silence in the Shadows

Gravekeeper

The Whispering Dead

The Ravenous Dead

The Twisted Dead

THE HOLLOW DEAD

DARCY COATES

Cover design by Stephanie Rocha/Sourcebooks
Series design by Faceout Studio, Molly von Borstel
Cover images © Pete Willis/Unsplash, shutterstock.com, Vecteezy.com

Published by Poisoned Pen Press, an imprint of Sourcebooks
P.O. Box 4410, Naperville, Illinois 60567-4410
(630) 961-3900
sourcebooks.com

Library of Congress Cataloging-in-Publication Data
Names: Coates, Darcy, author.
Title: The hollow dead / Darcy Coates.
Description: Naperville, Illinois : Poisoned Pen Press, 2024. | Series: Gravekeeper ; 4
Identifiers: LCCN 2023028437 | (trade paperback)
Subjects: LCGFT: Ghost stories. | Paranormal fiction. | Horror fiction. | Novels.
Classification: LCC PR9619.4.C628 H65 2024 | DDC 823/.92--dc23/eng/2024
LC record available at https://lccn.loc.gov/2023028437

Printed and bound in the United States of America.
VP 10 9 8 7 6 5 4 3 2 1

CHAPTER 1

"IT'S TIME FOR WAR," Zoe said.

Keira sat in the corner of Blighty's cozy café, sinking into a plush high-back chair as she hugged a mug of hot chocolate. She didn't feel very warlike.

Zoe was in the zone, however. She'd tied a bandanna around her neck and spread her binders of conspiracies out over the rough-hewn table. Mason, wedged between the two women, was trying to defend his small slice of tabletop from the overflowing piles of notes.

"Your binders get fuller every day," Mason said, trying to nudge blurry photos of pigeons away from his drink.

"Small details can still be important, even if it's not immediately obvious how." Zoe flipped through a folder, scattering diagrams and photos with each reckless page turn. "We're creating a tapestry here. *Everything* is connected."

Mason wordlessly held up a sticky note from the pile. It read:

BIGFOOT?? BIGFOOT'S GHOST???

Zoe snatched the note back. "Tapestry, Mason. Focus on the tapestry."

Keira chuckled, but she still felt a small ache on the inside.

It had been three weeks since Keira had discovered Artec and its cemetery. That was three weeks with very little progress made on what had turned into the biggest problem of her life. And that was saying something, considering how many catastrophes she was juggling.

Keira had arrived at Blighty with no memories except for her name and no possessions except for a small amount of money and an old photograph.

Her earliest memory was of being chased by masked men with guns and dogs. She didn't know who they were, but they'd made one thing clear: they wanted to kill her. She'd taken refuge in a cemetery. And that was how she'd discovered an unexpected gift of a second sight that allowed her to sense and see the dead.

She'd spent the following weeks hiding in the groundskeeper's cottage behind the graveyard, helping to clear some of the spirits that had become trapped there, while also becoming friends with two residents from the nearby town, Zoe and Mason. Together, they'd been attempting to piece together Keira's unknown past—with very little progress.

Then they'd had a breakthrough that allowed Keira to put a name to the group she'd always thought of as *the organization.*

Artec. A seemingly innocuous company that owned a graveyard just a few hours from her current home.

She'd been to the cemetery, though. And it was anything but benign.

And she'd understood why Artec was so intent on hunting her: Because she was the only one who could see what they were doing. And she was the only one who could stop them.

Weeks had passed since then. It wasn't that she'd achieved *nothing*. She'd made good progress with the ghosts in Blighty's own graveyard. She'd worked to clean up her home, the little cottage hidden at the edge of the forest. And she, Zoe, and Mason had held so many meetings that they were starting to feel like permanent fixtures at the café.

But they kept circling around the same sets of problems: Artec was powerful. It wasn't afraid to employ violence to keep its opponents quiet. And Keira and her friends had no real idea of how they were supposed to topple it.

Keira suspected she'd have a better idea of what she needed to do if she had her memories back. But they were locked up somewhere inside of her, buried so deep that she was starting to think she might never get them back.

"Look, here's the problem." Zoe leaned forward, her fingertips spread across the mountain of information. "I'm chasing rabbits down holes because I've exhausted what I've been able to dig up on Artec. I exhausted it in the *first week*. I don't know that we're going to get any major breakthroughs. I think we just need to make a leap of faith and see where it takes us."

Mason's mouth twisted. "I understand that. But...calling us underprepared would be an exaggeration. We still don't know where their central office is, what defenses they have, or even what we need to do to bring them down."

"You're bringing *my spirits* down," Zoe muttered.

Mason only shook his head. "If we get this wrong, the most likely outcome is death for all of us."

A figure appeared at their side. Marlene, the café's most efficient and least emotive employee, dropped a plate of hot fries on the table, sending newspaper clippings from the eighties scattering. "I have no clue what you lot are scheming about," she said, "and I really think I want to keep it that way. Just try not to die on company property. It would upset the other patrons."

"I'll do my best," Keira said, giving her a tight-lipped smile.

Zoe sighed, running a hand over her face as Marlene left. "I get what you're saying, Mason. I just don't know what more I can do."

"Let's lay it out on the table again," Keira suggested, setting the food to one side.

Zoe began shuffling through her stacks. Keira caught glimpses of zoomed-in pictures of meteors, esoteric symbols, a nautical map, a mandala of eyes, and inexplicably, an illustration of Dracula with tiny love hearts drawn around him.

"Ignore that," Zoe said, quickly shifting it aside. "That one's just for me."

When she was finished, the table held only the core information—everything they knew about Artec.

They had a map of Pleasant Grove, the cemetery they'd discovered. Even though the map was just black lines on white paper, Keira could still picture the scene easily. The rows upon rows of spirits chained to their graves. Screaming. Contorted. Fighting against their restraints.

Somehow, Artec had found a way to hold the dead in the land of the living. No one except Keira could see or hear them. No one else knew the kind of torment they were suffering. Families visited, unaware that their loved ones were still there, just feet away, voicelessly howling.

Next to the map was a brochure Zoe had managed to acquire: a sleek piece advertising Artec's renewable energy branch. That was the whole motivation behind the graveyard.

Ghosts were made of energy. Any action—materializing, influencing the temperature, attempting to interact with the living in any way—used up that energy. But they regained what they spent by slowly absorbing it from the atmosphere. Strong ghosts gathered energy quickly and could appear often. Weaker ghosts might only be visible every few weeks.

Artec had turned its ghosts into batteries. Wires ran underground, beneath the graves, harvesting electricity from the trapped spirits. They then sold it as renewable energy. It turned out that no one asked very many questions about where the power was coming from, so long as it was cheap enough.

Zoe had also collected four more cemetery maps, each with different addresses. That had been one of the worst discoveries. Artec hadn't stopped with Pleasant Grove; it was just one of five graveyards spread across the region, all established within the past few years, and all offering cheap burial packages. Keira hadn't visited any of them. They'd collectively agreed that the risk of being spotted was too great. But she could imagine what she'd find there.

A clone of Pleasant Grove. Rows upon rows of the howling dead.

Sticky notes were scattered over these papers, filled with the questions. WHERE'RE THE HEADQUARTERS? Artec had an office listed, but Mason had driven past it one weekend and found it was just a small corporate space inside a business park. That was where they sold their burial plots to the public, but it wasn't where the minds behind the company worked. Artec was shockingly good at keeping its business affairs private.

More sticky notes read: HOW DO THEY TRAP THE DEAD? POWER IS STORED—WHERE? CAN WIRES BE CUT?

In answer to the last one, Keira was fairly sure the answer was no. Or at least, the wires weren't what was keeping the ghosts in place. She could draw energy from the cables if she managed to touch them, though—enough to kill a person. But the company could easily replace any cables Keira managed to damage, with no impact to the business.

Finally, there was one last piece of paper. It contained a photocopy of the Artec business name in the process of being registered in four other countries.

"It's my professional opinion that we need to act fast," Zoe said, stabbing her finger at that final piece of paper. "If they start expanding into other countries, we'll have no way to reach any of the new graveyards. Even if we could afford the plane tickets, Keira doesn't have a passport. And without Keira present, there's nothing we can do."

"I know." Mason was patient as always, but worry lines were forming between his eyebrows. "But we still don't know where to even start."

Zoe dragged the first map forward. "We'll drive to Pleasant Grove and play it by ear. Keira's instincts led us where we needed to go last time. She'll be able to do it again."

Keira tried for something that was half smile, half grimace. "To be fair, I nearly got us all killed last time."

"We're still here," Zoe said pointedly. "And the fact is, we can sit and brainstorm and mastermind this for as long as we want, but the longer we take, the more of an advantage Artec gains. You *know* they're looking for you. If we give them enough time, they might just find you."

That was a horrible truth. They *were* looking for Keira. And they weren't going to give up, not after what she'd done at Pleasant Grove.

"Keira's carrying the worst of the risk, so it has to be her decision," Mason said. "But I would strongly, *strongly* advise caution. We might only get one shot at this. We can't afford mistakes."

Zoe looked like she wanted to argue, but then her expression softened. "You're right. I just… I'm starting to feel trapped."

"Hence the eight pages of werewolf fan fiction labeled *Highly Important*," Mason guessed.

"Hey, don't trash-talk my work. You won't believe the kinds of dark-web networks I had to scour to find—oh. Oh no."

Zoe strained as she stared toward the counter. The little bell above the café's door chimed whenever anyone entered or left, but it was such a constant presence that Keira had long since stopped noticing it. She stiffened, sitting forward in her chair, suddenly afraid that she'd lowered her guard too far. "What?" she whispered.

"Look." Zoe's voice was full of part reverent shock, part horror. "Dane's here."

Keira followed her gaze. Dane Crispin, the final heir to the Crispin estate, stood in front of the counter as he placed an order.

Keira slumped back, relief flowing through her. "Don't scare me like that. We like Dane now, remember?"

There was a time when she'd feared him nearly as much as she feared Artec. But then she'd discovered what had made the man so reclusive, sullen, and bitter. His ancestors, back to the town's founding, had continued to haunt the estate. And they had been draining Dane's energy and goodness to gorge themselves.

Dane was changing now that the spirits were gone. She'd seen him in town a few times since the purging of his estate, and from what she'd been told, that was more than he'd been seen in nearly a decade. His clothes were still shabby, but he was putting them together with care. His hair held premature rivers of gray, but he'd awkwardly cut and combed it.

And he seemed to be trying to reintegrate himself back into the town. He fumbled with his wallet as he placed an order with Marlene.

Zoe looked horrified. "They're flirting."

"What?"

All three of them craned forward. Dane dipped his head as he spoke to Marlene. Marlene leaned toward him, probably because it was hard to hear his request in the crowded store.

"I'm fairly sure they're just talking," Mason said, faintly amused.

"She's smiling." Zoe's eyes had narrowed. "I know Marlene. I've known her for *years*. And she's *never* smiled at me. Not even once."

Keira thought that might have more to do with Marlene's opinion of Zoe than her opinion of Dane, but she decided to bite her tongue on that.

Mason sipped from his drink. "For someone who hates the gossip mill, you're a surprisingly active participant."

"That's the cardinal rule of gossip." Zoe's owlish eyes didn't even blink as she tracked every minute movement. "It's awful when it's about you. Fantastic when it's about anyone else."

Dane made his payment, then stepped aside to the waiting area.

Three weeks hadn't been long enough to fully revitalize him—Keira suspected he might never completely shake the effects—but he had some color in his cheeks, and his papery skin seemed slightly softer. His roving eyes landed on the group of them, and he raised a hand in greeting. A small smile flitted over his mouth.

The three of them waved back. Keira sometimes saw him at her cemetery, paying his respects to his one remaining relative, but it had been a while since she'd gotten to speak to him properly. She was trying to give him space. She suspected she was too much a reminder of his previous life.

Zoe's phone buzzed. She pulled it out of her pocket and squinted at the number. "Huh."

"What is it?" Keira asked.

The look of confusion didn't fade. "It's my neighbor. She *never* calls me—hang on, I'd probably better take this."

Zoe hopped up and held the phone to her ear as she pushed through the café's doors, the bell chiming overhead.

Keira watched her go. She waited until Zoe was well outside, then leaned closer to Mason. "Do you think Zoe's acting…odd?"

He released a held breath. "You noticed it too? I wasn't sure if I should say anything."

Keira nodded toward the stacks of notes. Zoe had always been passionate about research, but her tangents had never been this wild before. It almost felt frantic. "When she said she was feeling trapped…"

"I don't think it's about Artec," Mason agreed. "Things aren't going well at home."

Zoe's mother was sick, and it was serious. That was as much as Keira knew. Zoe kept her home life close to her chest, but in the few vulnerable moments they'd shared, Keira had picked up that her mother wasn't seeking treatment.

Zoe liked to fix things. And it was in her nature to pour herself into work when she didn't know what else to do. Between her job as a cashier at the grocery store, caring for her mother, and working on the Artec situation, she was keeping herself almost uncomfortably busy.

"Oh." Mason nudged Keira's arm, his expression brightening. "Look at the cup."

Dane had picked up his to-go coffee. His long fingers wrapped around the cardboard cup, but Keira could just barely make out the writing on it: Dane's name. And a carefully scrawled heart next to it.

Dane seemed to feel their eyes on him. He quickly adjusted his hold on the drink to cover the writing, his lips tightly pressed together and his face flooding with color as he hurried past them and out the door.

"Wow." Keira slumped back, her eyebrows high. "Remind me to never doubt Zoe's instincts again."

"I'd recommend you continue to doubt them plenty," Mason said, grinning. He nudged one of the notes spilling out of the folder: **ARE THERE ANY LOCAL CULTS? IF NO—START ONE??** "But she's going to like this at least. The gossip mill lives to churn another day—oh."

The door chimed. Zoe had returned. She didn't hurry back to them the way she normally did, though. Instead, she stood just inside the doorway, staring at the phone held in one hand. Her expression was blank, her mouth open a fraction, her eyes wide but unseeing.

"Zoe?" Keira rose from her seat and reached toward her.

"It was my neighbor." Zoe took two unsteady steps toward

them, then stopped. Her voice was thin and strange and raspy. "She was visiting my mum. She says Mum fell. She thinks...she thinks it's almost over."

Keira's heart broke. She put her arm around Zoe's back, half comforting and half holding her up.

Mason snapped into action. He scooped the binders of notes up, cramming loose sheets of paper in anywhere there was a gap. "My car's outside. I'll drive you home."

Zoe shook her head, but it was a slow movement, as though she didn't have full control over her body. "I can walk. It's just... it's just a few minutes."

"I'll drive you," Mason repeated, gentle but leaving no room for argument. "Keira, are you okay to walk home from here?"

"Yeah, of course." Keeping her arm around Zoe, Keira supported her as they pushed back into the bright sunlight outside. "What can I do to help?"

"Probably nothing at this stage." Mason had a parking spot right next to the café and threw the binders into the back seat before opening the passenger door for Zoe. "But keep your phone nearby. I'll call you if anything changes."

Keira stole just enough time to press Zoe into a quick hug. Her friend's eyes were still wide and unseeing. She tentatively squeezed back in response to the hug, then let herself be lowered into the car. Keira stepped back as the doors snapped closed.

The car came to life and pulled away, turning quickly, and Keira was left standing alone outside the café.

CHAPTER 2

KEIRA SWALLOWED THICKLY AS she watched Mason's car vanish around the corner.

Mason was capable and kind. He was probably the best person to be with Zoe and her mother. He wasn't qualified as a doctor, but he'd gotten most of the way through a medical degree before dropping the courses. He'd known what to do each time Keira needed help, and she hoped he'd be able to do the same for Zoe too.

It hurt that Keira wasn't able to help, but she knew Mason was probably right. The best thing she could do was keep her phone in hand and wait to see if they needed anything.

A thought pinged in the back of Keira's head, and she patted her pockets. They were empty. She swore under her breath.

Mason had given her a new phone after her old model had started to fail her. The upgrade was modern, sleek, and full of icons she didn't fully understand *or* trust. And she'd used it so rarely that she'd forgotten it back in her cabin, where it was plugged in to its charging cable.

Part of her wanted to stay in the town center in case Mason came back for her, but she knew that wasn't likely. She needed to go home and wait it out there. And just hope her phone didn't ring for her in the meantime.

The walk had grown very familiar during the time she'd spent in Blighty. Some of the store owners even recognized her and gave a wave as she passed. Harry Kennard, the florist's son, was outside the Two Bees flower shop, morosely kicking at buckets of bouquets that Keira suspected he was supposed to be rearranging.

"Hey, Harry," she said as she passed him, earning a heavy sigh in response. "Bad day?"

His dyed-black hair was draped over half of his face to form a screen over his pallid skin and black eyeliner. He gave his bucket another unenthusiastic kick. "I am condemned to stay here until these are sold."

Polly Kennard never ran out of ways to force her son into socialization. Keira felt a twinge of sympathy as she reached into her pocket for money. "You know, I want to buy one."

"Of course. The graveyard needs flowers." If Harry had been capable of displaying any strong emotion, she suspected he would have looked relieved. Instead, he simply lifted three bunches of flowers out of the bucket and shoved them at her. "Free."

"No, seriously, I want to pay—"

"The store is now closed." Harry kicked the other bucket over, then slouched through the florist's doorway, swinging the little placard to display a rainy-weather *Closed* sign. "Goodbye."

Keira had no chance to respond as the door was closed in her face. She held three soggy bunches of tulips and carnations in one arm as she stared down at the money in her other hand, then sighed. Polly Kennard, eager to bribe people into spending time with her son, had said Keira could take whatever flowers she wanted. It still didn't feel right. Keira forced a few bills under the door to at least cover the costs halfway, then hitched her dripping bundle higher and turned back to the road.

Harry was one of the few people in town who knew about her ability to see ghosts. And he was right; the graveyard *did* need more flowers. Keira tried to leave a few at each grave that carried a ghost. Some of the stones had been there for more than a hundred years; friends or relatives who might have visited them were long gone. Seeing a spirit attached to a stone that had become cracked and covered by weeds seemed like a uniquely tragic thing. Keira couldn't save every ghost in her graveyard, but she could at least show them that someone still cared.

She'd barely left the florist's when her feet dragged to a halt. Two familiar figures stood on the opposite side of the road. Gavin Kelsey and his father were arguing.

Gavin was the doctor's only son, and he was a killer. Keira knew of two victims. He'd tried to make Keira his third, only she'd been able to get the upper hand.

She didn't have a good history with his father, Dr. Kelsey,

either. But at least Dr. Kelsey seemed determined to avoid her. She couldn't say the same about Gavin.

Their voices were too quiet to hear, but Gavin was flushed and his father appeared stormy. Abruptly, Dr. Kelsey cut off, and they both turned toward Keira, as though they'd been able to feel her gaze. Gavin's features were stony, while Dr. Kelsey's lips twisted into a grimace. He grabbed his son's arm and dragged him away, down a side street and out of Keira's line of sight.

She knew they didn't have a good relationship, but she'd never seen them arguing in public before. Her impression of Dr. Kelsey had always been that he cared too much about his position in town to let any of the family's dirty laundry be aired like that. Whatever they'd been talking about, it must have been serious. And, knowing that the doctor was already aware of his son's crimes and had even attempted to cover for them, that didn't bode well.

"Gonna file that problem away for some other day," she muttered as she adjusted her hold on the flowers. She left the town's center and turned onto the road that would take her back to the cemetery. "Shove it in the *huge problems* filing cabinet. There's got to be room in a corner somewhere."

The walk home normally took twenty minutes, but Keira cut it down to fifteen. It was a cool day, and the trees shading the path rattled dry branches overhead. Keira's mind wouldn't stop swimming, but she was no closer to any kind of action—either for Zoe or for Gavin—by the time she passed the church and entered the town's graveyard.

Blighty Cemetery spread ahead of her, surrounded by an old forest. The gravestones reflected the town's age. Keira had found some dating back to the eighteen hundreds, though they were mostly so worn and cracked that they were hard to read.

As she neared, Keira felt the light prickling on her skin that told her specters were nearby. She felt for the muscle that existed just behind her eyes and pulled.

It was like lifting a veil. Suddenly, the cemetery was no longer empty. Faint shapes bloomed into view, like clusters of mist suspended in the air. Their bodies were transparent white and weightless. Their eyes were inky black and endlessly deep. They stared at her like a silent audience.

"Hey, all," Keira called. She began to weave between them to reach her home. "Hey, Tony. Still not wearing clothes, huh? Hi, Marianne. Elizabeth. There are a lot of you out today."

The spirits were silent, as they always were. She'd made progress, though. They were starting to grow more comfortable around her. Previously, they'd often walk away or vanish entirely if she tried to talk to them. Now, some actually approached.

Shivers ran through Keira as spectral hands grazed over her arms and neck. It didn't feel like much—just a prickle of weak electricity and a deathly, hollow coldness—but she could feel shards of frost melting on her skin where contact had been made.

"Are you excited about the flowers?" she asked, trying to disguise how unnerving the touch was. "I got a lot today. You can thank Harry. Give me a minute to drop my bag at home, and I'll start splitting them up for you—"

Keira's voice died as she faced her cottage door. It looked almost exactly the same as it had when she'd left, but Keira's instincts, honed by a prolonged period of hiding from Artec, set up alarm bells.

She'd left the door open a crack when she'd gone out, so that her small black cat could leave and return when it wanted. Now, though, the door was closed, the small rock she'd been using as a wedge kicked out of the way.

"Oh," she whispered as ghostly fingers continued to flit across her skin, leaving frost in their wake. "You were warning me, huh?"

Someone had been in her home when she was gone. Keira carefully laid the bunch of flowers on the low stone wall circling her yard. She wished she had her phone. For all she knew, the intruder could still be inside.

"Am I going to find someone in there?" she asked the nearest ghost. The specter was a middle-aged woman with a pinched, sad face. Possibly one of the mill workers, judging by her clothes. Cold radiated from her form as she pressed close to Keira's side, her loose hair billowing weightlessly around her. Blood ran from her mouth, though she didn't seem to notice it. Her empty eyes were unreadable.

Keira drew a quick breath and stepped closer to the door. She couldn't hear anything inside. The windows were dark. From where she stood, the groundskeeper's cottage almost looked abandoned.

Whatever was waiting for her wasn't going to get easier, no matter how ginger she was about it. In one smooth movement, Keira unlatched the door, shoved it open, and stepped back, ready to leap out of reach of anything that came through the door.

Inside her cottage was still and silent. Couches were positioned around a fireplace that had smoldered down to coals. The kitchenette to the right was clean, the way she'd left it. The bed to the left was unmade. There was only one interior door: it led to the bathroom/laundry. Keira crossed to it in five quick paces and shoved it open.

Nothing. Keira spent a moment searching the very few nooks where something could hide—under her bed and in her wardrobe—before accepting that she was alone in her home.

Adage, maybe? The kindly pastor was letting her stay in the groundskeeper's cottage and sometimes dropped by to visit her. He could have accidentally kicked the rock aside without realizing.

Keira stood in front of her open wardrobe, staring at the rows of clothing, and the prickles of unease intensified. There was something different about the way they were hung. She scanned the items, but if any were missing, she couldn't pick which ones.

Adage wouldn't have any reason to search her wardrobe. No one did, really. They were all items donated to the church that Adage had passed on to her. They included Christmas sweaters with lopsided Santa Clauses, polka dots that didn't match anything else, and weaves that had worn thin. The point was, they'd been donated for a reason, and Keira couldn't imagine any of their previous owners wanting to take them back.

Keira turned to the kitchenette. Her phone was still there, and she unplugged it and switched it on.

No missed calls. No new messages. She hoped that was a good

sign, but realistically, she knew there was probably very little *good* to be found in the situation.

A new thought struck Keira. She hadn't seen her cat. She turned, her heart running fast. "Daisy?"

A small peeping meow answered her. She looked up. Daisy was on top of the wardrobe, her huge amber eyes staring down at Keira and her tail twitching. The cat was so dark that, except for her eyes, she would have been invisible in the heavy shadows.

"Hey," Keira said, carefully lifting the cat down. Daisy clung to her shoulder, claws digging in, as Keira carried her back to the kitchen and her food. "What happened? I bet you saw who was in here, huh?"

Daisy's fur was bristled with alarm. Keira placed her down on the floor and stroked her gently until her coat flattened out again; then Daisy, distracted by her food, trotted away.

"Well." Keira stretched, then rubbed at the back of her neck. Someone had been inside her cottage, and she doubted they were someone she'd *want* there. But nothing seemed damaged or stolen, and she didn't know what else she could do about it.

"Just another entry for the *huge problems* filing cabinet," she said. "Shove it in. Kick the door closed. Hope nothing in there festers too badly in the meantime."

She could make jokes about it, but that still didn't fully erase the creeping unease of having someone invade her home. She glanced toward the windows. Specters stared in at her through the glass, their forms going hazy at the edges and bleeding together. They could give her the answers if they wanted to. They never did. Silently, they watched.

It would be smart to wear warmer clothes if she was going back outside to talk to the ghosts. She crossed to the wardrobe again and, for the second time, examined its contents critically. Nothing seemed to have been removed or added. Though, she had to admit, her clothes were so chaotic that there was a good chance she wouldn't notice.

Her favorite item and perhaps the only truly sensible piece in her whole wardrobe—the jeans she'd arrived in town in—was in the pile at the wardrobe's base, waiting for its turn to be washed. Something pale lay on the floor beneath. Keira frowned as she took the object out.

They were two small newspaper clippings, rolled up and held together by an elastic. Keira stared at them for a second as memories flashed through her. On the same night they'd found Pleasant Grove, Keira had stumbled on a motel where, from what she could gather, she'd spent time before. She'd found a nest of items in the rafters: money, matches, a small amount of charcoal, and the clippings. There hadn't been time to read them; she'd shoved them into her pocket and kept moving.

And then, in true Keira style, she'd forgotten about them. In her defense, there had been a lot going on at the time. They must have fallen out of the jeans' back pocket when she threw them into the wardrobe.

Keira carefully pulled the elastic off and unfolded the scraps on her kitchen table. The papers were badly creased and held tiny tears around their edges. They looked old. Neither held a date, but Keira wouldn't have been surprised if they were from at least a decade back.

The first piece was about a new amusement park being constructed. It was going to be at the heart of a planned development. It was a typical puff piece, talking about the size of the land and the prospective number of jobs it would bring to the local community. There was only one notable thing about it: the name of the construction company, Brightwater, had been underlined.

The name meant nothing to her. Keira flipped to the second piece. It was even shorter but dealt with the same amusement park. The project was being scrapped after nearly eight years of being stuck in limbo. The planned development around it had fallen through, and investors had gotten cold feet. After failing to secure the remaining necessary funding, the park had been abandoned partway through construction.

Neither of the papers seemed to hold much significance, but they *had* to be important. Old Keira, the Keira from before she'd woken up outside Blighty, wouldn't have stored them in her hidden stash otherwise.

Zoe would be able to find the connection. Keira smiled at the thought, though there was a low ache of anxiety starting in her stomach. *Not right now, but...I'll save them.*

She changed clothes and tucked the clippings into her back pocket, vowing not to forget them again.

She gave her home another questioning glance, as though that would give her answers about who might have been in there. It didn't. There wasn't much else to do except check her phone for a final time, then pocket it and return outside to do her job.

CHAPTER 3

BLIGHTY'S GRAVEYARD WAS OLD. Many of the graves were crumbling, their stones tilted or cracked or sinking into the earth.

The town had a long history, and parts of it had been bloody. The cemetery held spirits who had died in work accidents at the mill, in disputes turned violent, or under circumstances that even Keira didn't know.

Ahead was a spirit whose head had been crushed. One half of his face showed a drooping eyebrow and stubble; the other was a pulp of mangled flesh, bone fragments, and things Keira didn't want to put names to. She didn't know which grave was his or why he lingered. Any time she approached, he'd fade away.

That was true of a lot of the ghosts. But some were growing to trust her. Small children ran past her legs, their bodies pure ice as they brushed against her, engaged in an eternal game of hide-and-seek with one another.

Mist lingered around the cemetery. It clung to the tilting gravestones and hid the winding paths. Sometimes, when the weather and time aligned, the graveyard would be entirely swallowed by it, turning the space into something that felt very like purgatory—a world of white, interrupted only by the dead.

That day it was easier to navigate. Keira moved between the graves, clearing dead flowers that had been left by visiting families or by her and replacing them with a fresh bloom from the bunches Harry had given her. She pulled weeds as she moved. The graveyard would never look as neat as a modern cemetery, but she could at least save it from being entirely neglected.

Movement blurred around her as the spirits alternately paced along their rows or stopped to watch Keira's work. She could hide them if she wanted, by releasing the muscle behind her eyes and letting them fade out of sight, but she preferred knowing they were there.

A man with a piece of rebar through his chest walked past, a thin trickle of blood falling from the metal rod's tip. A woman in a stained nightdress stared at Keira with hollow eyes, then faded into fog as soon as Keira looked back. Gaunt and grizzled faces watched from a distance, but they were so faint that Keira could barely see them through the trailing mist.

An ethereal cane tapped the ground ahead of Keira. She was crouched next to a grave, pulling thorny weeds from around its sunken marker, and looked up.

The severe Victorian woman stared down at her. She was an heiress from the Crispin line, and she looked it; brooches adorned her dark silk dress, and her hair was pinned up behind her head. Wrinkles hung heavily around her face, but her gaze was sharp and cold as she stared down at Keira.

"Hey," Keira said, rocking onto her heels. "How are you today, Josephine?"

She rarely tried to communicate with Keira, or even acknowledged her existence. But the spirit had helped Keira at one point when she'd dearly needed it, which Keira considered as good as being best friends.

Josephine Crispin didn't acknowledge the question. She just stared down at Keira with empty unforgiving eyes. Mist swirled around the skirts of her dress, tendrils merging into her form and then tearing away again.

"Is there anything I can help you with?" Keira asked. "I'll be leaving a flower at your grave, but…"

Again, Josephine didn't dignify the question with an answer. Instead, she tapped her cane again. It was a soundless motion but harsh enough that Keira still flinched slightly. Josephine turned and raised a hand in a single fluid motion. She was pointing toward the far side of the cemetery, to an area that pressed close to the forest bordering Blighty.

"Oh," Keira whispered. "Someone else needs help? Someone over there?"

Josephine turned aside. Her skirts sent flurries of mist roiling in her wake as she paced back toward her own monument.

"I hope that was a yes," Keira said, standing and dusting her hands on her jeans. "Because I can't really afford to spend an hour wandering in circles if you spontaneously developed a sense of humor and decided to play a prank."

The cemetery's layout was chaotic. Recent graves tended to be closer to the parsonage, but the older graves spilled out as far as Keira could see, some of them even disappearing between the forest's old trunks. Shrubs and leafless trees were spaced about, their gnarled branches rising out of the mist to reach toward the cold sky.

Keira tried to visit each area, but the spaces closest to her cottage naturally got the most attention. She could see the ghosts from her window and was slowly becoming familiar with each of them.

The farther she walked, the more unfamiliar faces appeared through the haze. Most of them only stayed for a second before fading away again, barely more than an optical illusion. Keira folded her arms across her chest as the unnatural chill bored into her bones.

A woman appeared through the swirling white ahead. Her dress had been drained of color by death, but it would have been black silk, Keira thought. She stood perfectly still, facing Keira, and unlike the others, refused to fade.

"Hello," Keira called as she neared. "Were you waiting for me? Josephine Crispin said someone over here might want help."

Very slowly, the woman nodded. Gray hair spilled out behind her, and it rolled like ripples on the ocean as she moved.

She was an old ghost. She came from the late eighteen hundreds or very early nineteen hundreds, Keira thought. Her dress was buttoned up to her chin and her hem trailed across the ground. The dress wasn't as expensive or elaborate as Josephine's, but she still looked as though she might have come from one of the town's wealthier families, compared to the farmers and mill workers in the graves nearby. She looked at least fifty, but, even in death, Keira had the impression that she would have been considered a beauty in life. Soft creases clung to delicate skin around a heart-shaped face.

She stood next to a grave. Keira moved closer to read the name there.

"Cora," she murmured, moving one hand to brush the mist away from the stone. "Cora Wentworth."

The grave marker said she'd passed in 1882.

Keira looked up toward her. "Do you have a reason to stay? Some kind of unfinished business?"

Cora clasped her hands. Her expression was stony as she dipped her head in a brief nod.

"Great." Many of the ghosts either didn't know or couldn't tell her. "I can't make any promises, but I'll do my best to resolve it for you. If it's okay, I can run through a few common scenarios. You can nod to stop me if I get it right. Do you have a message for a loved one? An inheritance you want to ask about? A secret you want shared? A—"

Cora waved one hand, cutting Keira off. She seemed frustrated. She moved forward, her form blurring like an out-of-focus photograph, and stopped in front of her grave. She raised one hand. With it, she covered the surname, *Wentworth*. The spirit was transparent and Keira could still see the writing beneath her long pale fingers, but the meaning was clear.

"Huh." Keira tilted her head. "Are you unhappy with your grave?"

A firm nod. The hand stayed hovering over *Wentworth*.

"Were you given the wrong surname on your marker?"

A harder, eager nod. The woman's face was still stony, but hints of hungry hope were shining through around her eyes.

"Oh." Keira raised her eyebrows. "Well, that's maybe one of the easiest requests I've had. If a mistake was made with your grave, that should be pretty simple to fix. Give me a day or two, okay? I'll find out what your surname should be, then I'm sure we can get the stone changed."

Cora straightened. A smile flittered over her mouth, tentatively, before she turned and stepped away. Watching her leave was like watching her walk behind an invisible wall—one second she was there; the next she was gone.

Keira shivered. Being this deep in the graveyard meant being surrounded by a permanent chill. The dead dropped the temperature, and there were a lot of them nearby that day.

A misspelled gravestone seemed like an odd reason to cling to the mortal world. Keira thought it over as she walked back to her cottage. Maybe Cora had a lot of pride in her surname; she looked like she might belong to a historically significant family. Or maybe she was a perfectionist and this was a mistake she just couldn't get past, no matter how much time she had.

Still...when she compared it to some of the other ghosts

she'd been helping—the ones suffering from broken hearts or murders that had never been solved—it seemed almost painfully insignificant.

To me, she reminded herself. *It feels insignificant to* me. *It's obviously upsetting her deeply if she's still here after all of this time. And she deserves to be free, just like the others.*

Keira pulled her phone out for what felt like the hundredth time and checked it. Still no messages. She chewed on the inside of her mouth as she tucked it away again. It had been hours; she couldn't tell if that was good or bad.

As the parsonage came back into view, Keira caught sight of a distant cardigan-clad figure. Adage, the pastor who'd given her the cottage to stay in, was sweeping his front step. He waved as Keira came up.

"How's the work going?" he asked.

Adage knew about her gift. They'd come up with a deal: room, board, and a small allowance in return for Keira's work in the graveyard. As Adage had put it, he shepherded souls during life. After death, Keira had to take over.

"I have a new case today," she said, leaning on the wall around his parsonage. "Odd question, but how difficult would it be to replace a gravestone?"

Adage considered it. "Unless the family pays for the stone, it would be the church's responsibility. And we normally only do that in cases of vandalism. You've already seen how many of the graves are in disrepair; unless someone close to the deceased is still alive in town, it's hard to justify changing old stones."

That was about what Keira had guessed. "What if the stone was given the wrong name or misspelled?"

"Well, that's something I've never encountered before," Adage said. He leaned on his broom and nudged his glasses further up his nose as he considered it. "I suppose I'd have to bring it up to the congregation, possibly for a vote. It would be their donations that would pay for a new headstone. Does one of our graves have a problem?"

"Supposedly," Keira said. "A woman under the marker *Cora Wentworth* is asking for a change."

Adage's bushy eyebrows rose. "The Wentworths! That's a name I haven't heard in a while. How remarkable."

"Oh?" Keira leaned forward. "You know them?"

"Phillip Wentworth was a poet in the second half of the eighteen hundreds. He was never rich, but his books garnered enormous critical acclaim and are still somewhat popular today. He moved to Blighty briefly, where he met and married a local girl called Cora. Cora… Cora…" He frowned, lost in thought, then perked up. "Yates! That's it. Cora Yates. She came from a well-off family in town. From what I've heard, there was a great deal of controversy around the match, but I believe the girl loved him and married him in opposition to her family's wishes."

"Huh." Keira chewed her lip. "And *Wentworth* is spelled the traditional way?"

"It is."

It seemed like the issue with the grave wasn't a typo, then.

"Do you remember what happened to Cora? Do you know how she died?"

"Hm." Adage shifted his weight. "It wasn't a particularly happy end, I'm afraid. Phillip and Cora Wentworth moved away from Blighty and I believe struggled significantly. Both Phillip and Cora passed away in poverty, during a cholera outbreak. Not a joyous end for such a notable poet or his wife. Cora's body was returned to Blighty at her family's wishes, since Phillip's estate did not have enough to pay for the funeral."

A picture was forming. "Was Cora a lot younger than Phillip Wentworth?"

"I believe so, yes. It wasn't unheard of at the time, but she was very young when she married, and he was at least a few decades her senior."

Keira could picture it: a young woman, sheltered her whole childhood and then swept up in a whirlwind of love, only to be trapped in a life far different from what she'd dreamed of. If her family had been wealthy, she'd likely gone from having her meals cooked and her clothes washed by staff to performing those chores herself. And if that early love had worn thin…

The woman in the graveyard had been at least fifty. She'd had plenty of time to regret a hasty choice.

Maybe that was why she wanted her surname changed after death. To erase even the memory of a husband she'd grown to resent with every bone of her body.

"Thanks for helping," Keira said. "I'm going to have to think about this one."

"Of course. I'm always here if you have questions." Adage lifted his broom and resumed sweeping. "I'm not exactly a local history expert, but it's hard not to pick things up. Gossip is a flaw according to the Bible, but you'd be amazed how many of the congregation treat it like a virtue. Take care, my dear."

Keira waved as she left him. She had a slightly clearer picture of what her ghost was asking for and why. Now, she faced a completely different problem: the ethics and challenges associated with rewriting history and renaming the dead.

CHAPTER 4

KEIRA'S PHONE STAYED SILENT for almost the whole day. And when a message from Mason finally arrived, it wasn't what she'd expected.

Come to main road. Urgent.

Keira frowned at the short message. Then she frowned at the pasta she was cooking on her stove, then back at the message.

Zoe could sometimes exaggerate, but Mason never did. If he said something was urgent, then that meant it was *really* urgent. *On my way*, she texted.

Keira dragged the pot away from the stove and turned the heat off, then crossed to the door in loping steps. "I'll be back later," she called to Daisy, even though she was mostly certain the cat couldn't understand her. Daisy slept on the couch, draped so that both of her front legs and head hung off the edge in a pose that would have looked uncomfortable except for how content the cat actually seemed. Her eyes were barely closed and the tip of a pink tongue extended from her mouth. She didn't react to the words.

Keira kept the phone in one hand as she jogged through the graveyard, being careful to avoid stepping on any graves. It was approaching dusk, and color spread across the distant sky. She half expected Mason to send another message explaining what was happening, but her phone was quiet. Which meant he was probably traveling to meet her.

Thoughts swirled. The message didn't bode well. She couldn't offer much help to Zoe or her mother if she was unwell. That was Mason's arena. But death—death was Keira's.

Please, no. It would devastate Zoe. She'd mentioned she had a lot of siblings, but Zoe was the only one who'd chosen to stay with their mother. They were close, Keira knew.

If she'd passed, Zoe might want Keira to make sure her spirit had moved over. But it didn't explain the *urgent* at the end of the message. Unless something had gone very wrong.

She broke into a sprint as the driveway led downward toward the main road. She heard the engine even before she reached the drive's base. Mason's car skidded dangerously as it got near, and Keira's first instinct was to think that it couldn't possibly be Mason driving. He was there, though, gripping the steering wheel with white knuckles, his eyes wild.

Keira didn't wait for an invite. She threw the back door open and leaped inside. The car skidded forward before she'd even found her seat.

None of this was like Mason. He was the most cautious driver she knew and somehow even more tentative behind the wheel than the gentle pastor, Adage. He normally refused to move unless everyone had their seat belts locked in place. Now, though, the tires screamed as he pushed his car back onto the road.

Mason wasn't the only one acting out of character. Zoe—bubbly, happy Zoe—sat in the back seat next to Keira. Her normally expressive face was flat and drawn. Her eyes were the kind of red that only came from hours of crying.

That was the moment Keira knew—Zoe's mother was gone.

"Tell me what you need," Keira said.

Zoe sucked in a shaking breath. She was hunched, her hands gripping the edges of her seat so tightly that her tendons looked close to popping. Her eyes were red, but they were also desperate. Terrified. "I need to ask something from you," she said. Silent tears trailed down her already wet face. "Something a friend should never ask."

"Anything."

Zoe's eyes were locked on Keira's, and they burned like coals. "I need you to save me."

The car rocked as they raced around a corner. Mason was going way over the speed limit, possibly for the first time in his life.

"Zoe's mother passed earlier this afternoon." Mason's gentle tone was at odds with how recklessly he was driving. "The neighbor, Mrs. Gould, called Dr. Kelsey, and Dr. Kelsey issued the death certificate."

Keira remembered seeing the doctor arguing with Gavin.

That must have been right before he visited Zoe's mother.. Her stomach twisted. "What did he do?"

"He was fine." The car ran over the center lines as Mason cut a corner. "He called the nominated funeral director. About twenty minutes ago, they arrived to take Zoe's mother away. And—"

"I didn't even see it until the van was pulling away." Zoe was quivering so badly, she could barely talk. "Their uniforms were plain. I didn't see the logo until I saw the van driving away..."

Horrible realization crashed over Keira. "Not Artec."

"Artec," Mason confirmed.

"She bought a funeral plan." Zoe choked on the words. "She knew it was coming so she bought a plan, and she told Mrs. Gould and she told Dr. Kelsey but she didn't tell me. She didn't tell me so I didn't even imagine... She's been trying to save money lately and Artec's plans are all cheaper than their competition because..."

Because of what they did to the dead. Because of the hellish, eternal chains locking them in place. Keira felt sick.

Zoe had never told her mother about what they'd experienced in Pleasant Grove, just like Zoe's mother hadn't told Zoe about her plans.

Both of her friends were watching her. Mason's anxious gaze flittered to meet hers in the rearview mirror, and Zoe's sore red eyes were fixed on her with painful desperation. They didn't know what to do next. That was why they'd come to her; if anyone was going to pluck answers out of the ether, it had to be Keira.

"Can you catch up to the van?" Keira asked.

"I'm doing my best." The car's odometer ticked further upward. "There are only a couple of roads leading out of Blighty. I think they were driving toward this one, but..."

He trailed off, and Keira understood. He didn't know if he was on their trail or chasing shadows.

Keira swallowed thickly as she tried to think. Despite three weeks of research, she still knew far too little about Artec or how it worked.

She knew the spirits were locked into place once they were in their graves. She knew she didn't have the knowledge or the skills to free them once they were there. She'd tried, and it had nearly killed her, even though the howling ghost hadn't so much as quivered.

She didn't know at what point that locking happened. She didn't know if it was already too late. But she knew, if she had any chance of doing anything, it had to be now, before they arrived at one of Artec's facilities. Before Zoe's mother was locked behind any kind of guarded area.

"There," Zoe gasped, rocking forward in her seat and pointing.

They'd entered the narrow twisting roads that led through the mountains around Blighty. There were almost no other cars on the road except for them...and the sleek white van that had appeared on the road ahead.

It was almost identical to the van Keira had seen when she'd stopped at Cheltenham's hospital, the first time she'd begun to understand what the organization was. There were no rear windows, but the van's back had two doors that would open out sideways. The company emblem—a hexagonal design of twisting leaves—was painted in faint gray on the white surface. Just the sight of it infused her with cloying dread.

The van disappeared around a bend in the road, then slid back into sight. A horrible, reckless idea was growing inside Keira. "How long until we reach the freeway?"

"About ten minutes." Mason flexed his hands on the wheel. "What do you want me to do?"

"Get as close to that van as you can."

He gave a short nod as he pressed on the accelerator.

"Zoe, what's her name?"

There was terrible hope in Zoe's wide eyes. "Kim. Kim Turner."

"Kim. Good." Keira unbuckled her seat belt as their car crept up on the van. Twenty feet between them. Ten. The van's back was wide; the driver would have trouble seeing them in their mirrors.

Then there were just five feet separating them, the road no longer visible between the vehicles. She took quick shallow breaths as she judged the distance. "Hold the car as steady as you can, Mason."

"Okay—wait!"

Keira opened her door. Wind buffeted around her, sending her hair flying.

She didn't know much about who or what she'd been in her past life. But she had some clues. She had sharp reflexes, could move fast, and was good at hiding. She wasn't afraid of physical obstacles: climbing trees, scaling fences, or running long distances. She'd never tested out her skills to see just how far she could take them, but now, she dearly hoped they weren't going to fail her right when she needed them.

"Keira," Mason called as she crept out of the open door. "Keira, no!"

"Keep the car steady," she said, and inched around the door, finding a grip on the driver's side handle to pull herself forward. She caught a flash of Mason's panicked face as she passed, then she hauled herself onto the car's hood.

The wind rippled around her, sending her hair and clothes flapping. The hood was hot under her hands from a combination of the setting sun and the engine. Mason had let the gap between them and the van widen; they were back to ten feet. Keira slid around so that her legs were ahead of herself and her feet braced on the bumper.

Mason was barely visible under the glare on the windshield. She could see his set jaw and the frightened sheen to his eyes. He gave his head a very slight shake. He didn't want any of them to be doing this.

Stay with me, Mason. We don't have much time. Keira used a beckoning motion to tell him to speed the car up again. His lips pressed into a tight line. The car's engine grew louder, and the space between the car and the van began to narrow again.

The road twisted. Keira braced her hands on the hood to hold herself in place. Mason was taking the curves as gently as he possibly could, but Keira had very little to grip and her muscles burned from the effort of holding herself in place.

Eight feet to the van. Six. Four. Keira leaned forward as they drew closer. She reached behind and made a circular motion with her hand, asking Mason for slightly more speed. Three feet, then two. That was close enough. Keira pressed her heels into the car's bumper and arched forward before leaping.

Her muscles knew what to do, even if she had no memory of practicing any kind of stunt like it. She landed on the back of the van, her hands hooking on the handle and her shoes barely finding purchase on the step.

The van rocked slightly from her impact. She felt it slow down and squeezed her eyes closed, desperately clinging to its back. *Please don't stop. Please don't stop—*

The van coasted for a moment, then picked up speed again. The driver must have thought he'd hit a pothole or something. Keira let out a held breath and opened her eyes again.

There were no windows, so she couldn't see what might be inside. She just had to hope that the rear doors didn't have any kind of alarm system as she hooked her fingers under the handle and pulled.

CHAPTER 5

ONE HALF OF THE double doors clicked open. Inside the van was windowless and dark. There was no kind of beeping alarm, and Keira thanked whatever luck she was clinging to as she slipped through the open door and into the vehicle.

Mason's car continued to trail behind the van as close as he could manage. Keira didn't want to lose sight of her friends. But she also couldn't leave the door open; it would bang with each turn, and she couldn't afford to draw any more attention to herself than she already had. She made a pushing motion, indicating for Mason to increase the gap between them again, then pulled the van's door closed.

Darkness swallowed her. Something metal nudged against Keira's hip. She couldn't hear anything except for the engine's faint rumbles.

But she could feel it. The presence of a spirit. The hairs on her arms rose as the achingly low temperature sent ice into her lungs. There was a ghost here, and the ghost was agitated.

Keira reached into her back pocket and pulled out her phone. Her fingers were turning numb as she switched on its flashlight, and the van's insides were bathed in a cold white light.

Metal rails ran along the walls to hold trays with bodies. Keira suspected, if the van was at capacity, it could have held at least six sets of remains, and there wouldn't have been room to stand. As it was, only one stretcher was in the van, pressed against the right-hand wall.

That stretcher held a body bag, its zipper closed. In Keira's pale light, the body inside seemed to shift slightly each time the van rocked.

Keira exhaled through her mouth, and a plume of thick condensation spread from her lips. She didn't know what she was going to find when she opened her second sight. A shade, the twisted, broken form of spirits? A ghost, as pale and voiceless as the spirits in her own graveyard?

Nothing?

That last option would be the worst of all. She could help ghosts. She could sometimes even help shades. She dreaded finding the van was empty. In the corner of her eye, the covered body rocked, and rocked, and rocked.

Keira braced herself, then felt for the muscle behind her eyes and pulled on it. A pale shape shimmered into view, and Keira could have cried from relief.

She was a ghost, not a shade. Not yet twisted into a monstrous form of black smoke. That was a mercy. And she was visible, which meant Keira still might be able to help her. Perhaps.

"Kim?" Keira asked, keeping her voice quiet so that it wouldn't carry to the van's cab.

She was a small woman. Even with the color drained out of her, Keira could still see traces of Zoe in her face: the fullness of her cheeks, the roundness of her eyes. Her dark hair, which Keira guessed might have been steel gray in life, was cut into a bob with bangs. A patterned button-up shirt and slacks flowed about her, moved by an invisible current. She was backed as far away as she could in the small space and watched Keira warily.

"I'm Keira." Her mouth was dry and her fingers shook. The air was so cold that she thought she could see frost forming around the metal rails. That wasn't good; Kim's spirit was burning through her energy too fast. She might not be able to stay visible for long. "I'm a friend of Zoe's."

At her daughter's name, Kim's empty eyes fluttered.

"We don't have much time," Keira said. "But I'm here to help you move over. Is there anything holding you on earth? Any kind of unfinished business?"

For a second, the ghost didn't react, and Keira was afraid she might be as aloof and unresponsive as some of the spirits in the graveyard. Then Kim gave a very small shake of the head.

"Okay." Their luck was holding, but possibly not for much longer. Each breath stung Keira's throat as the temperature dropped below freezing. "I'm going to try to forcibly move you on. It won't hurt. It's just…it's important that we do it now."

She didn't want to have to explain to Kim what would happen if her ghost was still tethered to the earth when she arrived at Artec's institution.

Kim hesitated again, then gave a very small nod.

Keira didn't need her light to see what she was doing, but she still held it up resolutely, as though the white glow could protect her from the softly rocking body or the Artec employee who was only feet away in the driver's seat. She reached toward Kim's chest, blindly feeling for the bright thread inside.

In her time at Blighty, she'd learned a few ways to remove ghosts. The first was if they knew what was holding them in place—some regret or some kind of business that needed to be resolved. If she could help a spirit deal with it, then the ghost would often release themselves, fading away into fog.

The second method was for stubborn ghosts who were causing harm, either by sucking the life from anyone nearby or causing spectral rot to spread. Ghosts were made up of the same energy that Keira held inside her. Provided she had enough to spare, she could force it into a ghost to overload it, causing it to split at the seams and collapse. It was taxing and dangerous, especially since feeding it energy but failing to overload it would leave it far, far more powerful than it had been before.

The third method was for the peaceful ghosts who didn't know why they were still on earth. Either they'd forgotten their unfinished business, or had never had any to begin with, and simply didn't know why they remained. When that happened, Keira could feel inside each spirit for the tangled thread that hung in their chests, close to where their hearts had once been. Unraveling it would release the spirit.

Chills raced through Keira as her fingertips plunged into Kim's form. Kim's eyes—nothing but empty black holes—were turned toward her, watching warily as Keira felt for the tangled strand.

Like a gift from the Three Fates, Keira thought as her fingers closed around the loose end. *Meting out thread for the living. Cutting it upon death. But what happens when cutting the thread isn't enough?*

Fizzing electricity ran through Keira's fingers as she tightened her grip on the thread. She pulled.

The knot tightened.

A lump formed in Keira's throat. She pulled harder. The sizzling thread felt as if it were burning the tips of her fingers, but it refused to shift.

Normally this was enough. When a ghost was ready to leave—and Kim seemed ready—the thread would unravel with a slight pull. The only ghosts she'd met whose threads she wasn't able to untangle were the ones who were fighting to stay: the shades or ghosts who were clinging to something important.

She pulled harder. Electricity fizzled along her fingers. The knot refused to budge.

Keira let go and stepped back, her breathing ragged. "Are you sure you don't have any unfinished business? Nothing that could be keeping you here?"

Another shake of the head, this time slightly more resolute.

Keira could see it in her face. Kim's disease had been ravaging her for months. She'd known where her path was leading; she'd made plans. She was ready to go.

She just *couldn't*.

Keira bit her lip. It had to be related to Artec. In Pleasant Grove, she'd been shocked not only by the condition of the spirits—billowing, smokelike shades, all of them—but by the number. Most graveyards only held a handful of spirits. In Pleasant Grove, every single grave had an occupant.

Which meant Artec had a way to bind ghosts to their bodies before they even arrived there. Their scheme was reliant on each grave carrying a spirit that could act as a battery; they couldn't afford to let any move over to the next life before they were interred.

Kim wasn't a shade. Not yet. But she was moving closer to it, Keira realized. The temperature was so chilled that every raspy breath was a plume of mist through the air and every metal surface bore a thin sheen of frost. Temperature was related to a ghost's disposition: angry and upset ghosts made the world colder. But Kim was calm. Anxious, yes. Confused, yes. But nowhere near emotional enough to conjure this kind of chill.

Artec was doing something to her.

What? How? They were the same questions Keira had been battling with for weeks. *How* did they hold the ghosts? How did they make them shades?

And how could she stop it?

"Did you see them do anything to you?" Keira asked the spirit. "The people who collected your body. Did they…I don't know…perform any kind of ritual?"

But Kim's spirit was sinking away from her again, huddling back in the farthest corner of the van, and refused to even look at her any longer.

The van's rocking motion changed subtly. The speed picked up. Keira realized what that meant: they were on the freeway. Their time was running out.

Bubbling desperation heated Keira's stomach, even as the rest of her became numb from the cold. She turned toward the body bag. It had been shifting slightly with each turn and change in speed, but now lay still as the freeway gave the van an easier path to follow.

Keira clenched her teeth and reached for the bag's zipper.

CHAPTER 6

SHE'D SEEN PLENTY OF ghosts. She'd even seen a dead body once before, in Cheltenham's hospital morgue. But that had been a sanctioned visit, with Adage at her side and the mortician watching over. This felt wrong somehow. Keira could only mutter a soft apology as she dragged the zipper back to expose Kim's body.

The woman on the stretcher was vibrant compared to the colorless ghost in the van's corner. Her hair was steel gray, like Keira had suspected, but still held streaks of the same glossy black that Zoe had. Her shirt was covered in a geometric pattern of reds, blues, and greens.

Even with her face sunken and hollowed out by disease and death, there were just as many laugh lines around her mouth as crease lines around her eyebrows. Keira felt a sudden pang of sadness that they'd never met in life. She thought she would have liked Kim.

She kept unzipping until the body was fully exposed. Kim's shoes had been taken off, but the rest of her clothes were still in place. Keira searched the inside flaps of the body bag, hunting for anything that might be used to keep a spirit in place. What, she didn't know. Her brief time at Blighty had been spent learning how to move ghosts over to the next life, not hold them.

There were no pockets or secret zippers in the bag. Keira's desperation increased. She could feel the road vanishing under them like a ticking clock, counting down to the point where Kim would be beyond saving.

Then she saw it. A hint of something white peeking out from under the shirt's collar. Kim's skin had turned pale in death, but the white line was a shade lighter still.

"I'm so, so sorry," Keira whispered, and undid the top two buttons on the shirt.

The fabric dropped away, and Keira sucked in a sharp breath.

Someone had drawn a rune on Kim's chest, right in the center of her sternum, close to where her heart was. It looked to have been made with a white ink pen.

Keira had a very limited knowledge of runes. She had one under her bed to concentrate energy into her and recharge her as she slept. She was fairly sure Old Keira had been far more familiar with them.

This was a very different shape. It was spiky, with arrows pointing inward. Keira frowned and tilted her head as she stared at it, trying to understand it.

The mark was faintly familiar. Like an itch at the back of

her mind or like a whisper that was forgotten before it was even finished. She tried to clutch at it, but it was gone before she could even begin to feel its shape.

She'd seen the symbol before, though. And it wasn't as familiar or as welcome as the rune that drew energy. This was an uncomfortable memory, like the edge of an unsettled dream right before it tipped into a nightmare.

"Okay," Keira whispered, one hand hovering over the marks. "Okay, what now?"

Get rid of it, her subconscious whispered.

Keira pressed her thumb against one of the white lines. Kim's body was cooling—not yet fully cold, but no longer holding on to the warmth of life. The ink sizzled under Keira's fingers, like touching a live wire. It was powerful. She tried to smudge the line, to break it, but the paint wouldn't move.

She spit on her thumb to wet it, then tried again. Kim's paper-thin skin dragged as she rubbed against it, and the hissing power from the sigil stung her hand, but the marks still wouldn't budge.

Keira had a distant sense that this was related to her. Maybe once, long ago, she'd broken the rune on a body very similar to this. Maybe that had been enough to force Artec to use a more permanent ink, something that couldn't be smudged away or washed off with just water.

Think! Keira grit her teeth. The van rocked slightly as it changed lanes. Kim's ghost watched with dead eyes. *The lines can't be erased...but what else can I do?*

A thought snapped through her. *What would happen if, instead of erasing the rune, I changed it? What if I turned it into a different rune entirely?*

She cast around for something to draw with. It wouldn't need to be permanent—just enough to break the rune's hold and let her free Kim. The back of the van was empty except for the stretcher, the body, and the spirit hunched in the back corner.

Keira searched her clothes, hoping for some kind of pen. She hadn't brought any. There was just the crinkle of the newspaper articles in her back pocket.

It doesn't have to be much. A bit of grease from the van's axel, maybe. Or a piece of chalk. Just enough to draw a few lines—

The van shifted again. The speed slowed, and Keira staggered into one of the rails. They'd left the freeway. She hoped Mason and Zoe were still behind her, but she couldn't waste time checking. If they'd left the freeway, it meant they were close to their final destination. And she absolutely couldn't afford to be found in the back of the van.

But she also couldn't afford to leave the pale frightened spirit to a fate worse than death.

Keira glanced down at her own hand. All she needed were a few drops.

She put her thumb between her teeth and bit down as hard as she could.

Her skin was hard under her teeth, then a canine punctured through as she tasted hot blood and stinging nerves. Keira raised her seeping thumb toward the body.

Please. Please. Show me what to do.

She touched down near the sigil's center. Tentatively, she drew a line outward, crossing one of the sharp arrows.

Her first movements were uncertain, but the second stroke became more sure. Her subconscious remembered the runes, even if she couldn't. She painted shapes that felt both distant and familiar. Like old friends whose faces had long ago been forgotten. The pointed arrows were softened into squares. Circles were added. And finally, a long line through the center.

It was no longer a rune of holding. It was…it was…

She squinted. A thought floated through her mind: *a rune of peace.*

It was impossible to know if that was the truth, but she wanted to believe it. More than anything, she wanted Kim to find peace.

"We're going to try again," Keira said. Blood seeped from her thumb, but she ignored it as she stepped toward Kim's spirit. "Please don't be afraid. If this works, you'll be free to step into the next life."

The spirit's expression was still wary, but now it held a hint of longing, barely visible beneath the fear. She took a half step forward.

Keira reached for the small tangled light inside her chest. Kim's hand came out and gently touched her wrist before she could find the thread, though.

"What is it?" Keira asked, trying not to show how the contact was bleeding the last of her warmth away.

Kim's eyebrows furrowed as she thought. She wanted to say something; she was just incapable of speech.

"Do you have a message?" Keira guessed.

Kim nodded. Her other hand, thin and bony, stretched past Keira to point behind them.

"Zoe?" she guessed. "Do you have a message for Zoe?"

This time the nods were emphatic.

The car rocked as it took tight turns. They were nearly out of time. Keira tried to focus and tried to repress the impulse to drag the thread free right then and there. "What did you want me to tell her? Can you write it out on the wall or…?"

Kim didn't try. She brought one hand up and thumped it into her chest, twice, then pointed behind her.

Keira's throat tightened. She blinked moisture from her eyes. "You want her to know you love her."

Emphatic nods answered the question. Kim released her hold on Keira's hand. That was the only message she had left for the world of the living.

"She loves you too," Keira said, and her voice shook. She dipped her hand into Kim's chest to find the thread. "She loves you so much."

Kim closed her eyes and tilted her head back. A barely visible tear trailed down the side of her face. Keira's fingers tightened over the loose end of the thread and she gave it a gentle tentative pull.

This time, it unraveled effortlessly, as though the knot had been waiting to come undone all of this time. As the thread floated loose, Kim's ghost faded, breaking away in wisps like fog on a cool morning.

Keira stood there a second longer, breathing deeply, as the van's chill began to fade. The prickles were gone. Kim's spirit had passed over. Now, her body was nothing but that: a collection of muscles and tendons and tissue. Keira had nothing to wash away the blood across the rune. She rubbed it with her sleeve, though, hoping to make it at least a little less obvious. If she was lucky, Artec might think the smeared blood had come at the point of death, not from Keira's meddling. It was the best she could do in the time she had. She rebuttoned the shirt, then zipped the bag closed again.

The van was slowing down. Keira crossed to the door and bit her tongue as she pulled on the latch to open it. She'd been in the van for longer than she'd thought. The sun had set; the sky was dark. She couldn't make out much except for the van's taillights, painting a trail of red behind it—and two headlights twenty feet beyond that.

Zoe and Mason were still following.

The van was going slowly enough that she thought she could jump off. She balanced on the back step, one hand clinging to the thin seam around the door's edge as she shut the door she'd left through.

Then she turned to the road, took a quick breath, and leaped.

CHAPTER 7

KEIRA STRETCHED HER LEGS ahead of herself. It was hard to judge the distance in the dark. As soon as her feet touched ground, she rolled. Loose stones bit into her as she flipped over them and came to a stop on her back, facing the dark sky and the earliest budding stars.

Tires scraped across dirt as Mason's car veered off the road to avoid her. He came to a halt just a few feet away, the headlights washing over where Keira lay, and within seconds Mason was out of the car and scrambling over to her. "Keira!" He kept his voice at a whisper, even though the van's engine was fading into the distance. "Are you hurt?"

"Mm. No." She ran a quick mental inventory. A few bruises. A couple of scrapes. No broken bones.

She took Mason's offered hand and let him pull her to her feet. Zoe was at her other side, her face pale in the wash of blinding headlights.

"She's gone," Keira said.

Zoe's whole body shuddered as she sucked in air. She clutched at Keira, and they ended up with their arms wrapped around one another.

"Thank you." Zoe muttered the words into Keira's shoulder like a prayer. "Thank you, thank you, thank you."

"It's okay." Keira ran a hand over Zoe's hair. The same shade as her mother's. "She…she had a message. Just one. She wanted you to know how much she loves you."

The shudders grew far worse. Zoe didn't seem able to stand any longer, so Keira let them both collapse back to the dusty dirt strip off the side of the road as Zoe rocked and cried.

Mason wordlessly left. He came back a moment later with blankets from the back of his car, which he draped over them. Then he sat at their side, his long legs pulled up to his chest as he stared down the road.

They stayed like that for a long time. Slowly, Zoe's tears softened. Tiny moths fluttered around them, attracted by the headlights. A few cars passed, but no one stopped.

Zoe tilted her head back to stare at the sky. There weren't many lights in that stretch of the road, and the stars above them were clear. She took a ragged breath. "I'm sorry. About all this."

"What?" Keira shuffled slightly closer. "Why would you be sorry? None of this was your fault."

"That was so dangerous, though. So reckless."

"I thought *recklessness* was your middle name."

Zoe managed a watery smile. "Yeah. It is. But when you

disappeared into that van and Mason started having a panic attack—"

"I didn't," Mason protested weakly.

"Oh, you did. And it just hit me. How dangerous that was. How we'd promised ourselves we'd be more careful, and then..."

"She was your mother." Keira leaned her head against Zoe's shoulder. "We can get a bit reckless when it's for family."

Zoe scrunched up her mouth as she tried not to cry. Fresh tears spilled out anyway. "I knew it was bad, but I didn't think... She didn't tell me how close it was to the end. She was getting thinner every day, but I thought I had more time. Even just another six months. I didn't think..."

They fell into silence for a moment. Then Zoe sucked in a painful breath.

"Okay," she said. "Okay, we've still got work to do. We still... We were going to..."

"Zo, it's okay," Keira whispered. "It's okay to let it hurt."

"No, this isn't me." Zoe pulled herself free from Keira and stood unsteadily. "Mum's gone. And it's ugly and it hurts like hell, but it could have been a thousand times worse. At least she got to pass over. So now, now we need to..."

She faltered, and the rigidity in her expression faded. She stared into the distance without seeing anything. "What do we do now?"

Mason glanced at Keira; then he unfolded himself and stood too. "Now, we're going to get off the side of the road before someone calls the police on us. We'll get something to eat. There's got to be a place that serves food around here somewhere."

Zoe nodded, and some focus came back into her eyes as she moved to the car. Keira took the rear seat next to her. As the engine came to life and Mason pulled them back onto the road, Zoe turned to Keira. "You were in the van a long time. We were starting to think something had gone wrong. What happened?"

Keira hesitated. She wasn't sure how much Zoe really wanted to hear and how much would just hurt her. But Zoe's gaze was unwavering and demanding, and Keira realized she was doing exactly what she did every time she felt trapped: she was looking for some kind of work to focus on.

Briefly, Keira told her about what had happened. Zoe's expression turned thunderous as she heard about the rune on her mother's chest, but she didn't interrupt. When she'd finished, Zoe simply said, "So it all comes down to the runes."

"As far as I can tell." Keira hadn't had much of a chance to think about the implications of what she'd seen in the van, but it was feeling increasingly likely that some kind of rune was responsible for keeping the twisted spirits held captive—not just for transportation, but once they'd been interred into their final resting places too.

"That might be good," Zoe said. "Bodies don't stay whole forever. If the bodies decay, the runes will rot away too, right? Eventually they should get weak enough that the ghosts won't be held there any longer—even the embalmed ones." She hesitated, then turned to Mason. "You did a bunch of studies on dead stuff, right?"

He frowned slightly. "I was a medical student."

"Yeah, exactly. How long does an embalmed body last?"

"I wish I didn't know the answer because it's going to validate your bias, but..." Mason sighed. "Depending on the ground where it's buried, it could be years. Or decades. Or longer. With the right conditions, a body can essentially become mummified in its grave."

Zoe grimaced. "Not ideal."

"The marks might not even be on their bodies," Keira said. "Those could just be there to keep the ghost tethered until the funeral, then something more permanent is added. Possibly marks on the coffin or casket. Or even a piece of metal that's placed over the remains, so that it never fades."

"Good point. There's no chance Artec would want their batteries to go dead after a few years. Considering how big Pleasant Grove is, they've been doing this for a while, and probably have a system." Zoe chewed her lip. "I really hope we're not going to have to resort to mass grave exhumation to fix this thing."

Mason turned into a parking lot. An old stone pub stood ahead, with lights shining through narrow windows. It looked as though it held hotel rooms on the second floor. He turned in his seat to face them both. "Is here a good place for dinner?"

"It says it's karaoke night," Zoe said, staring at a sign by the door. "Sounds horrendous. Let's go."

The music could be heard well before they opened the door. Not only was it karaoke night, but the pub was packed. Keira took a quick look around, and she thought they might be the youngest people there by at least two decades. It suited her, though. They weren't far from where they'd split from the van, which meant they weren't far from Artec, and the noise and constant movement would help disguise her in case any employees happened to be karaoke enthusiasts.

"Ah," Mason gasped as the lights washed over them. He reached for Keira's hand. "You're hurt."

She'd become good at pushing pain to the back of her mind. The bitten thumb had turned into a distant ache. It had taken a while to stop bleeding, though, and lines of red ran down her wrist, and blood from the modified rune was smeared on her sleeve.

"Hang on," Mason said, turning. "My kit's in my car."

"Don't you dare." Keira tugged his arm to pull him back. "It looks worse than it is, and we can fix it up later. I'm hungry now."

He hesitated, looking torn.

"Later," Keira insisted, and led the way to the crowded building ahead.

CHAPTER 8

THEY MANAGED TO GET a table in the corner. Keira wrapped a napkin around her hand to hide the worst of the blood. She wasn't entirely sure what she ordered; she just pointed vaguely at a spot on the dinner menu and the server scribbled something down before rushing to the next table.

Badly off-tune karaoke songs floated over them. Zoe stared through the window, her eyes red. Mason folded his arms on the table ahead of himself and rested on them. He looked tired.

One thought was digging at the back of Keira's mind, and she couldn't stop herself from bringing it up with Mason. "You said Dr. Kelsey was at Zoe's house."

"Ah, yes." Mason lifted his head and gave her a wry smile. "He was Mrs. Turner's physician. She'd prepared an end-of-life directive. He was able to show it to us. The funeral home was listed there, though it was under a name I didn't recognize.

I wouldn't be surprised if Artec uses shell companies to hide themselves."

Zoe, still staring through the window, shifted uncomfortably. "The directive said not to admit her to hospital. No matter what. She...she didn't want to die somewhere that wasn't home, I guess. And Dr. Kelsey said there wasn't anything that could be done. Though I could throw him about twice as far as I trust him."

"No, I think he was right in this case." Mason's voice was very gentle. "I'm sorry. You might have been able to delay it another few hours. But the end would have been the same."

Zoe was quiet. Keira could only imagine what it must have been like, trapped at home with a doctor she didn't trust and with no choice but wait for her mother to pass away. It must have been horrendous.

"We should talk about what comes next," Mason said.

Zoe stared at a spot on the opposite wall. "About Mum."

"Yeah." He ran a fingertip across a small section of the table, tracing the wooden grain. "Keira was able to clear her spirit, but Artec still has her body. I'm sorry to bring it up when everything is still so raw—"

"You want to know whether I'm going to fight to get her body back," Zoe said. She was blinking hard as she battled with her tears. "And I don't know. It's...it's just a body, right? It's not Mum anymore. Not really. It shouldn't matter. It *shouldn't*." She paused, breathing heavily.

Keira reached across the table, finding Zoe's hand and holding it. "You're allowed to let it matter, you know."

Zoe blinked harder. "Yeah. I want her back. She should be buried at Blighty. I want to be able to visit her, and not in one of those hellish cemeteries either."

"It should be as simple as canceling the burial plan," Mason said. He glanced at Keira. "Does that seem safe to you? Is Artec likely to connect it to you at all?"

She thought of the state she'd left the van, with thin traces of blood still streaked across Kim Turner's chest. She swallowed. "I don't know."

"It would be safer to do nothing, wouldn't it?" Zoe said. Her lips were pale but her eyes had taken on a steely quality. "Having one of their ghosts vanish and then having that same burial plan canceled…it's going to draw more attention than we need, isn't it?"

Keira desperately wished she could say no. Zoe deserved to have a grave to visit. The best she could do was say nothing.

"We have time," Mason said. "She won't be interred without a funeral, and since you were listed as next of kin, that needs your approval to go ahead. Let's wait a day or two and see if anything happens. In the meantime…"

Keira nodded, guessing his thoughts. "We need to stay careful. Artec might put the pieces together. Or they might have no idea. There's not much we can do except wait to find out."

The server, rushing, stopped to drop food off at their table. Keira discovered she'd ordered the potato soup.

Zoe picked at her own meal. Keira wished she knew what to do to help, but she also knew the answer was probably *nothing*. Grief wasn't something that could be washed away in an afternoon.

"Thank you, by the way," Zoe said abruptly. The karaoke songs were heading into the disco territory and none of the pub's patrons seemed to want to change that. "Both of you. For stopping Artec from getting my mum. Not just because of the whole...graveyard situation." Her smile was toothy and pained. "Mum was always religious. She loved Adage's sermons. Never missed them. He visited a lot in the last few weeks and...well, if there's an afterlife, she deserves to get there."

Keira nodded. The spirit at the back of the van had seemed confused and anxious. Kim Turner had been ready for death. But the fate that she was being dragged toward was far, far different from the one she'd believed in.

"I'm surprised she didn't want to be buried in Blighty," Mason said.

Zoe grimaced. "She became really money conscious the last few weeks. If I knew I was dying, I'd want to live it up. But it was like...she became very aware of what she was leaving, I guess. She probably saw the prices at Pleasant Grove were so much cheaper and thought it would be like a gift to me. A little extra to add to the nest egg to see me through." Zoe's breathing had turned ragged. "Guess I have to figure all of that out now. What the rest of my life looks like. Do I keep living in her house? Is that allowed? I don't..." She blinked. "I don't..."

"Why don't we stay here tonight?" Mason suggested softly. "They have rooms upstairs. I'll rent one. We can deal with all the rest come tomorrow."

Zoe seemed to relax a fraction. "Yeah," she said. "Yeah, that sounds nice."

A strange prickling sensation passed over Keira: the feeling of being watched. Moving carefully to avoid drawing attention, she tried to glance around the room. It was just as crowded as before. No one seemed to be paying any attention to her. She turned to the window. The parking lot was lit faintly by streetlights; a few figures hurried across it, but none seemed to be looking toward her.

As quickly as the sensation had come, it was gone again.

Keira wet her lips. She knew better than to ignore her instincts. "Maybe we shouldn't stay here."

"Did you want to go home?" Mason asked.

Keira hesitated. She didn't feel comfortable claiming they were being watched when there was a very good chance she was wrong about it. But it still didn't feel safe to stay. "I don't love the vibes here."

"Bad vibes." Zoe nodded, as though that made complete sense to her. "Sure, let's go back to Blighty. It's probably safer that way anyway."

Keira's relief was almost immediately doused by guilt as she saw the redness around Zoe's eyes. Zoe had looked so relieved at the thought of staying at the hotel that night. For Zoe, going home meant going to an empty house with a lot of new, painful memories attached to it.

"Let's stay at my cottage tonight," she suggested. "We'll make it a sleepover."

"Yeah?" Zoe perked up a fraction. "That sounds nice."

"It does. I mean, my cat will lick your face, but if you can get past that…"

"I've never said no to face licking before, and I don't plan to start now," Zoe said. She folded her napkin on her table. "Let's go."

Mason paid for dinner, and they filed out of the pub. As they crossed the parking lot to reach their car, Keira felt the same prickling, uneasy sense of eyes on her back. She turned, scanning the darkness ringing the edges of the parking lot's perimeter, but if anyone was there, she couldn't see them.

She didn't feel comfortable until they were in the car and back on the road. Even then, she found herself obsessively watching the cars behind them, paranoid that someone might be trying to follow. When they peeled off the freeway to enter the rural roads leading to Blighty, though, they were alone.

Mason put some music on for the drive. Zoe spent most of it staring through the window and watching the landscape rush past. By the time Blighty's familiar lights shone through the windshield, it was growing late. They stopped by Zoe's house—a pretty suburban not far from the town's center—so that she could pick up a change of clothes, a sleeping bag, and a toothbrush; then they stopped at Mason's—a larger house at the edge of town—for the same. Finally, they pulled to a halt near the old church as the car's headlights washed over the fog-shrouded graveyard.

"Any ghosts out tonight?" Zoe asked.

"Yeah," Keira said, meeting the sets of empty eyes staring back at her from the gloom.

"Good."

They followed the winding path to the groundskeeper's cottage. As they neared the stone wall bordering its garden, a dark shape frisked out from between the graves. Daisy, fresh from a night of exploring her domain, wove between their legs and darted into the cottage ahead of them.

"Make yourselves at home," Keira said as she switched on the lights. "Spare blankets and pillows are in the wardrobe."

"I'll make some hot drinks," Mason offered, crossing to the kitchen, "if someone else can look after the fire."

It was cold, and Keira knelt by her hearth to revive the coals that had burned down while she was gone. Zoe began unrolling their bedding, her efforts hampered by the small black cat that was intent on climbing through and disturbing every layer.

"Hey, magic cat," Zoe said, pausing to scratch Daisy's head. Daisy arched into the pats, looking pleased.

The flames rose as they caught on the added wood. Keira took her jacket off and felt the crinkle of old papers in her jeans' pocket. She pulled out the two newspaper clippings she'd been saving.

"What're those?" Zoe asked, draping her coat over the back of the couch.

"Yeah, these. Remember how we found some newspaper cuttings in that hotel we stayed at a few weeks ago? Because I didn't."

Zoe's eyes lit up. "Bread crumbs from Past Keira."

"They don't mean much to me," Keira said, passing them over. "And I don't expect you to do anything about them right now, obviously—"

"No, no, this is exactly what I need." Zoe snatched up the slim pieces of paper and held one in each hand, her eyes darting over them hungrily. "If I sit and think too long, I'll implode. I need to be *doing* something. This is perfect."

"Glad to hear it," Keira said.

Mason returned from the kitchenette and placed three steaming mugs on the small side table next to the couch. "Is it information on Artec?"

"I genuinely don't know," Keira admitted.

"Huh." Zoe had finished reading the cuttings and began a second pass. "These names don't mean anything to you, do they?"

"No, not at all. The construction company, Brightwater, is underlined, though, so it's got to be significant, right?"

"That's what I'm thinking." Zoe chewed on her lip. "It feels vaguely familiar, but I just can't pin it down. The name Brightwater is so generic that it's going to be a nightmare to research, I bet. I might need to spend all night on it."

"Sorry—"

"Like I said, it's perfect." Zoe already had her phone out. She began texting without taking her eyes off the cuttings. "I have some contacts. Let's see what they can rustle up."

CHAPTER 9

MASON HAD BROUGHT HIS medical kit from his car and placed it on the small side table as he sat on one end of the couch.

"Hand," he said to Keira, and nodded to the seat next to him.

She'd forgotten about the puncture in her thumb. It throbbed slightly but didn't seem too bad. "It's fine. Seriously."

He gave her a pained look.

"It's just got a bit of saliva on it," she insisted. "And…I rubbed it over a dead body… Okay, good point."

Mason took his time working over it, cleaning out the cut with burning antiseptic, and then covering it with cotton and a wrap, while Zoe paced behind them. Her strides were growing longer and more energetic until she abruptly came to a stop.

"Are you kidding me?" Zoe muttered.

Keira glanced at her. "What's happening?"

"My prime contact is off-grid at a UFO-abduction-support-group-and-yeti-abduction-celebration-group joint convention. Don't ask."

"But there are so many questions," Mason whispered.

Zoe flicked a hand to wave his comment away. "I'm going to have to start making phone calls. You guys stay put."

Zoe stepped out of the cottage. Keira watched her go as the low sense of dread resurfaced. She hadn't had the time or the tools to properly cover her presence in the van. She was hoping no one would look too deeply—it was just one body out of thousands that were being shipped into Artec's cemeteries—but if someone there *did* connect the missing spirit to Keira, it would lead them straight to Blighty. "I'm not sure we should be splitting up."

"I agree." Mason's focus was still on her hand as he trimmed the edges of the bandage. "But I think Zoe needs to keep moving right now."

Faintly, Keira could hear the murmur of her friend's voice as she spoke into her phone. The conversation grew louder and softer in cycles as Zoe paced around the garden.

As long as she stays within hearing distance.

"That was brave, earlier." Mason finished with the bandages and began packing his kit away. "Reckless and dangerous. But still brave. Thank you."

Keira chuckled as she leaned her bruised shoulders against the couch and shuffled around to face Mason. Daisy leaped onto her lap and immediately flopped over to prepare for a nap. "It's not like I can claim all the credit. You got me there."

"Ha. I sent a text message and drove a little fast. I'm not sure that's on the same level as conducting a spontaneous high-speed séance in the back of a moving van."

"You make me sound a lot cooler than I actually am."

"Mm. Hard disagree on that."

Mason's smile was warm and gentle. His gaze lingered, and Keira found it increasingly hard to look away. In her lap, Daisy stretched, all four legs reaching out and quivering before she wrapped herself back into a tight ball.

"Do you ever imagine what your life might look like once this is over?" Mason asked. He shifted, pulling one of his long legs up underneath himself. "If or when Artec is no longer a problem, I mean."

They were close enough that their knees grazed. She could feel the warmth radiating not just from the fireplace and from the now-sleeping Daisy, but from Mason as well. A reckless, dangerous thought rose: *I'd like something just like this.*

In that moment, it felt almost possible. There was an incredible amount of tenderness in his eyes. His hand, inches from hers, twitched, as though wanting to close the distance.

There was a short rush of longing, immediately broken by panic.

"I want to keep collecting cats," she said, faster and louder than she'd meant to. "Lots of cats. At least twenty."

"Oh?" His eyebrows rose. "That's ambitious."

"Yep." They were still too close, so Keira shuffled back slightly, causing Daisy to droop off her lap like a melting candle. "I already have that cross-eyed cat sweater but I'm thinking of expanding the collection. Everything I wear will have a cat on it. I'll make my entire personality about cats."

Mason was laughing now, and it was so kind and good-humored that it made her chest ache. "You have a plan at least. I'm really not sure what I'm going to do. I mean, I'm committed to this. As long as it takes. But it's hard to imagine who I'll be when it's over."

"You could finish med school," Keira said.

He shrugged lightly. "I guess I could. But I'm not sure I'd want to be away from Blighty for so long. Especially not now that I have friends here."

"We'd survive," Keira said, the panic still hot and tight in her chest.

Mason's smile vanished entirely. The look he gave her was utterly unreadable; then the muscles in his face twitched again and the smile was back in place. "Yeah. I guess so."

Keira felt as though she was suffocating. "Bathroom," she said, and rolled an unconscious Daisy onto the couch before rising and crossing her cabin in long steps.

She locked the door behind herself and turned the tap on.

I shouldn't have said that.

She dipped her face under the flowing water again and again, in a failed effort to cool the burning.

Why did I say that? Why do I always *pull away? What am I afraid of?*

Her face, dripping wet, stared back at her through the mirror. It was *her* face, and she'd grown familiar with it in her time at Blighty, but some mornings it still felt like looking at a stranger.

Her eyes were haunted. Strands of wet hair clung against skin that seemed unnaturally pallid in the harsh light.

She tried to smile at herself, but it looked unsettling, like an animal baring its teeth.

No matter how comfortable or happy she felt at Blighty, she could never overlook the fact that she had a past. A past that she couldn't remember. A past that she couldn't vouch for.

She looked down at her hands and imagined them crushing the life out of someone. She'd nearly done it once; when Gavin Kelsey had attacked her, she'd had the chance to kill him, and she'd come close to taking it. What frightened her the most was how easily the thought had come.

She didn't want to be a murderer. But that might not be her choice. Not when so much of her life was still unaccounted for.

The cottage's door creaked as Zoe returned. Faint voices came from the main room. Keira turned the tap off and sunk low over the sink, trying to build up the will to rejoin them. Then a hand knocked against the bathroom door, its raps harsh enough to rattle the wood.

"Whatever you're doing in there, speed it up," Zoe called. "I have *news*, and I think you'll want to hear it."

Keira pressed her face into the hand towel to dry it. Then she counted to ten and opened the door.

Zoe had crossed the room to lean on the kitchenette counter. Her eyes were red around the edges, and Keira thought she might have stepped out for more than just privacy to make her phone calls. Any traces of tears had been wiped away, though, and her attention was wholly focused on her phone, where she furiously tapped messages. Mason was still on the couch, his medical kit fully packed away. He had Daisy on his lap and gently, affectionately stroked around her jaw. Her whiskers quivered happily with each brush.

"Hey," he called as Keira approached. "She's a heavy sleeper, isn't she?"

He was going to act like nothing had happened. Like always. And Keira was going to go along with it. Like always.

"Sometimes I think she just pretends to sleep so that she can listen in on conversations," she said. Instead of sitting next to Mason again, she took the third seat and folded her legs up underneath herself. "What's this about news, Zo?"

"Yeah, I'm still crowdsourcing feedback," Zoe said. "But I think I have a clue about why Old Keira hoarded those clippings. Brightwater Construction has a *reputation*. Supposedly, it's used been used by a whole bunch of companies that have ties to money laundering and more."

"Old Keira was incredibly excited to launder her money," Keira said.

"Well, someone was." Zoe flashed her phone around, though Keira was too far away to read the tiny text. "The clippings only talk about the amusement park, but it's more than that. You can break it into three parts: the park, the beginnings of a town close by it, and supposedly, a major hotel built inside the park. From what people are telling me, the whole thing was shady from the start. We don't know exactly who benefits the most from it collapsing, but it's believed *someone* made a lot of money."

"It's so strange to live in a world where having a business fail can be more profitable than having one succeed," Mason said.

"Do we think Artec was behind the laundering?" Keira asked.

"Not necessarily. I've spoken to someone who lives near the failed development. Fish Face Guy." She raised a finger. "Before you accuse me of bullying, that's what he calls himself. His handle on all the niche conspiracy forums is, quite literally, Fish Face Guy. He even has an image of a weird blobby fish as his profile picture. I met him once, and you want to know the weird thing? He looks nothing like a fish. More like a horse, really. But I'm getting off track."

Mason looked pained. "Does…Mr. Guy have any helpful information?"

"Fish Face, as his friends call him, fosters many niche interests. He collects model trains. He volunteers to run book clubs at retirement communities, provided the books are about fish. And, most notably, he has a fascination with the development. He's spent some time poking around what little of the town was built. The problem starts when he tries to get into the amusement park." Zoe leaned forward. "There's a huge fence around it. The place has been abandoned for nearly two decades and yet someone is still paying for security guards to patrol the outside. Fish Face has experience sneaking into restricted areas but he's found it impossible to get inside. All of the best conspiracists agree there's something hidden there."

"They would, though." Mason gave an apologetic smile. "I don't want to sound contrarian, but they're conspiracists. It's their lifeblood. Have you ever heard a conspiracist say, 'Don't worry about that, it's just a coincidence'?"

"*It's just a coincidence* is the language of cowards." Zoe fixed him with a hard glare, her eyebrows arched high. "Anyway, this is more than a coincidence. Who locks up a half-built amusement park and hotel? Who has security guards patrolling it around the clock?"

"People who have an investment they want to preserve," Mason said. "That's exactly what they would do."

"Please. It's been empty for nearly twenty years."

He shifted forward in his chair. "When a major development fails far into construction, there's usually millions or even billions invested into the infrastructure. Selling a development like that can be difficult, but it's not impossible, and a lot of investors cling to that hope of regaining their money. Hiring a security guard or two to ensure it's not subject to arson, water damage, or graffiti can pay huge dividends if a buyer eventually comes along. And compared to the money at stake, the cost of a guard is insignificant."

Zoe drummed her fingers on the back of the couch. She spoke as briskly as ever, but Keira was sure she could detect thick emotions wavering at the edges of the words. "I need you to stop being practical for a moment and let me get swept up in the fantasy, please."

Mason hesitated for barely a second, then nodded. "Sorry. I *do* believe it's worth investigating."

"*Thank* you." Zoe rallied, her smile back in place.

"If nothing else, the fact that Keira saved those clippings makes it significant."

"Oh, so you'll take Keira's word on something but you won't believe my friend Fish Face Guy?"

Mason let the silence hang for a second. Then he said, very clearly, "Yes."

"Mm." Zoe tilted her head. "Yeah, that's fair."

"If we believe something really is being hidden there," Keira said, "what's it likely to be? And how would it be connected to Artec?"

"That's the question." Zoe sank into the chair between them. "People have been sending me their thoughts. You get the usual theories—nuclear weapon stockpile, UFOs, secret society of lizard people—but there's also a handful of more niche ideas. Jenna thinks they're breeding Loch Ness Monster clones in an indoor swimming pool, and Brian is one hundred percent certain that there's a portal to a new, slightly louder dimension contained in the basement."

Mason looked like he was suffering. "Are they all like this?"

"Oh, no, don't worry. Most of them are much, much worse."

"Great. Love it."

"The key thread is that no one's ever been inside the amusement park," Zoe said. "Or even close to it. Apparently, there's a chain-link fence that runs around the intended parking lot. It creates something like a moat that keeps anyone from getting within a hundred feet. We only know a few things for certain. Mainly, it's believed power and water are still connected."

"That's reasonable," Mason said. "Power for lights in case someone needs to search for vandals. Water for the sprinklers in case of a fire."

"I'm going to keep digging," Zoe said, ignoring Mason. "Fish Face Guy is asking around his local network too. But I think this is the path forward we've been looking for over the last three weeks."

"How far away is the development?" Keira asked.

"Nearly five hours."

She grimaced. "Not a quick trip, then."

"No." Zoe watched her phone as still more messages spilled in. "I'd have suggested we go tonight, but…"

"We suspect it's connected to Artec, and we know Artec is dangerous. Even a few days of preparation could make a huge difference," Mason said. He nodded to the clock above the fireplace. "Besides. It's late. Let's reassess tomorrow."

Keira moved her mattress to the floor so that she could sleep next to her friends. Even with the lights out, the fireplace's glow kept the cabin lit. It was strangely comforting to have company that night. As Keira'd promised, Daisy took her turn with each of them, sitting on their chests and licking their chins until she was suitably happy that they were clean. She ultimately fell asleep in the space between Keira and Zoe.

Keira didn't find sleep quite so easily. Neither did Zoe. Her friend stared blankly toward the ceiling. Zoe's phone occasionally buzzed, and she would pull it out, glance at the message, frown, and shove her phone back under her pillow.

When Keira finally fell asleep, her dreams were spotted with the sensation that she was being watched from the shadows. She woke repeatedly. Finally, when the clock above the fireplace read five and the first hint of dawn showed through the windows, Keira gave up on trying to sleep and crept out of bed.

Mason and Zoe were still asleep, Mason curled up on one side, Zoe with both arms flung overhead. Keira let them be.

She shivered as she approached the window. The fog was thick that morning, nearly drowning the sunken gravestones until they looked like ghosts themselves.

In the middle distance stood Josephine, the severe Victorian woman who'd directed Keira toward Cora Wentworth and her grave. She faced the cottage and Keira, as though waiting. Slowly, she raised one arm, a single finger pointing away, toward the darkest and coldest part of the cemetery.

"Now's kind of a bad time," Keira muttered, but she was already reaching for her jacket.

CHAPTER 10

KEIRA HUNCHED LOW IN her thick coat as she marched through the cemetery. Even with everything else happening, she couldn't ignore the spirits' requests. She'd promised them that she'd help if she could.

And they'd been waiting a long time for it. More than a hundred years in Cora Wentworth's case.

Only, she still didn't know exactly what she was going to do. Adage was reluctant to use the congregation's donations to pay for a new headstone unless there was a good reason for it. And as far as Keira understood, Cora's reason came down to resentment. She'd been buried under the correct name. She just didn't like it.

Maybe there's some kind of compromise we can find. It's not like ghosts ever get irrationally stubborn about anything. Keira chuckled at her own joke, and the laughter emerged as plumes of drifting mist, fading behind her like a steam train's trail. *Nope, never met a stubborn ghost in my life.*

The weeds grew more spindly as she trailed deeper into the space. A fresh spiderweb hung from a dead tree and gathered dew on its strands like baubles, and Keira ducked to avoid disturbing it. Blank faces stared at her from the fog as the spirits moved between the graves.

And then she reached Cora.

The woman stood exactly where Keira had last seen her, next to a stone that came up to waist height. It wasn't elaborate like Josephine Crispin's, but it was more expensive than many of the other markers around her. Her family had cared for her enough to give her a good funeral, even if her last years of life had been spent in poverty.

Dawn was still so thin that Keira could barely see any of the spirit's details against the dark, tangled forest backdrop.

"Hey," Keira said, awkwardly raising one hand as she neared Cora. "I'm back. I just need to ask a couple of things."

Cora's expression was as hard and unreadable as granite.

"The name's spelled correctly, isn't it?" She waited for a response. Cora gazed down at the headstone but gave no other response. Keira cleared her throat. "I know it's not the name you want, but there's no spelling error, is there?"

After a second, the ghost shook her head.

"Okay. Yeah." Keira hunched her shoulders high and shuffled her feet, trying to keep some warmth in them. "Were you hoping to change the surname entirely?"

This time, there was a forceful nod. Cora clasped her hands ahead of herself. The angles around her face seemed to grow harder, more urgent.

"Your maiden name was Yates," Keira said. "Was that the surname you wanted?"

A deep, eager nod.

"Did you want it changed because you dislike Phillip Wentworth? You don't want to carry his name any longer?"

Another firm nod.

"Okay." Keira rubbed at the back of her neck. Until then, she'd held some doubt that maybe she'd misunderstood the spirit's request and the name on the gravestone held more importance than simple resentment for a husband she'd fallen out of love with. It looked like her first guess had been right, surprisingly.

I really don't know what to do about this. I suppose it doesn't matter if the stone carries her legal name or not, as long as she's happy, right?

Only, Keira had no idea how to go about it. There was no kind of justification Adage could present to his congregation for updating a grave marker for someone who had been gone more than a century…especially not if the update was technically incorrect.

Keira supposed she could change the stone herself. Visitors rarely came this deep into the cemetery, and none of them would notice if an old stone was abruptly taken down and replaced.

But gravestones were expensive. Her allowance was barely covering the food she and Daisy ate; she didn't want to think about how long she'd need to save for a proper marker. And she doubted the severe, rigid Cora Wentworth would accept a hand-carved wooden cross in its place.

"Please don't take this the wrong way," Keira said. She dropped her hands to her sides helplessly. "But I'm having trouble understanding why it's so important. It's the name you had when you passed away. There shouldn't be any shame with having his surname on your grave, should there?"

Keira knew she'd crossed a line the moment the words left her mouth. The spirit ahead of her didn't move, but the mist deepened, swelling around Keira until she couldn't see anything except the sharp, glowing specter ahead and the grave between them. Frost spread out from Cora's feet, wrapping over the grass and creeping up the headstone.

She was furious.

"I just want to know if there's anything else we can do," Keira said, taking a hesitant step back. "Maybe we could have the graveyard's official records updated. Or..."

The frost had overtaken the headstone, bleeding into the deeply carved words. It was creeping closer to Keira. Cora's long gray hair whipped behind her as the gentle breeze that seemed to surround every spirit turned into a storm.

Every other ghost in that section had vanished. The fog spread, overwhelmingly heavy, until every distant shape and even the sky were blotted from sight. Keira and Cora were very much alone.

"Give me more time," Keira said, raising her hands placatingly as chills ran through her and ice crystals burned her lungs. "I know what you want now. And I get that it sounds like a simple request, but it's difficult to complete. I'm trying, though."

That wasn't enough for Cora. She was advancing toward Keira, and with each step the frost bloomed farther and the mist grew thicker. Keira felt as though she were drowning in it, as Cora's dangerously hollow eyes fixed on her.

She staggered, trying to escape the cold. The back of her heels hit an overturned headstone. Keira fell with a gasp, landing hard on the spongy ground. Pins and needles traveled through her limbs as the chill invaded her bones.

Keira had encountered angry spirits before. But there was something about the way her whole world had become swallowed up by the mist, until the only thing she could see was the rippling spirit advancing toward her, that robbed any ability to think. Cora loomed far above, seeming to swell as her anger multiplied. She stretched her long pale hands toward Keira.

She lurched to her feet and ran. Dead branches scratched her arms. She tripped again and again as the smothering fog left her blind.

A small dark shape frisked through the white void ahead of her. Daisy, awake and inexplicably outside, darted between the graves.

Keira had long since learned to put trust in her cat. She made jokes about how Daisy was secretly magic, but the truth was she'd started to believe it. Daisy, the cat that had turned up outside the cottage on the night Keira had arrived at Blighty, always seemed to find her whenever she needed help the most.

Keira clambered to her feet again. Daisy was already moving away, nearly swallowed into the swirling white. Keira followed the frisking black tail as it teased the edges of her vision. Daisy was moving fast, and Keira said a silent prayer that her shins would miss the grave markers dotting her path as she raced to keep pace.

And then, abruptly, Daisy came to a halt. Keira staggered to a stop next to her, breathing hard. Daisy's body language changed. Her eyes turned wide and dark as they fixated on something in the distance. Keira tried to follow her gaze but couldn't see what had caught her cat's focus.

"What is it?" she asked, her voice a whisper. "What can you see?"

The tip of Daisy's tail twitched. Faster than Keira had thought possible, she sprang. And landed very awkwardly as a tiny moth fluttered away from her paws.

"Oh," Keira said, slumping. Daisy continued to leap, teeth bared and paws swiping, as she fought to catch the moth. It wasn't moving fast, and yet none of Daisy's attacks brought her close to catching it.

"At least one of us is having a good time," Keira said, and chuckled. Her laughter faded as a faint sound caught her focus. She turned, staring into the thick fog. In the distance, she could barely make out the forest's edge. Tree trunks rose like an impenetrable wall. And something…

Something moved between them.

Keira's mouth turned dry. She stared, her eyes burning, willing the shape to become clear.

She'd seen deer around her cottage before. But this didn't look deer shaped. If anything, it looked like a human. A human, half-hidden between the trees, staring down at her.

"Hey, Keira!"

Zoe's voice floated through the fog. Keira flinched as she turned. The edges of her cottage were barely visible through the ocean of white.

Daisy had managed to lead her back home after all.

She looked back toward the forest. The thing she'd thought she'd seen was gone. Now there was nothing but the distant trees, their branches heavy with dew, perfectly still and silent.

"Keira!" Zoe called again.

"Coming!" Keira bent to pick up her cat, who was still battling the moth. She carried Daisy close to her chest as she ran for the open cottage door and the relative safety it offered.

CHAPTER 11

"I WORRIED WHEN I woke up and found you missing," Zoe said as Keira stepped past her and into the cottage. "Leave a girl a note, won't you?"

"Sorry, sorry, just trying to tie up some loose threads with a ghost." Keira lowered Daisy onto the floor, and the cat immediately trotted toward her food bowl, which Mason had already filled.

He was in the kitchen, preparing breakfast. Her friends must have woken up not long after she left. They were still bleary and mussed from sleep, but Zoe had already rolled up most of the bedding, and three steaming mugs sat on the table, waiting for them.

"They don't give you much of a rest, do they?" Zoe's phone pinged. She pulled it out, made a face, and put it back in her pocket. "Anything we can help with?"

Keira pulled out a chair at the table and drew one of the drinks close to herself as Mason dished out scrambled eggs and toast. Once the spectral chill invaded her bones, it was hard to get past, so she hunched around the hot mug. "Have you heard of Cora Wentworth?"

"Married to the poet?" Mason asked, taking a seat opposite her. "I have one of his collections. He was a big deal in his day."

"That's the one," Keira said. Daisy had already finished her bowl of food and leaped into Keira's lap. She held her cat with one hand as she funneled food up to her mouth with the other. "Cora's not loving her grave marker, though. She wants me to change her surname."

"Seriously?" Zoe frowned. "How long has she been waiting for this to happen?"

"Since the 1880s."

"Wow" was all Zoe said.

"Was she able to tell you why?" Mason asked. "As far as I know, she was still Wentworth at her death."

"That's what I've gathered too. My best guess is she resented her husband. She'd come from a rich family and he never earned much money. That's the only possible motive I've been able to find."

Mason raised his fork. "Small correction there—he earned a good amount of money, both from his inheritance, his writing, and the grants he won. He just lost it quickly and frequently. Mostly to heavy drinking and gambling. It's the thing he was best known for, other than his writings. He was able to examine the human condition in ways that were considered heartbreakingly beautiful, and yet he himself fell victim to some of the most common vices of the time."

"Oh." Keira raised her eyebrows. It was adding another piece to the puzzle. A wife, not just frustrated by their lack of means, but because whatever money they had vanished as quickly as it arrived. "From what I can tell, Cora resented him. Enough to want her gravestone changed. The anger must have built up over the decades they were married."

"Hm." Zoe tilted her head. "I thought they were only married for, like, two years."

"That's right," Mason said. "It was very brief."

Keira hesitated, her fork poised over her scrambled eggs. "The ghost I'm talking to is at least fifty."

They all exchanged glances. Mason frowned. "Are you sure? Cora married young—she wouldn't have been over twenty when she passed."

Keira pictured the spirit she'd been speaking to: steely-gray hair, papery creases across her delicate skin. That didn't match the description she was hearing.

"The mother," Zoe said abruptly. She threw her fork down, apparently too excited to keep eating. "I bet it's the mother. Henrietta Yates."

Keira drew a breath. "You mean—"

"When Cora Wentworth passed away, Henrietta had her daughter's remains returned to Blighty for burial. She joined the family plot. Apparently, Henrietta hated the marriage. She'd tried to stop it before it happened and tried to have it erased from the history books after her daughter's death. She saw it as a huge stain on the family reputation, I'd wager."

"I didn't know you were interested in poetry," Mason said, faint admiration in his voice.

"I'm not." Zoe waved dismissively. "Can't stand poetry. But I *am* into historical family dramas and all the skeletons they try to hide in their closets. Blighty has *loads*."

"Ah."

Keira sat back in her chair, faintly stunned. She'd thought she had an easy case this time around. Instead, she'd completely misunderstood what she was looking at.

Maybe the marriage *had* been one of love. Maybe Cora, stifled by her family's expectations, had tasted true freedom with the soulful but troubled poet. They'd lived in poverty, but it was possible Cora had continued loving her husband until both of their untimely ends.

She hadn't seen Cora's spirit in the graveyard. Only her mother's. A mother who was so bent on getting her way that she'd clung to earth after death in a mission to erase her daughter's perceived betrayal.

It didn't make the solution any simpler. Was she going to have to remove Cora's gravestone, presumably against Cora's wishes, just to appease the mother's ghost?

It might be possible to forcefully remove the spirit. But somehow that didn't seem right, either. Keira might think that Henrietta's reasons for staying were petty, but they were obviously important to the ghost. It felt like an overstep to pass judgment on someone else's feelings. Especially when a hundred years of lonely contemplation hadn't been enough to change them.

She didn't like the idea of leaving a request for help unanswered, but she was starting to feel like that might be the most likely outcome.

"Imagine getting so offended by your daughter's husband that you just refuse to die properly," Zoe said, biting the edge of her toast. "What a weird family."

Zoe's cell phone beeped again. She pulled it out, grimaced, and put it away.

"Are those updates on the abandoned development?" Keira asked.

"I wish. It's my siblings."

A wave of cold guilt fell over Keira. Zoe was so bright that morning that it had almost been possible to forget what she was going through.

"Are they messaging about the funeral arrangements?" Mason asked.

"*Every* kind of arrangement." Zoe's expression darkened. "*When's the will reading? Do I need to be in town? Can't we have her grave closer to the city? Let's change the funeral date; I have a dentist's appointment.*"

"Oh," Mason said softly.

Keira hesitated, then said, "You were living with her at the end. You get to make the choices. In your own time. If you need anyone to run interference for you..."

"Thanks." Zoe's smile was thin. "They're at least somewhat right, though. I need to figure stuff out. And quickly."

"Everyone's timeline is different. It's fine and even normal to wait a week or more to finalize funeral arrangements," Mason said. "And when you're ready, you'll have us to help."

Zoe stabbed her fork into the remains of her breakfast. "Kind of wish we could just go back to talking about the ghosts. They're way less scary than irritable siblings."

Her phone's ringtone began playing. Zoe looked ready to throw it across the room. "I told them not to call—"

She saw the number displayed, and her face went blank. Wordlessly, she stood, turned away, and answered the call.

Keira and Mason exchanged a look. Zoe's words were low and careful. "Yes. I am. Yes. Okay… Okay. Okay. I'll do that."

The call ended. Zoe stood there for a long moment, staring down at her phone. Then she said, her voice choked, "That was Artec. Or…whatever funeral home name they were operating under. They said there was an issue with the contract and they can't fulfill the agreement. They said they're going to return my mother's remains to Blighty's local funeral parlor and I need to make arrangements elsewhere."

Mason, his arm draped over the back of his chair, watched Zoe sadly. "They must have realized they couldn't use her in their cemetery."

"Apparently."

"It's good news, isn't it?" He leaned forward a fraction. "You wanted to have her buried here, at Blighty. I think she would like that."

"Yeah. She would." Zoe finally lowered the phone. She turned back to them. She didn't look relieved. She didn't even look sad.

She looked furious.

"I want to end these people," she said, her voice hoarse from the emotions choking her. "I want to burn their buildings to the ground. I want to erase their names from history. I want to watch them boil alive."

"Oh" was all Mason could manage.

"We saved my mum," Zoe said, her knuckles turning white around her phone. "We got her out of their grasp, and I'm never going to stop being grateful for that. But you know what I couldn't stop thinking about all last night? Everyone else's mums who never got rescued. Or their dads. Or siblings. Or—or *anyone*."

"Yeah," Keira said softly. On her worst nights, she dreamed of the twisted cemetery. Rows and rows of faces, screaming, howling, begging for mercy. They had been people once. No different from the people she passed in Blighty's streets.

No one deserved what had been done to them.

"We saved my mum, but it doesn't stop what they're doing." Zoe blinked at angry tears. "More souls are being carted in there every single day. I can't—I can't just sit here and build diagrams and map out plans and *think* about it for even another day."

Mason's breath was unsteady. He glanced at Keira, watching for her approval. She gave a small nod.

"Okay," he said. "I know I've been holding us back. I know I play things cautiously. But…I also understand what you're saying. Let's go to the abandoned development."

"I want to go today," Zoe said.

Again, Mason glanced at Keira. Again, she nodded.

"Then let's go today," he said.

CHAPTER 12

THEY PACKED UP QUICKLY. The drive to the abandoned amusement park would take five hours. Factoring in stops, they'd be working with limited daylight hours once they arrived.

"We'll go today," Mason said, watching Zoe. "But I want to make sure we're also prepared."

"Yeah, obviously." A vicious, bitter smile formed as she shoved her sleeping bag back into its case. "We'll need weapons. And something for a distraction. Most of those things we can get at my house, but some we'll need to pick up at the general store too."

Movement flickered in her peripheral vision, and Keira found her eyes drawn to the window. A ghostly pale face stared out of the fog at her. One of her spirits, wandering close to the cottage. They very rarely passed the stone fence that formed the edge of the garden. It seemed to be something like a sign of respect, in the same way Keira avoided walking on their graves. This one was nearly at the window, though.

"One of my ghosts is visiting," Keira said, bundling spare clothes into a backpack in case they needed to overnight at their destination. "I'll check what he wants before we leave."

Zoe glanced toward the window. A choked scream escaped her.

"I can see it," Zoe yelled, pointing. "The ghost! I can see it!"

"What?" Mason stared at the window, shocked, then his shoulders dropped as he began laughing. "Oh. No. That's not a ghost. It's just Harry."

Keira stared out at the pallid face. It stared back. Mason was right; she was looking at the florist's sullen son.

He came to the door when she opened it and slowly shambled in. Droplets of condensed mist clung to his flat black hair. Heavy smears of dark liner ran around his eyes, accenting them. He didn't smile, but he did raise one hand in a morose wave. "It's awful weather out," he said. "Which is nice."

"Sorry, Harry," Keira said, kicking the door closed behind them. "I thought you were a ghost."

"I'll cherish that knowledge for the remainder of my life." His voice held no inflection, and when he gazed at the gear they were gathering in a pile in the room's center, there was no sign of curiosity in his features. "My mother sent me to invite you to lunch, but I can tell her you're busy." He paused, then added, "*Please* let me tell her you're busy."

"We actually are," Keira said. "We'll be gone for the rest of today. Maybe tomorrow too." She didn't add the final part: *maybe forever, depending on how badly things go.* "But thank her for us. Lunch sounds lovely."

"It really doesn't," he said. Daisy wove around his legs, and Harry bent, his hand outstretched, to let her rub against it. "I heard you say something when I was outside your window. You said you needed a distraction."

"Ah." Keira worked her jaw. Harry knew about her gift with ghosts—inadvertently—but she hadn't told him about the organization hunting her. She was trying to keep that as close to her chest as possible. Whispers reaching the wrong ears could have disastrous consequences.

"We need to break into an abandoned location," she said, opting to give him an abridged version of the truth. "It's dangerous, and there are guards. We're trying to figure out a way around them."

"I can be your distraction," he said. "I can start a large fire."

Keira, Zoe, and Mason all exchanged a glance.

"I can start *multiple* large fires," Harry added, as though that would sell them on the idea.

"That's an incredible offer," Mason said with something very near sincerity. "But we can't accept. When we said this was dangerous, we meant *actually* very, legitimately dangerous. We're not talking about jail time. We're talking about injury or even death."

For the first time, Harry looked intrigued. It was a subtle shift—a very slight brightening of his eyes—but he was so un-emotive normally that it was impossible to miss. "Let me come," he said, his voice as empty as always. "I am willing and prepared to beg if necessary."

Zoe laughed even as Mason shook his head. "Your mother would never forgive us," he said.

"She said she'd never forgive me when I dyed my hair black," he responded. "And yet, it turns out she forgives easily."

Before Mason could say anything else, Zoe grabbed his arm and beckoned for Keira to follow. "Private conference," she said. "Quick."

There wasn't much privacy to be had in the tiny cottage. They ended up huddled in the room's opposite corner, no more than six feet from Harry, who watched with mild curiosity as they talked in rushed, hushed tones.

"You're not seriously considering—" Mason started.

"Listen. We got in trouble last time because we didn't have a getaway driver. I'm not suggesting he goes into the development with us. But I'm suggesting it would be smart to have someone on the outside to watch the car and pick us up if we need to make a quick escape."

"I could watch the car," Harry agreed from across the room. "I have no experience but it feels like the type of thing I would be good at."

"Hey." Zoe glared at him. "This is a secret meeting. Pretend you can't hear us."

He obediently turned away.

"I thought he couldn't drive," Keira whispered, keeping her voice as low as possible.

Zoe shrugged. "He doesn't have a license. But I'm pretty sure he knows enough to coast down a street or two if necessary."

Mason rubbed his jaw. "I don't think it's fair to involve Harry. He doesn't know what we're doing. Or why. I'm not even convinced he actually understands how serious the risks are."

"It's a forgotten amusement park in the middle of a forgotten development," Zoe said. "We don't know what connection it has to Artec, if it even has one. As long as he doesn't actually try to break in, anyone who sees him will assume he's no different from Fish Face Guy: someone with a casual interest in abandoned locations. And Fish Face Guy has gone poking around that development dozens of times without any issues."

"Who's Fish Face Guy?" Harry asked.

"Seriously," Zoe said, turning on him. "Private meeting! Zip it!"

Mason chewed his lip as he thought through what Zoe had said. "It's hurting me to admit this...but you have a point." He glanced at Keira. "How are you feeling about it?"

She looked at Harry. He stared at the opposite wall, appearing bored. "You've both seen how bad it can get. You've seen the guns and the tasers; you've had to climb walls and run. When you offer to help, I know you're prepared for what that means. It feels different to bring an outsider into it...especially when they don't have that experience."

"But...?" Zoe prompted, eyebrow raised.

Keira sighed. "But we need help. As much of it as we can get. Especially if this is five hours from Blighty. Having someone just a couple of minutes away who can bring us a car or call the police would be invaluable."

"Yeah," Mason said. "Okay. But let's at least visit his mother first.

Polly loves him more than anything in the world. Even if we can't give her the details, she should at least know where he's going."

"Agreed," Keira said.

They turned back to Harry. He shuffled around to face them, his shoulders slumped and arms limp at his sides. "Can I go on the death mission now?" he asked.

"Yeah," Keira said. "Welcome to the death mission."

She almost—almost—believed she saw the corners of his mouth twitch up.

"And can I light multiple large fires when we get there?"

"That's a negative." Keira clapped her hands. "Let's go."

CHAPTER 13

IT TURNED OUT TO be surprisingly easy to get Polly Kennard's permission. They piled into the florist's, surrounded by intensely fragrant bouquets and racks of gift cards, and faced the shrewd, pince-nez-wearing woman behind the counter. She was decked out in so many floral prints that she almost vanished into her stock as she cut ribbons.

"I am leaving on a journey, Mother," Harry said at the head of the group. "I may not return."

Polly blinked once; then her expression transformed into one of delight. "You've been invited on a camping trip!"

"Uh…" Keira and Mason said in tandem.

Polly wasn't listening, though. She clapped both hands together. "Yes, yes, go! Go and socialize! It's been *weeks* since you've spent any time around another person your age. Oh, this will be so good for you…"

Harry was already slouching his way to the store's exit.

Mason leaned forward, his voice low and serious. "We'll do our best to look after him, but—"

"Oh, I don't care about that. My boy got invited on a camping trip! I'm just happy to see him get out of the house. Keira, dear, will you be there?"

"Oh, uh, yeah."

"*Excellent.*" Polly beamed as she placed a little too much emphasis on the word. "It's not unheard of for sparks to fly on a trip. And once Harry figures out how to access his rugged outdoorsy personality…"

"Yeah, great," Keira said, fighting off the bunches of flowers Polly was trying to push toward her, as well as the unwanted mental image of Harry in a beard and a flannel shirt. "We'll see you tomorrow. Hopefully."

Polly either didn't catch the ominous note to the farewell or didn't care. She was still beaming and waving at them through the window as they piled into Mason's car.

Keira ran through her mental checklist. She'd asked Adage to keep an eye on Daisy when she left the cottage. The car's trunk was full of supplies from the general store.

"We need a few things from my house," Zoe said, obviously processing a very similar list. "Then we're good to go."

"Hooray," Harry said dully. When they looked at him, he said, "My mother wants me to try more positivity."

"It's not working, buddy," Zoe said gently.

"Good."

Mason navigated the roads through Blighty and pulled up outside Zoe's house. A soft, sad tenderness crossed her features as she looked up at it. She was probably seeing a thousand memories with her mother, Keira knew. The house had to be saturated in them, from the curtains to the welcome mat to the flowers lovingly planted around the driveway.

Then Zoe squared her shoulders and unbuckled her seat belt to get out of the car. Keira hesitated, worried that she'd be intruding on something private if she followed, only to be fixed by a sharp look from Zoe through the passenger window. "Come on. You may as well see my room. It's in the basement."

The house wasn't large, but it had been made comfortable with decades of care. Handmade crafts hung from the walls—some seemingly done by Kim, others by her children. Zoe paused in the hallway.

"The house feels weird when it's this empty," she said, then shook herself slightly and turned toward a door. "This way."

The basement felt worlds apart from the warm tones and cozy atmosphere of the house's main parts. Dark concrete stairs led downward, lit only by a single overhead bulb. Keira strained to see what was ahead of them, but it was only when Zoe flicked on multiple switches, turning on rows and rows of string lights draped around the place, that she could see her friend's room.

"Wow," she said, and she meant it.

The basement had been turned into an open-plan living and work area. Rugs, a riot of color and unmatched styles, were strewn across the concrete floor. Zoe's bed was pushed into one corner, unmade. One wall was taken up by a computer system with no fewer than six monitors and two keyboards. Each screen bore something different: maps, scrolling numbers that appeared to belong to the stock market, and a dozen stacked windows filled with images and phrases in foreign languages.

Zoe's passions didn't stop at her computer screens. Mismatched bookshelves were stuffed so full of binders and folders that they looked ready to collapse from the weight. Corkboards were strung haphazardly across the walls. They were covered in a riot of posters, maps, images, and scraps of paper, all crisscrossed with hundreds of feet of red string. It surrounded the room in something that felt like a massive web.

The space was so intensely, quintessentially Zoe that Keira almost had to laugh.

"I haven't been down here since we were assigned a school project together back when we were kids," Mason said, a hint of fondness in his voice. He tilted his head back to admire the decorations spanning around them. "There are fewer dead things, which is nice."

"Yeah, I was kind of into taxidermy back then," Zoe admitted. She crouched by her desk and began pulling crates of equipment out. "Turns out trying your hand at taxidermy and being eight years old with no proper tools or training are not the best combination. We only need a couple of things from here. Short wave radios to start—ah, got 'em."

Mason accepted an empty crate, which Zoe dumped her gear

into, including something that looked like a hard drive with several cables spilling out of its side and a tiny screen.

"I got this from a friend in Tasmania," she said, pointing at it with evident pride. "It's supposed to override any security system. Allegedly. I haven't actually tested it out yet."

"There's no time like now, I suppose," Mason managed.

"I wish I'd splurged on those night vision goggles from the flea market," Zoe muttered, sifting through piles of cables. "Most of my work happens at a computer, so I didn't really think I'd need them."

"I'm impressed," Keira admitted. "I knew you kept busy, but I didn't think it was this extensive."

"And I'm impressed a grocery store salary can support all of this," Mason added.

"Some people keep tropical fish for a hobby," Zoe said, grinning. "I track the bear-people's secret hideouts. Turns out the budget for both of them is surprisingly similar."

Zoe had promised she only needed a few things, but the crate was nearly full when they left. She backed out of the house's front door, closing and locking it in her wake, only to freeze as a voice came from behind them.

"Looks like I found you at last."

Keira turned, her muscles tight, ready to bolt.

I knew it. Someone's been following us. I shouldn't have ignored it—

The thought cut off as she faced the stranger at the end of the driveway. He didn't look like he was a part of Artec. He would have only been a few years older than Keira, but he wore an impeccably tailored suit. One hand rested in a pocket while the other hung casually free. Sleek, expensive glasses were pushed high on his nose, and a luxury black sedan was parked on the street next to Mason's own car.

"Hey, Tyler," Zoe said with a grimace, and the pieces fell into place.

Now that she knew what to look for, Keira could see the family resemblance: Tyler's jawline was sharper and more defined, but he had the same expressive eyebrows and the same glossy dark hair. While Zoe left hers in a chaotic short cut, Tyler's was styled so perfectly that Keira suspected he was on a best friend basis with his barber.

A small smile flickered, but it didn't reach his eyes. "You haven't been answering my texts."

"There's been a lot going on." Zoe finished locking the door and put the keys in her pocket. She didn't invite Tyler in. "Give me some time to breathe, and I'll send you the details once I figure them out."

"I was passing through town on the way to prepare a client for deposition," Tyler said, the cold smile unflinching. "I thought it might be wise to check in and make sure a schedule's being set."

Mason took a half step forward. His smile was warmer than Tyler's, but his tone was just as firm. "I'm sure she's grateful for your help, but she's already been very clear that you should wait for her update."

Tyler hesitated. His eyes skimmed over Mason—tidy and well-dressed—and then Keira, wearing a badly stitched Christmas sweater even though it was nowhere near Christmas, and finally Harry, who was decked out entirely in black clothes and wore more makeup than the rest of the street combined. His mouth twisted a fraction.

"Look." Tyler sighed, ignoring Mason and speaking to Zoe. "You've got your little hobbies and your oddball friends and that's…fine. But the rest of us are juggling tight schedules. We can't just take time off. Not even for a funeral. Maybe we should ask Ali to handle it; she could organize the service in Cheltenham. It's closer to the rest of us, and I know we'd all appreciate less travel time—"

Color spread over Zoe's cheeks. She hefted the crate as she pushed past him. "We're having the service here, at the church Mum went to every week, with the friends she spoke to every day. I'll send you the details when I know them. I very much hope you can find time in your packed schedule to make it."

"Hey, Zo!" Tyler called, hands spread in frustration as Zoe marched to the car, Keira, Mason, and Harry striding beside her. She didn't stop to reply.

"That's your lawyer brother, huh?" Mason said as they opened the car doors. "From the way you talked about him, I was expecting someone more professional." He spoke just barely loud enough for Tyler to hear.

They were rewarded with an exaggerated sigh from Tyler and a small pleased smile from Zoe. They bundled into the car without looking back, and Mason pulled out, skirting around the expensive black sedan Tyler had arrived in.

"Are we all ready to go?" Mason asked, glancing at Zoe in the rearview mirror.

"Yes," she answered without hesitation. "Yes, I am so ready to get out of here."

CHAPTER 14

THE ROAD VANISHED UNDER them as they left Blighty. Zoe slumped back in her seat, her eyes closed. Harry, who had been silent through the whole encounter, finally said, “You don’t like your brother.” His voice was so monotone, it was impossible to know if he was asking a question or stating a fact.

“He’s…fine.” Zoe squirmed before settling into a shrug. “He’s under a lot of stress. You could say the same for all of them. Overachieving nightmares that they are.”

Keira, sitting in the front seat, tuned to see Zoe better. “Sounds complicated.”

“It always is. I almost don’t know them these days. And I never see them except at Christmas.” Her voice dropped. “Mum never saw them except at Christmas.”

“Tyler was still in town when I was younger, but I didn’t recognize him at all,” Mason said.

“It wasn’t always like this. I liked them all best when we were kids, back when we built sandcastles together and chased each other with gross bugs we found in the garden. But now Tyler is a wunderkind at some big legal firm in the city, and Ali is halfway to being a surgeon, and Andy is gunning to become CEO at a bank, and…I continue to be the only underachiever in the family, working at a convenience store by day and pinning photos of Bigfoot onto my wall by night."

Mason was silent for a moment, chewing that over, then took a deep breath. "We all have different measures for a successful life. For some people, it's earning a lot of money. Or becoming famous. Or owning a lot of homes and cars. But you were with your mother on the afternoon she passed away. And you were with her every day leading up to that, even if your relationship wasn't always the smoothest. You were there for her. And a lot of people would consider that a life well spent."

Zoe stared out the car's window. She was quiet for so long that Keira began to imagine she wasn't going to answer, and then she said, "Thanks, Mason."

"You know I'm on your team," he said.

She smiled faintly. "I'm still not going to stop calling you a nerd, though."

"I think I'd be heartbroken if you did."

"Nerd."

They chuckled. Keira found herself relaxing back in her seat.

Mason was good at that. At putting people at ease, and smoothing over discomforts, and seeing the best in people who might not always show it. Just like with the moment they'd shared the previous night. The moment that Keira had ruined. She clenched her hands in her lap. Words bubbled up inside of her. *I like you. I like you a lot. I want to hold you sometimes, and I don't think I'd want to let go.*

But it was like there was an invisible band in her throat, choking the thoughts before they could be spoken. She turned toward her window so that she wouldn't have to see Mason's clean jawline or strong nose or kind eyes any longer.

Misting rain set in as they drifted farther from Blighty, and it gradually thickened the more they drove. The rhythmic thud of the wipers became a strangely comforting sound. Car lights blurred around them, sparkling off the wet roads.

This is really happening, Keira realized as they moved through the twisting freeways. *After all the talks and all the planning, we're actually doing something.*

It was terrifying. She still felt so unprepared. They didn't know what the abandoned development might hold for them, or if it even held anything. A dead end. Certain death. Or anything in between.

They stopped briefly for lunch in a small town. Even just running back to the car was enough to leave water dripping from Keira's hair. They turned the heater up high and watched as condensation fogged the corners of windows.

"Less than an hour to go," Zoe said. She'd been scrolling through her phone intently, and her eyes had turned bright. "Fish Face Guy just sent me a dossier of info, and his timing couldn't be better."

"Yeah?" Keira glanced back at her. "Anything good in there?"

"Well, he's asked for a monument, but that's nothing new."

Mason squinted. "He asked for a…?"

"Oh, yeah, it's kind of a whole thing for him. He wants a monument. I'm not really sure why, but every time he helps someone on the forum he says they can pay him back with a monument."

"That sounds very reasonable," Mason said, his voice dry.

"That's not the exciting part, though," Zoe said, tapping her phone. "He's gotten us the whole history of this place. Let me see if I can summarize. Remember how the newspaper clippings were about an amusement park?"

"Yeah," Keira said.

"Right. Everything starts there. It was planned to be huge and act as a multiday event for families, using a very popular brand as its draw. The thing with amusement parks, though, is that they cost an incredible amount and take up an incredible amount of space. Developers often look for cheap land parcels in remote areas to not go over budget. And that's exactly what our subject, Five Suns Amazement Park, did. An attraction of this size wouldn't be relying on foot traffic to support it. It was banking on national and international tourists coming exclusively to experience what it offered."

"Having it somewhere remote probably saves on local council complaints too," Mason said. "I'm sure no one wants to live in a quiet town only to have a theme park open right behind them."

"Bingo. And Five Suns was going to be a big deal. The council was talking about putting in an airport for tourists. A luxury hotel was being built on premises with plans for others not far outside. And, well, at a certain point the plans started leapfrogging prudence. The local council sold parcels of land around the park for developments. Some were commercial, but lots were going to be residential. A mall was planned. This was spiraling from being just a theme park and was quickly becoming a mini-city centered around the anticipated tourism."

"But…" Keira prompted.

"*But*," Zoe replied, with emphasis, "it turned out the negotiations for the IP hadn't been finalized. Investors, contractors, and the local council were all told the papers were as good as signed, but the truth was anything but. Negotiations stretched out for years. Allegedly, neither side could reach a compromise. That didn't stop the construction on the park, though. Buildings went up; paths were paved; rides—the ones that didn't require the IP—were built. From what I'm told, the park was closing in on eighty percent finished when the agreement fell apart."

Mason whistled. "You'd think, with so much money already spent, the park would have found some way to make the deal work."

"This is hearsay stacked on hearsay," Zoe said. "But some people involved in the construction believe the park never wanted to use the IP at all."

Keira frowned. "Explain that."

"Licensing rights are expensive. Unless a theme park owns them outright—like a movie studio building a park based around the films they make—the annual fees can be huge. But Five Suns guessed, probably correctly, that it would only get the major investors if it had a major brand backing it. The rumors claim that Five Suns deliberately waited until late in the process, and even built rides that weren't attached to the IP, before canceling the deal. The theory was that investors would feel it was too late to withdraw their funding at that point, and Five Suns could have its park without paying for an expensive license."

"I sense some hubris on the horizon," Keira said, grinning.

"Impeccably correct. The project had already gone over budget. When investors heard the beloved and famous property that had lured them in was no longer attached, they began to back out. First one, then another, then an avalanche of them, until Five Suns had no funding left. Five Suns tried to find other investors to complete the park, but it was already earning a reputation as a failure that threatened to drag down anyone involved, and no one wanted to touch it."

"So it was never finished?" Mason asked.

"No. The park stalled at about eighty percent complete when Five Suns could no longer pay the contractors. It tried to claim—to the local mayor, to the press, to anyone who would listen—that it was a temporary setback until they could get the final infusion of funding, but most people realized that was never coming. The shopping mall pulled out first, even though they'd already laid their foundation. The airport was canceled next. And finally, the suburban development was put on hold, even though more than a hundred houses were complete and some people actually lived there."

"Ouch," Mason said.

"Ouch indeed. Imagine buying a house next to an amusement park, with the promise of a bustling large town and all the amenities and investment opportunities that comes with it, only for everything to be abandoned shortly after you move in."

"It sounds nice," Harry murmured.

He'd been so quiet that it had been possible to forget he was there. Keira craned her neck to see him through the rearview mirror. "Yeah?"

"Decay is underrated" was all he said.

"Do people still live there?" Keira asked Zoe.

"Apparently. Every few years someone on the council comes up with new ideas to revive the area, but none of them have gone anywhere."

"I'm amazed I haven't heard of it before," Mason said.

"Yeah, I was going to say the same," Keira added, "except my memory can be measured in weeks, so it's less of a surprise in my case."

"Eh." Zoe shrugged, her hands up by her shoulders. "The whole thing collapsed before any of us were even born. I'm sure it was a big deal in its day, but except for rare and increasingly improbable rumors that it might be revived, most people don't remember it anymore."

"We should work out a plan," Mason said. "Considering the clippings Keira saved were for both the park and the development surrounding it, we actually have a huge amount of ground to cover."

"Agreed," Zoe said. "We need a plan, and therefore the plan is to let Keira loose and follow wherever she wants to wander. Like a supernatural sniffer dog, except for sinister locations with dark secrets."

"Uh…" Keira smiled, but she was pretty sure it came out looking like a grimace. "While I'm fully on board with the comparison, you have too much faith in me. I was able to lead us last time because past me had spent a lot of time in the area. I can't promise the same for anything here."

"Sorry," Zoe said, and reached forward to squeeze her shoulder. "You're right, that's a stupid amount of pressure to put on someone. Let's build a plan B."

"I vote we start with the suburbs surrounding the park," Mason said. "And work our way inward. The suburbs sound like the least risky area to begin but might still give us clues about what we're looking for. If Keira gets some insights she wants to follow, we'll go with her, but otherwise we'll cross the area methodically."

"Predictably boring and predictably safe." Zoe sighed. "Sure, let's do that."

"Yes, let's," Harry said flatly.

The other three occupants of the car sent him a shrewd glance.

"Hooray, team," he offered.

"The plan involves you staying with the car," Mason said. "Where, I hope, nothing deadly can befall you. Okay?"

"Disappointments shouldn't surprise me after all this time, and yet this happens" was all Harry said. Keira guessed that was the closest they were going to get to an agreement.

"We should be coming up on it soon," Zoe said, watching her phone. The land they'd been driving through had been nothing but hilly countryside for the last hour. "Take the next left."

The turn looked nondescript: a simple two-lane road weaving off the main path and seemingly into nothing. As they crested the hill, though, an unexpected scene spread out below them.

They'd arrived at their ghost town.

CHAPTER 15

THE LAND, WHICH HAD been nothing but green grass and shrubby trees, was transformed inside the valley. Streets wove through the landscape. Not just rural streets, either, but suburban roads with curbs and drains and sidewalks.

There were no houses, though.

Keira's stomach curled as she stared down at the grid-like mesh of roads, designed to provide accommodation for thousands of people but left utterly barren. It was almost possible to see where the buildings had been intended to go, but there were no driveways, no letterboxes, nothing except blocks of overgrown, weedy ground surrounded by faded asphalt roads.

That afternoon, there was very little sun to brighten the development. The rain had eased, but the air was heavy with moisture and low clouds gave the sense of perpetual twilight.

The street they were on would funnel them straight into that surreal maze. In the far distance, Keira thought she could make out the form of something larger. *Five Suns Amazement Park?* The air was too thick with condensation to be sure.

"There are homes over there," Zoe said, a hint of reverence in her voice. "The few that were built before the whole thing collapsed."

Keira craned to see to their right. A cluster of small suburban houses ran along two streets. There were no more than thirty of them. Some were simply outdated, with cracked driveways and plants that clung to tenuous life. Others seemed purely neglected: broken windows covered with cardboard and bare earth lawns.

"What do we think?" Mason asked, holding the car at a slow pace as they crept into the valley. "Start with the houses? I can see a few cars. There might be people who can tell us more about the park."

"I'm on board with that," Keira said. She wasn't sure she wanted to speak to the people living in the struggling forgotten subdivision. It looked like a grim, cold place, and gooseflesh rose over her arms. But it might be their best chance to get more information about what had happened there.

Mason turned down toward the houses. They'd been built closest to the town's entrance. The developers must have gotten the streets, water, and power installed in bulk but intended to build the houses in groups. From the looks of it, they'd never gotten past the first batch.

Everywhere Keira looked, there were hints of what could have been if the development's story had taken a better direction. The houses were uniform and modern in contrast to the buildings in Blighty, but the yard sizes felt almost uncomfortably small compared to the amount of space spreading around them. Tight fences carefully contained a dream of suburbia. Many letterboxes were leaning. Sickly trees had been planted along the unused sidewalk.

In a different universe, this would have flourished into a comfortable but inexpensive neighborhood. The streets would have been places for kids to practice roller skating and to ride bikes. The backyards would have been filled with washing lines and trampolines, and the small garden beds around the houses' fronts would have been bright with flowers.

Instead, the whole space felt on the verge of death.

Mason parked at the start of the occupied street. As the four friends climbed out of the car, they surveyed their prospects.

The first two houses along that stretch were both clearly abandoned. One even had a foreclosure notice taped to its front door, though it had been there for so long the ink had faded and the paper had crinkled.

They walked past those buildings. The ground was dry and dusty, despite the spitting rain, and the grassless yards felt inhospitable to any kind of life.

The third house held someone. A pinched, narrow face stared at them from behind a window. Mason smiled and raised a hand in greeting only for the figure to draw their curtains with such force that Keira swore she could hear the rattle of the metal rings even from their distance.

"Maybe not that one," Mason whispered, and Keira hunched against the uneasy chill that had settled over her.

As they kept moving, more and more of the houses appeared empty. In some cases, vestiges of their former owners' lives remained: hoses draped like enormous snakes across the dead yards, ladders leaned against the walls, and empty planter pots stacked about, like a tribute to someone's forgotten dreams. Each time they tried to approach one of those buildings, though, they were faced with dark windows and empty rooms beyond.

Zoe gasped and grabbed for Keira's sleeve. A door creaked behind them. On the other side of the road, a woman emerged from her home, carrying a bag of garbage for her bin.

Mason was the most professional looking and the most engaging. Keira let him take the lead as they crossed the road.

"Good afternoon!" Mason called, and the woman looked up, her gaze piercing. Mason, undeterred, stopped politely on the sidewalk. "I'm so sorry to bother you, but we were hoping to talk to someone who knows the area."

"You don't look like reporters," the woman said, her sharp eyes darting over them. She assessed Keira's Christmas sweater and Harry's long, black hair in a fraction of a second. "You ghost-town tourists?"

Her voice was husky. Her pose remained wary, the garbage bag clutched close as though to create a barrier between them.

Mason hedged his bets. "Not really. We were just curious about this area in particular. I don't want to take up any of your time, but I'd be immensely grateful if we could ask you some questions."

"Ha." The woman's face remained cold. "You've got a silver tongue. Nobody but reporters and thrill seekers come through anymore. And the thrill seekers have blogs, and those blogs send more thrill seekers here. I'm tired of it. I'm not going to be on your show, whatever it is."

"No shows." Keira, sensing their opportunity was on the verge of slipping away, stepped forward. "We don't have any cameras or blogs."

"I have a blog," Zoe whispered, and Keira tried to subtly shush her.

"I'm sure you're tired of curious people treating your home like a tourist attraction," she said, "but we're not going to do that. We have personal reasons for wanting to be here."

The woman's eyes narrowed a fraction as she regarded Keira. She didn't speak, but she wasn't yet retreating. Keira pushed her luck.

"I think I have a connection to here," she said, choosing her words carefully. "I...I lost some of my memories. And I'm trying to fill in those gaps. I think this place is significant somehow. I just don't know why."

"That's the weirdest excuse I've heard yet." The woman squinted, then looked up at the darkly rolling clouds above. She sighed and placed the garbage bag on the ground. "I can give you two minutes. No more. What're your questions?"

Thank you. Keira clasped her hands. She was aware of their limited time, but she still opted for a safe opening, afraid that any of the harder queries might make the woman lock them out again. "How many people live here?"

"Me and eight other families now," she said. "Used to be more. People drop away as the promises fail. This was meant to be a nice place. The artwork showed parks for our kids, a pond. None of it ever happened. The people who don't leave are the ones who can't."

"I'm sorry," Keira said. "It's because of the amusement park, isn't it? The construction failed."

"Yep. I bought in—we all did—before the park was done. The houses were cheap, and we thought it would be easy to get a job with all the people that were going to be coming to the area. Then the park shut down before it ever opened. Sheer malice on their part, ruining lives like it didn't even matter to them. I suppose it didn't."

Keira frowned. "Malice? I heard the park shut because the IP agreement fell through."

"Oh, it fell through all right. They made sure it did." The woman turned aside and spat on the ground. "They were supposed to be partnering with a big brand. It was popular back then. Not so much now. And the brand was keen to make it happen. Every demand the park made, the brand eventually agreed to. But the park's owners just kept asking for more, and more, and more, until they sank their project."

"Because it would have been cheaper to run a park without the licensing deal," Keira said, remembering what Zoe had told her.

The woman's gaze was steely. "No. Because they never wanted to open the park at all."

Keira and Zoe shared a look. "But I thought—"

"*The deal fell through* is the pretty lie they presented to the world, but the whole thing was rotten from the start. They knew the investors would pull out if the brand canceled. And they did nothing to prevent it. There's only one possible reason for that: they wanted the park to fail. The whole thing was dead before they even broke ground."

"Huh." Keira frowned, trying to absorb this new information. "Why, though? It makes no sense."

"No, it doesn't." The woman spat again. "I'm sure they have their reasons. Tax write-offs. Money laundering. Whatever caused this whole abomination, I don't care. They got what they wanted, and everyone else is left to scramble for crumbs."

Keira gazed along the street and at all of the houses left to slowly decay as the elements ate away at them.

"It's why people say the place is cursed," the woman finished.

Harry shifted forward a fraction. "I like curses," he said simply.

The woman stared at him for a second, then broke into short cracked laughter. "You'll love this place. I never believed in cursed land until I moved here. Nothing grows right. Animals don't like hanging around. People don't feel comfortable here."

Keira sensed she was close to something. The uneasy prickling she'd felt since entering the town's border was growing stronger. "Does anyone know what caused the curse?"

The woman sighed. She looked like she was close to being done. "There's an old story that the park developers dug up an entire graveyard and built their foundations over that land."

Keira took another half step forward. "Really?"

She snorted. "If you want to believe it. I don't. Why would there be an ancient graveyard all the way out here? Before the park, no one's been settled here for as long as anyone remembers. But that's the story if you want some extra morbid details to add to your blog."

"No blogs," Keira promised. "But I'm curious about why people would come up with that idea. Does anyone in the development claim to see ghosts or…?"

"I gave you two minutes, and we're well past that," she said, bending and picking up her bag. "I'm done."

Keira bit her lip. She felt like she was on the edge of something important, but the woman turned her back to them as she dumped the bag into her bin and then retreated to the house.

"She didn't like that," Zoe whispered. "The talk about ghosts. I wonder why."

Yes. Keira turned back to the street. The prickling on her skin was strong enough to make her shiver. Until then, she'd discounted it as discomfort from the spitting rain and grim surroundings, but now she could finally recognize it for what it was. The memory of death.

She reached for her second sight. The veil lifted.

Spirits stood about the street, staring at her with hollow, dead eyes.

"Oh," Keira whispered.

Mason watched her closely. "What is it?"

"Ghosts." Another shiver wracked her. "Hundreds of them."

CHAPTER 16

SPECTERS STOOD IN THE lawns. In the street. On the sidewalk, just paces away. Their forms were pale and washed out. Their clothes and hair rocked in an invisible current. Cold radiated from them, dampening the weather and sending chills through Keira.

When she looked toward the empty houses, she could even see the flickering spirits inside the windows. None of them moved. They just stood there, staring at her.

Keira raised a tentative hand in greeting toward the nearest cluster. There was no response. Not even a twitch of recognition in their faces. Compared to the ghosts she'd met before, they were uncannily static.

And that wasn't the only part of them she found unsettling.

"That woman was right." Keira's voice caught. "This doesn't make any sense."

Mason kept his voice soft so that no one would overhear them. "What's wrong?"

"These aren't the dead from some ancient, forgotten graveyard." She saw modern haircuts. Jeans. Sundresses. "They're all recent dead. From the last few decades. I can't see any that would be more than forty years old."

Zoe pressed a hand over her mouth, frowning. "I guess that answers our core question," she muttered. "This has got to be related to Artec. It's too much of a coincidence otherwise."

"Normally I'd bring up that thing about conspiracists never believing in coincidences," Mason said, "but in this case I think you're right."

Harry made a very faint, slightly pleased noise in the back of his throat. Keira turned to him. He didn't smile, but he sounded almost content as he said, "A ghost town with real ghosts. I've been looking for one my whole life."

"Hey, yeah, that's a good point," Zoe said. "Could any of these spirits come from the housing development? Like, maybe Artec was luring people here only to kill them off and turn them into ghosts?"

"I don't think so." Keira couldn't drag her gaze from the figures around her. The spirits were unnerving in how still they were; except for the flowing hair and clothes, they could have been statues. "There are too many. If the entire subdivision had been built out? Maybe. But there just aren't enough houses."

The farther she looked, the more dead she could see. They didn't end with the houses. Even the vacant streets and empty lots held wispy, motionless forms.

Then something in the distance caught her eye. Hills surrounded the valley, hiding it from the outside world. At the top of the hills, standing on the same road the four friends had arrived on, was a lone figure.

He wasn't wispy. He wasn't transparent. He was silhouetted against the heavy clouds as he faced the valley. Keira's breath caught. "Hey. Can you see that person up there?"

Mason squinted. "On top of the hill? Yeah."

"Maybe it's someone who lives here?" Zoe offered.

He wasn't moving, though. He stared toward them. And Keira didn't think she was overreacting to think he was looking directly at her.

There was no escaping it any longer. "I think someone's following me," she said. "I've felt it for the last few days. And I think that's him."

Zoe swore under her breath. "Artec?"

"I don't know. I feel like they would have *done* something by now if it was. They've never exercised much restraint before."

Mason worked his jaw as he watched the distant figure. "What do you want to do? We could try to get closer. If we could just see their face—"

"Hold up," Zoe whispered. "That's not the only person watching us."

Keira swung to follow Zoe's eyeline. All she saw were the blank-faced, staring dead. She relaxed the second sight, letting them fade.

A man stood beside his house, disguised by its shadow. He held a hose in one hand, though no water ran from it. He looked old; papery skin hung from his thin form, and his head no longer carried any hair. His eyes seemed to flicker as he watched them. Keira couldn't tell if it was her imagination, but he almost looked hungry.

She turned back to the hill. The figure was moving away. Even as she watched, he disappeared over the hill's horizon. It would take at least ten minutes to get there by foot; they wouldn't have any chance to catch up to the figure, even if Keira was certain she wanted to.

Which meant just one alternative. She turned back to the man. He'd taken half a step out from behind his house. He twisted to glance over his shoulder, as though nervous that someone would see him, then gave a very small discreet beckon for them to come closer.

Her instincts warned her about getting any closer to someone who clearly didn't want to draw attention, but she wasn't in a position to turn down any kind of help, no matter where it came from.

"This doesn't feel ominous at all," Zoe whispered, apparently reading Keira's mind as they crossed the street in a tight huddle.

The man was pressed close to his house's brick wall, the hose clasped in a brittle hand, the house's side gate open behind him.

"You were talking to Gina," he whispered as they came within hearing distance. He glanced along the street, toward her house. "She doesn't like when people come around and ask questions."

"That's what she told us," Keira said. "But we just wanted to know about the area."

He worked his lips, his voice small and nervous. "She wouldn't have told you about the trucks."

Zoe's eyes lit up. "No, no she didn't."

He hesitated, glancing behind himself again, then back to the main road, as though watching for something. "I shouldn't, either."

He turned and began shuffling away, along the side of his house, his hand tracing the bricks' patterns as he moved.

"Wait!" Keira looked behind them, but the street remained bare. "What trucks?"

The man hesitated at his side gate. "Gina doesn't like it when we talk to outsiders."

"It's okay," Keira said gently. "We're not reporters. We're not bloggers. We just want to know the truth."

"The truth…" he whispered, then shuffled to face them again, his breathing wheezy. "The truth. No one knows that. But I do know about the trucks. I see them. Every Monday and every Thursday. They drive past us. The Five Suns park gates open and the trucks go inside and they don't come back out again for hours."

"Oh…" Zoe craned forward, eager. "Do the trucks have any logos?"

"Just white trucks," he said, then covered his mouth with his sleeve as he coughed. When he surfaced, his eyes were watery. "Gina doesn't like us telling people about them."

"You said they stay for hours," Keira prompted.

"Two." His hand twitched as he frowned. "Three hours, maybe. They unload something. And then they leave again."

Keira's heart ran fast. She kept her voice low, matching the man's volume, as she asked, "Gina said some people believe the land is cursed. Have you felt, or seen, anything like that?"

The man looked up, past their shoulders, and his eyes flashed. He turned away, hose still clutched in his hand, as he shambled through his house's side gate. It rattled as he shut it behind himself, blocking the four friends out.

Keira turned. The woman they'd first spoke to, Gina, stood in her house's open doorway. Her lips were pressed into a narrow line, and her eyes were frosty as she stared at them.

"Time to go, I think," Mason said.

"Yeah." Keira kept her head down as they returned to the sidewalk. "I don't think Gina wants us talking to anyone else."

They crossed back to their car as quickly as they could. As Mason started the engine, Keira looked back behind them, toward the only street out of dozens that had been given any houses. Gina still stood on her front porch, her arms slack at her side and her features unforgiving. She watched them until they were out of sight.

"That was creepy," Mason said, flexing his hands on the wheel. He looked like he was already waiting for the moment they could leave.

From the back of the car, Harry whispered, so softly that Keira almost missed it, "This might be the best day of my life."

She was glad at least someone was having a good time.

Mason drove slowly, coasting along roads that were designed to carry thousands more cars than they ever had. Sometimes he took a turn at random, but the landscape never looked any different.

"It's got to be Artec," Zoe said at last, echoing her earlier thought. "You don't get hundreds of ghosts in a place like this without any reason."

"No," Keira agreed. Not even Blighty's cemetery could come close to the number of spirits she'd seen standing in the very streets they now drove through. Her skin continued to prickle. She didn't want to open her second sight again.

"But they're not shades," Zoe continued. "Not like the ghosts in Pleasant Grove."

"No." Keira frowned. "But they don't look happy, either. I mean…no ghost is every really *truly* happy. That's why they're here. They have some old wrong they want to right usually, or else they want to pass over. But…"

She remembered the ghosts back outside her cottage. They were standoffish. Sometimes more mistrustful than she thought was really warranted, almost like they didn't fully identify with the living any longer. But they paced their rows, and sometimes stood together as though they were friends, and the children played tag.

They had life, despite their physical lack of it. They looked and behaved not entirely unlike the people they'd once been.

The ghosts here…they seemed hollow. They wore the clothes they'd died in, but otherwise had seemed indistinguishable. It was as though the life and personality had been sucked out of them.

"Can we stop the car for a moment?" Keira asked.

Mason put the indicator on to pull over to the curb, as though there were anyone around to see or care.

Keira needed to know more about the ghosts. She braced herself and opened her second sight.

A woman stood directly in front of the car. She was so close that Keira felt compelled lean away.

Her arms hung limp at her sides. Her hair was straight down to her shoulders, and it floated limply in the invisible currents. Based on her clothing, Keira doubted she'd been dead for more than ten or twenty years.

Her eyes had the emptiness of death, but unlike the spirits at Blighty who could still express emotions with a gesture or the slant of their eyebrows and the creases around those empty pits, the woman's expression was entirely blank. She stared at Keira, but it was like she didn't see her.

Or didn't care.

Keira reached her hand forward. She was still inside the car and couldn't go past the windshield, but even so, the woman was so near that she should have reacted. Keira waved.

The ghost just stood, unresponsive. Empty.

"It's happening, isn't it?" Zoe's eyes were wide and bright. "You're communing with them. *You're speaking to the dead.*"

"Ehh." Keira pulled a face. "If it can even be called that. I mean, I'm giving them attitude and they're giving me nothing in return."

"Still, though." Zoe's enthusiasm could not be dampened. "I'm watching a spirit medium ply her trade."

"I told you it wouldn't be very exciting."

"It's excellent," Zoe said at the same time as Harry said, "Go on."

Keira couldn't smother a smile. "I don't usually have a cheer team for this."

She turned to look through her side window. More ghosts were spaced through the barren patch of land.

They all faced toward her. None showed any flicker of emotion.

"This is weird," she muttered.

"What?" Zoe tapped her shoulder, a bubbling cauldron of energy. "What's happening?"

"Shh," Mason said. "Give her space. Let her work."

Keira shook her head. "No, it's fine. It's just…the more I look, the stranger this is. All of these people are from approximately the same window of time. I mean, it's not a *small* window of time—but some of Blighty's ghosts are centuries old. These people all passed within a few decades of one another. And that's not all."

"Yes," Zoe whispered, enraptured. "Tell us more."

"They all died around the same age."

The woman ahead of her had to be around thirty or thirty-five. Keira looked to her side. She saw a man around thirty. A woman in her late twenties. A man who might have been in his forties.

"No children," she said. "No elderly."

Mason's face worked as he processed that. "What does Blighty's ghost population look like?"

"A mix of everything." She thought back to her restless dead; there was a slight bias toward elderly ghosts, but every age was represented.

"I know it's not my place," Mason hedged.

Keira, without taking her eyes off the road, nudged him with her elbow. "You already know I want to hear your thoughts. Spill them."

"Can you see their cause of death?" He tilted his head. "I know you've mentioned it for some previous ghosts. Are there any correlating factors?"

It was a good question. Keira narrowed her eyes as she scanned the group. The woman ahead had barely perceptible bruise marks across her chest and a small cut on her forehead. Behind her was a man with a gunshot wound through his temple. Still farther back she saw a sliced throat. A head twisted to one side from a broken neck. Blunt force trauma.

"Violent deaths mostly," she said. "Which isn't too surprising if they're young. Some look like accidents. Some might be murder. I can't see any big similarities."

She hated looking at them. Even more, she hated the way they looked back.

"Let's keep moving," Keira said.

Slowly, Mason coasted the car forward. Keira flinched as the woman passed straight through them. She made no move to step aside or fade. Through the rear window, Keira watched as her smoky form swirled before stabilizing again.

The ghosts slowly turned, their shuffling footsteps minuscule and numb, to keep Keira in view. She dropped her second sight so she wouldn't have to watch the car pass through more of them.

"It's got to be Artec," she said, agreeing with Zoe. "I just don't understand why, or how, or for what purpose."

The empty streets seemed to last for ages before the asphalt roads turned to compact dirt. Realistically, Keira knew the planned development couldn't be as large as it seemed, but the looping pattern did something strange to her sense of space.

They entered another patch of relative wilderness, following the only road left. A gently sloping hill rose ahead, but it didn't seem natural. Someone had constructed a rise in the earth that ran the length of the valley. And they'd done it to hide what lay on the other side.

The car crested the hill. Keira felt her heart squeeze.

"It's here," Zoe whispered. Her breath caught. "And so is *he*."

CHAPTER 17

THE AMUSEMENT PARK SPREAD out ahead of them.

At least, what there was of it.

The sky was still heavy with rain clouds. In the hazy distance, Keira could see a massive Ferris wheel rising into the sky, its sharp metal angles and collapsing baskets cutting through the gray. Tracks for what looked to be a partially built roller coaster arched away to the right. Buildings were scattered about—gray concrete slabs not yet painted or decorated with the branding that had never made it onto them.

Ahead of everything else were the park's gates. They were enormous, intended to be the first thing any prospective visitor saw. At least three stories high and wide enough for fifteen queues to move through them, the arched metal was decorated with five 3D, yellow-painted suns adorning it like gems on a crown.

The suns were fading, though. The paint was peeling. One

of the spiky shapes had collapsed entirely, showing the cold gray metal innards as its face drooped, held up only by cabling that must have been intended to light it up at night.

There was one more obstacle between them and the gateways, though. A chain-link fence that had been erected to keep trespassers out. It ran around the outside of what must have been an extensive parking lot. Bizarrely, the parking lot lights were all running, bathing the wet concrete in sickly yellow light. Some sections of the tarmac had parking spaces painted in, the job abandoned partway through when the funding was withdrawn.

Zoe had talked about the fence, but it was only when she was seeing it that Keira understood exactly what she'd meant. It was like a moat—a broad expanse between where they stood and the park's main gates. An impassable distance where they would have nowhere to hide from watching eyes.

The park wasn't the only thing waiting for them.

A car was parked off to one side of the road just a dozen meters ahead, shielded from the amusement park by a cluster of wild bushes. A tall, incredibly thin man stood beside it. He stared at them, then beckoned, pointing to the space next to his own car.

"Pull over," Zoe said. She was bubbling with excitement.

Mason sent her just one dubious glance, then steered his car off the road to park near the strange man. "Do you know him?"

"Yeah." Zoe already had her seat belt off and door half opened even before the car came to a complete halt. "I can't believe he came. This is Fish Face Guy."

Keira and Mason shared a glance before getting out of the car.

Zoe had run ahead of them. She and Fish Face Guy exchanged some kind of muffled greeting; then she turned to beckon them close.

"Guys," she called. "Meet the man with all the knowledge. Fish Face, these are my friends."

"Hello," the man said. His voice was very soft and a little hoarse. He towered over them, easily six feet five, and his eyes were small and bright behind a set of enormous square glasses. He looked at least forty. His face was long and so deeply creased that he could have been much older, but his hair was so thick and dark that it was hard to be sure.

As Keira gazed up at him, she found herself forced to agree with Zoe's earlier assessment. He didn't look like a fish at all. More like a horse, really.

Mason extended a hand as he smiled. "Nice to meet you. Is there, uh, something you'd rather we call you, Mister…?"

"Just Fish Face," Fish Face Guy said bluntly. He took Mason's hand in both of his own and gave it two quick pumps before letting go and immediately pulling a bottle of antibacterial gel out of a pocket in his coat.

"Well, it's nice to meet you," Mason said, followed by, "Oh, no thank you," as Fish Face Guy offered him a serve of the gel.

"I'm told you have a particular interest in Five Suns Amazement Park and the development around it," Fish Face Guy said, getting down to business even before the gel dried. His eyes darted over them, never lingering on one person for more than a second. That whole day Keira had felt faintly judged by anyone who gazed at them like that—by Zoe's brother, by Gina in the abandoned town—but there was no twinge of distaste or uncertainty in Fish Face's expression. He took in the Christmas sweater and Harry's heavy makeup with a simple casual interest, nothing more.

"We absolutely do," Zoe said. "Thanks for the dossier. It's been invaluable."

From another pocket in his coat, Fish Face whipped out a large folded sheet of paper. He spread it out over his car's hood. Keira leaned closer only to realize she was looking at a hand-drawn map.

"The park is here," Fish Face said, gesturing. "The park walls are tall, and the secondary chain-link fence goes right around them. Your best option will be to slip in through the main gate, here."

One long finger stabbed into the map, marking the entrance.

"Most of what's beyond that is unknown, even to me," Fish Face said gravely. "Very little is visible over the walls, just those largest attractions and the hotel that was built to extend from the park's farthest end. That is of particular interest to me. It seems abandoned, but sometimes a light can be seen inside, only ever for a minute or two at a time."

Keira took a step past the shrubby coverage to get a clearer view of the park. She thought she could faintly make out the hotel in the far distance. It existed as barely more than a vague blur.

"Don't get so far into the light," Fish Face said. His eyes looked almost feverishly bright behind the heavy glasses. "Stay back here. They're less likely to see you."

Keira took a step back. She hadn't noticed them on the first look, but now she realized a guard paced along the inside of the chain-link fence. Their dark uniform and cap blended into the growing late-afternoon gloom. They were too far away for Keira to make out what they carried on their utility belt, but some kind of silver metal glittered in the distant lights.

"There are four of them," Fish Face said in answer to Keira's unspoken question. "One for each wall. No angle unguarded."

"Even overnight?" Mason asked, frowning.

Fish Face nodded bleakly. "Even overnight."

Keira's stomach turned. There was no longer any question of Five Suns being a dead end. Whatever she was looking for—whatever she needed to free the chained spirits—was hidden here.

"I've never been inside," Fish Face said. "But not for a deficit in trying. I swing by a few times a year, at least, but this isn't a solo job. You'll need a distraction. Today, that will be me."

"Oh?" Mason lifted his head. He was starting to look concerned.

"I know these guards. And they know me." Fish Face adjusted his glasses. "I'm certain I can create enough of a fuss to draw at least some of the guards and keep them busy for a few minutes. Say, three or four. You use that lapse in their focus to slip through the fence and get into the park."

Keira could feel her nerves thrumming. This wasn't just some abandoned building they were breaking into. The stakes were rapidly escalating. And she didn't like it.

"I'll hold them as long as I can," Fish Face said. He swallowed thickly, his back straight. "Even if it means death."

"It shouldn't, though," Mason said weakly. "We don't want death to be on any kind of table tonight, please."

"All I ask is that you construct a monument to me," Fish Face said gravely. "Preferably a big one. But whatever you can manage will be fine."

"Uh..."

"Are you sure you want to do this?" Zoe asked, brushing past the monument request. She was still bent over the map, even though it only held a handful of shapes.

"Of course." He blinked slowly. "I've found many sites of interest in my time, but this location has become a thorn in my side. If we can learn even a little about what it is and why it was built here, this will all be worth it."

"Okay." Zoe straightened from the map. Her face was tightly focused. "A distraction provided by Fish Face. The three of us will try to get in by the western side; that's the shortest stretch of parking lot before we can get to cover. We'll signal you when we need to break back out, Fish Face."

"What is my job?" Harry asked. He held up a long pale hand before any of them could answer. "Please remember my offer to light many large fires."

"That's, like, plan F," Zoe said. "Every plan except that will have you staying with the car. Mason will give you the keys; move it somewhere it can't be seen from the roads. And have it ready to pick us up on short notice if we need to get out in a hurry."

Harry shrugged, his un-emotive face unreadable.

"Relax. You've got snacks, plus we'll be staying in touch,"

Zoe said. She crossed back to Mason's car and opened the trunk, then pulled a handful of items out of her crate. "Shortwave radios. These things will let us talk and should have the range to cover the park as well. I bought them for fun, and I'm honestly a bit shocked to actually need to use them. There's one for each of us."

Keira took hers, and Zoe briefly showed her how to press the button to speak and which knob to turn to mute it.

"We should establish call signs," Fish Face said. "For covert communications. I'll be Fish Face Guy."

"Can my call sign be Hello?" Harry asked. "I want everyone to be confused when they try to talk to me."

"Absolutely not" was Mason's cheerful response.

Harry sighed. "Dead Man Walking, then."

"Are there any rules against my call sign just being Keira?" Keira asked.

"That sounds fine to me," Mason said. "And I'll be Mason."

Zoe scowled at them. "Just as long as you know you're wasting an amazing opportunity for drama. At least Dead Man Walking has some style to it. I'll be Blackbird."

"We're really doing this, aren't we?" Mason frowned down at his own radio. He took a shallow breath; then his familiar smile was back in place. "Sorry. It didn't feel quite real until now."

Keira stepped closer to him, her own radio held tightly. "You can stay here," she said. "I wouldn't blame you. You could stay with Harry and keep the car ready. Just say the word."

He gazed down at her, and his face softened a fraction as the anxiety melted. "No," he said. "I'll be with you as long as you need me. No question about it."

They'd somehow drifted too close. Keira's hand brushed against his. His fingers twitched against hers.

"Ready?" Zoe asked, snapping the trunk closed.

The spell broke. Keira pulled back as Mason cleared his throat.

"Ready," Keira said, and hoped the tightness of her voice could be mistaken for stress about the job ahead.

"Okay." Zoe slung her backpack over her shoulders. "No time like the present. Let's break some laws."

CHAPTER 18

KEIRA, ZOE, MASON, AND Fish Face slipped back behind the hill and then circled the park's perimeter. The man-made rise had been constructed to keep prying townspeople eyes away from the park, but now worked just as well to keep the park's eyes off them.

They split up at the development's end, where the open earth rose into forested hills. Fish Face gave them a thumbs-up before clipping his radio onto his belt and hiding it beneath his coat. Keira, Zoe, and Mason kept moving, crouched behind the low shrubs and relying on the thickening gloom to help disguise them.

They came to a halt facing the western fence, two hundred yards from where they'd left Fish Face. Zoe unzipped her bag and passed out thick fabric gloves. She drew out a large set of wire clippers, then pressed the button on her radio. "Fish Face. It's Blackbird. Ready on your signal."

The handset crackled. "Thirty seconds, Blackbird" came his tinny voice from the speaker.

Keira craned forward. From their vantage point, they could see two lengths of the chain-link fence: the side they were closest to and the side facing what would have been the main road.

Fish Face approached from that second side. He started at a walk, which turned into a lope, which then broke into an all-out run. She pressed one hand over her mouth in horror as he hit the wire fence and began doggedly climbing, shoving the tips of his shoes into the holes for purchase.

"Get down from there," a guard yelled, jogging toward him, one hand on the ominous silver part of their belt.

"You can't keep me out forever," Fish Face yelled, his voice crackling from the effort as he reached the fence's halfway point.

"We definitely owe him a monument," Zoe whispered.

"Freedom!" their odd friend yelled. "Release your secrets! Unseal your doors!"

A second guard jogged the length of the western fence, drawn by the noise. Zoe nodded. "That's our cue."

They crouched as they ran, covering the bare ground in just forty steps. Zoe dropped to her knees by the fence while Keira and Mason stood guard on either side of her.

Fish Face had reached the top of the fence and had slung one arm over, though he didn't seem able to complete the climb. He continued to yell inspirational quotes to help mask the snap of Zoe's clippers. "Know the fish, become the fish!"

The two guards stood below him, hands on their hips, as they yelled at him to get off their fence.

A final length of wire snapped, and Zoe pulled back a flap just large enough to crawl through. "Quick," she hissed.

Keira lunged through first and felt the sharp metal tips snag her clothes and hair. Then she rolled over the parking lot curb on the fence's other side and put out a hand to help Mason through.

"Just show me what you're hiding!" Fish Face screamed. He was dipping, his grip on the fence wavering as he slipped back toward the ground.

Zoe scrambled through the hole last as Keira held the wires back for her. Then she pushed the cut section back into place. It would be obvious if anyone looked closely at it, but Keira could only hope the guards were jaded enough by their job that they wouldn't notice.

Then she, Mason, and Zoe got their feet under themselves and set off at a run, moving as quietly as they could as they aimed for the shadows around the park's walls and the gaping entrance.

They hit the concrete and pressed their backs to it just as Fish Face dropped off the wall entirely.

"You've won this time," he yelled, his voice wobbling as he adjusted his coat. "But I'll never give up. Never!"

"Just go home, man," one of the guards called back. They were already backing away from the fence.

Keira beckoned for her friends to keep moving. They skirted around one of the massive pieces of metal holding up the five decaying suns. The space beneath would have been turned into ticket-reading turnstiles for the park's opening, but all that was left of that plan was a rope suspended between two metal balustrades. The rope was rotting and swung mournfully as they slipped under it.

They sidestepped, putting their backs to the park's internal walls, where they would be out of sight of the guards. Then they waited. Five seconds. Ten. Twenty. There were no raised voices, no shouts, no alarms. Distantly, Keira thought she could hear the crunch of footsteps as the guards returned to their posts.

"It worked," Mason whispered, seeming utterly shocked by that fact.

"Stage one down." Zoe pushed her clippers into her backpack and then hefted it back onto her shoulders. The park, made windless by the high walls, was doused in thick mist from the recently fallen rain. "Stage two: figure out what we're doing next."

"Getting away from the gate sounds like a wise idea," Keira said, keeping her voice low. The guards were still too close for comfort, but the park was large enough that they could easily vanish into it. Mason gave her a small nod, indicating that she should lead, and they set off at a half jog.

Concrete structures rose out of the fog, indistinguishable from one another. The path under them was wide enough to accommodate summer crowds, but now spindly grass grew out of the cracks that had formed.

Keira kept them moving for more than a minute, until she thought they had enough space between them and the entrance that their presence wouldn't be easily noticed. Then she let them stop, their backs to a building, and gazed up at the remnants of Five Suns that towered around them.

Up close, it was easier to see just how badly neglected the park had been. The Ferris wheel, drowning in distant mist and thickening shadows, looked to be on the verge of collapse. To her right was a roller coaster, and she could barely make out the stretches of track that had crumbled away.

This isn't right, is it?

The park had been abandoned for decades and the machines left without maintenance, but…fair park rides were built to last. They had to be. Any ride that could become derelict so quickly would be a massive loss of money and a massive liability to the riders' safety. Even without use and without maintenance, they shouldn't have rotted so severely and so quickly.

Unless they were built by a company that knew they'd never be used. A company that was happy to put up an imitation of the real thing and shave some money off the budget.

Keira squinted to see the space around them. More of the concrete buildings loomed through the heavy fog. They had no signs and in many cases no doors to cover their dark entrances. Weeds and shrubs and even small trees grew in any place they could find purchase. The main paths had already been put in—solid concrete blocks that curved languidly between the structures—but in other areas, it was clear a footpath had been planned but never installed.

Uncomfortable prickles ran over Keira's skin, like chilled air grazing across her.

That meant there were more spirits inside Five Suns. She didn't want to have to look at them again. But she *had* to know how many there were.

She opened her second sight. Figures emerged from the fog. Blank-faced. Hollow. Staring at her. *Surrounding* her. Keira's breath caught in her lungs.

The spirits had felt overwhelming in the empty streets of the development, but there were more here. Too many of them. They seemed to fill the space as thoroughly as if the park's gates had opened on a warm summer day and welcomed in a throng of visitors.

Maybe that was what Five Suns had been designed as: a theme park for the dead.

Only, none of these visitors were happy to be here. They didn't touch the rides; they didn't admire the empty buildings.

They just stood, vacant, unseeing, and unresponsive.

"There are more of them here," Keira whispered, as though the ghosts could hear her, as though they would *care*.

Zoe, shoulders pressed to the concrete wall, sent her a hard glance. "More spirits?"

She just nodded.

"Maybe it's a good thing the park never opened." Zoe put her arm through Keira's, offering her some warmth. "Imagine coming here for a nice day with the family and spending it walking through dead person soup."

Keira let her sight drop, and the spirits faded again. It didn't entirely stop the shivers running through her.

"So we're looking for *something*. We just don't know what," Zoe said. "And it's in here *somewhere*, but we don't know where."

"That's about the size of it," Mason said, next to Zoe. "Keira, did you have any preference for where to search?"

She took a deep breath, drawing the fog into her lungs. She was searching for any hint of her old life: a vague sense of familiarity or an invisible thread drawing her in a particular direction or a warning from her subconscious. She couldn't feel anything. "Sorry, Past Keira is silent on this one."

"In that case, we'll pick a direction and see where it takes us." Zoe hugged her closer. "We should focus on significant buildings first. The exhibition hall. The larger restaurants. The hotel. Let's see what we can find."

They moved forward, following the main path again. The park hadn't been given any signage, so they had to guess what each building was.

It wasn't hard to identify the exhibition hall. The building emerged through the fog like a hulking gray monster. It had been built close to the park's entrance and was one of the larger structures. Its door, wide enough for six people to pass through at once, had been covered with a sheet of thick tinted PVC. The plastic had a split down the center to enter through, but it looked old. Dust and mildew clung to it.

They stopped outside, squinting as they fought to see through the rippled and discolored PVC curtains; then Zoe took a shuddering breath.

"Nothing ventured, nothing gained," she said, and swept her arm into the plastic to push one of the flaps aside.

They ducked into the building. It was too dark to see more than the barest sheen of the concrete ground near their feet. Zoe fumbled for a moment; then a flashlight clicked on.

The space was massive. Even with the flashlight, Keira couldn't fully see the other side. Every small movement they made echoed back to them from the distant corners, and dust motes spiraled in their light.

Zoe's beam flitted over shapes Keira couldn't fully identify. Massive boxes, made of metal, all locked. There were stacks of them. Some were positioned on metal shelves. Others were left in piles on the floor.

Keira took a step deeper into the space as Zoe's beam illuminated the ceiling far above their heads.

A frantic flapping noise made Keira twitch back. A bird exploded past them, wings beating furiously as it tried to escape, only to vanish into the rafters.

"Geez," Zoe muttered. "What is all of this? Leftover storage from the construction?"

"I was thinking that too at first…" Mason took a step closer to one of the metal boxes. "But this looks more recent, doesn't it?"

Keira came up beside him. The box was about two foot square, and more solid than she'd first thought. She tried prying the lid up, just in case, but it was locked in place. The padlock rattled as she tugged at it.

Every Monday and every Thursday. Trucks come in. Trucks come out.

The box was covered with dust, though. She doubted it was as old as the rest of the park, but it still wasn't entirely recent.

"Wait. Bring the light over here." Keira tilted the box. There were markings on the side, just below the lock. A tiny plaque was attached to the metal, letters punched out of it.

15021, Bianca Walton

Keira's mouth dried. She set the box back down, her hands burning. "I think..."

She didn't want to voice it. And she didn't want to open her second sight.

But she did anyway.

A woman stood immediately ahead of her. Her jaw hung open; swelling spread across her face. Shards of skull poked free from her broken skin.

A car crash, Keira thought. A bad one.

Despite the damage, the same blank stare filled her face. Keira extended a hand. Her fingers shook as they neared Bianca's form. A sense of coldness, of emptiness, rolled off the woman. Keira's fingertips entered her body, but still the woman refused to respond. Blood seeped from around the wounds. Blank eyes stared. There was no reaction, even when Keira swiped her hand through the ethereal form.

"What is it?" Mason, close by her side, kept his voice soft.

"I think these boxes are cremated remains." Keira withdrew her hand.

When she turned, she saw walls of spirits. They were more tightly packed here than anywhere else, to the point of overlapping. Each stood beside one of the metal boxes. And each metal box bore an identical padlock and an identical plaque. Only the names and numbers punched out of the identifying tag were different.

Keira turned back to the woman ahead of her. Bianca Walton, her box said. There was so little of her left that Keira doubted there was any way to help her. Except for one. She reached her hand back into Bianca's chest, past the fractured ribs and crushed organs, to feel for the small delicate thread each ghost had.

Her heart skipped a beat. There was no thread. Her questing fingers were normally drawn toward its light and its electric hissing power. Now, her hand stretched out into nothing.

Just a cavity where a thread belonged.

She took her hand back again and let her second sight drop. Nausea filled her. She stumbled to the nearest wall and pressed her back against it as she waited for the shivers to stop.

Mason was immediately at her side. "What's wrong?" He pressed a hand to her neck, feeling her temperature. "You don't look well. Did you want to go outside?"

"Just need a minute," she mumbled.

What have they done to the ghosts here? No thread...what does that mean? No soul? Nothing to pass over to the next life?

Zoe stayed close, but she kept passing her light across the boxes, her lips twitching as she counted them. The space was too large to get a complete count. Her light faded before it could fully reach the other side.

"I think the town's residents were right in their own way," Zoe said at last. She turned back to Keira, and perspiration dotted her forehead. "There might not have been a graveyard in this valley before the construction took place, but there's certainly one here now."

"Is this what we're looking for, do you think?" Mason asked. "Is this why you held on to those newspaper clippings?"

"No." Keira straightened, her arms folded around her torso to preserve the little warmth she had left. She knew she was right, even if it was hard to put into words. "This is just storage. The plastic sheet over the door was to keep dust out, but it was grimy. Barely ever touched. It can't account for the trucks coming each week. There's something else going on here. And I think these boxes are just a symptom."

Rejects, maybe. Spirits that didn't suit Artec's purposes, shifted outside to be forgotten.

Keira turned back to the plastic-covered doorway. "I can't help any of the ghosts here. Let's keep moving."

CHAPTER 19

KEIRA KEPT HER SECOND sight up and active as they continued to pace through the abandoned park. The world was growing darker, entering that uncomfortable stretch between twilight and night, but they didn't dare use their flashlights.

Any kind of light would be like a beacon to the guards outside. They'd have to explore by moonlight alone.

Large stretches of the park had been left bare, ostensibly for rides that had never materialized. They passed by a row of stalls that might have been intended for food, next to a courtyard that had never had its seating installed.

They passed bathrooms and ducked inside to confirm they were empty. They paused underneath the partially fallen roller coaster. Rusted metal bars jutted out at crooked angles far above their heads, threatening to plunge free and pierce them through at any moment. They moved on quickly.

Two large restaurants had been built in the park. They stopped by the first. Unlike the showroom, its doors had been installed, and they were sealed closed with a chain.

Large windows overlooked a cobblestone square. Strips of blue tape crossed the windows in an X shape, an effort to keep them intact but without fully blocking them. Zoe pressed her flashlight against the glass and clicked it on, and Zoe and Mason squeezed in either side of her to see.

The glass was grimy. It speckled dark spots through the beam, making it harder to see distinct shapes beyond. Keira could make out a dusty tiled floor, a service counter that had never had its top installed, and a dining room that was empty of seating but filled with two-foot-square metal boxes.

"More storage," she whispered, her heart sinking. "More remains they wanted to hide."

Zoe turned her light off again and pulled back. "This might be the case for every large building we go to. We still have the other restaurant and the hotel, plus a handful of midsized buildings."

"We should check them all at least," Mason said. "If Keira thinks there's something more hidden here, I'm inclined to believe her."

They moved away from the restaurant and pressed deeper into the park. True night had set in. Clouds smothered the moon, and even with her eyes adjusted to the darkness, Keira found it nearly impossible to see.

Mist swirled around her legs. Distant shapes teased at the

edges of her vision. The roof of the hotel, hidden at the park's farthest reaches. The Ferris wheel. And the massive walls that encircled the park, containing them. Trapping them.

They passed through a long street that might have been intended for carnival games. Another bathroom, empty. Plants grew thick and tangled past it, and they had to backtrack to weave around them.

Something kept pulling Keira's eyes toward the wheel. She couldn't understand why. At first she'd assumed it was just natural—it dominated the skyline—but when she found herself staring at it for the fourth time, she realized there had to be something more drawing her to it.

"This way," she said, crossing behind rows of scaffolding that had been left for a partially complete building.

"Aha," Zoe whispered, jogging in her wake. "Bloodhound Keira has found something."

"Bloodhound Keira has a preoccupation with carnival rides, and she doesn't know why," she replied. "Maybe Bloodhound Keira just likes the pretty lights."

Bulbs had once been affixed across the wheel's metal surface. At night, it would have become a spectacle. Now, most of the bulbs were broken. Multicolored glass fragments shimmered across the concrete ground, and Keira had to tread carefully as she neared the structure and climbed onto the platform.

The wooden boards groaned under her weight. Red ropes were draped across the surface, the last remnants of a queue that was never used. Ahead was the entrance to the wheel. One of the carriages waited in the platform's dip, ready for boarding, except that one of its pins had come out and it hung at a dangerous angle.

Why am I being drawn here? Keira crouched on the platform as she waited, giving her subconscious room to speak, but it was frustratingly quiet. She began to circle the enormous poles bolted into the ground to hold the wheel's structure upright. Above, the baskets swung slightly, their rusted hinges groaning. Small dark shapes were hung like icicles from some of the crossbeams far above her head. Bats, she thought, choosing the derelict monstrosity as their home.

And then, her gaze turned down, as though it new exactly where to go. Hidden behind one of the support beams, near the section where guests would have been ushered into their baskets, something had been carved into the wooden floor.

Time had worked to disguise the shape under grime and dead leaves, but Keira swept them away to expose it. A symbol had been whittled there, possibly with a knife, formed from a series of jagged lines.

She knew the shape. It was the rune she used to gather energy. To recharge herself when she grew too tired.

"I was here," Keira said, kneeling to trace her fingers across the jagged, hastily scratched markings. "A long time ago."

As she let her hand rest over the symbol, she felt the very soft whisper of energy traveling along her arm. It wasn't much. The rune wasn't powerful; it couldn't supercharge her, no matter how many of them she tried to use. The most it could do was bring her back up to her normal operating levels when she was worn down. But she'd take every scrap she could get at that moment.

"Why here, I wonder?" Mason asked. He squinted as he gazed about them, from the concrete buildings to the distant lights of the parking lot. "You could have put it anywhere. Inside shelter. Hidden in a dark corner. Why here, out in the open?"

"Maybe I really did just like the pretty lights," Keira said. "I'd have to sit here for a while for the rune to make much difference. Maybe I wanted something nice to look at."

She gazed up at the structure above: a kaleidoscope of broken bulbs spiraling into the darkness. When she squinted her eyes, they blurred together, interrupted by the heavy, groaning passenger cars.

And past the Ferris wheel…

"Wait a moment." She crouched down and scooted forward until she was sitting on the damp wood, directly over the rune.

That part of the platform was sheltered on two sides by the metal support bars. Their shadows covered her. She'd be almost impossible to spot there, especially if she kept still.

But from that position, she had a perfect view of the distant hotel.

"Oh," Keira whispered. "Look."

Zoe and Mason huddled in at her sides. She pointed. The hotel was a large building, constructed on the amusement park's border. It was at least twenty stories tall. The windows were all dark, creating a grim, unrelenting pattern of dense glossy blocks interrupting the gray walls.

It didn't look like a fun place to stay. Even if it had eventually been painted, the stark and rigid form left it looking vaguely hostile—as though the concrete slabs could come crashing down to chew up anyone who dared enter.

"Ugly building," Zoe said. "Maybe Past Keira was into the brutalism design style, as well as shiny lights."

"No, seriously, just watch a second."

They did. Drips of water fell from the Ferris wheel to trickle through their hair and chill them further. With each exhale, Keira's breath plumed, and she knew they had to be surrounded by the dead.

But then it happened again. A light blinked on. Only for a second, and only in one window, on the fourth floor.

Then it was gone again.

"This is why I sat here all that time ago," she breathed. "This is why we had to come to the park. Whatever we need, it's in that hotel."

CHAPTER 20

MASON LEANED FORWARD, ONE hand braced on the massive support bar beside them. His eyes stayed fixed on the hotel. "What does that light mean?"

"No idea." Keira didn't even let herself blink as she waited. "It could be automatic. Or it could be triggered by someone inside. But it's got to be significant. Power was run to the parking lot lights, but we haven't found a single working bulb inside the amusement park yet. Even if that light's automatic, it means power was connected to the hotel. And I don't think it would have been done by accident."

As she finished speaking, the light came on again. A single red bulb, high up in its room, blinking out at them for one second before vanishing again.

"They never imagined anyone would notice it," Zoe said, her jaw set. "It's so far away. Even if someone broke into the park, what are the odds that they would stop at just the right place and just the right time to see it?"

She was right. They'd had to climb the Ferris wheel's platform, putting them at the right angle to see the light over the park's high walls. Keira doubted she would find many other similar vantage points. At least, not without climbing onto one of the concrete structures' roofs.

"It looks like we have a destination," Mason said. "Now, we just need to get to it. It's outside the main park."

"But not unguarded," Zoe noted. "That's why they have four guards. Two to watch the main gates. Two to watch the hotel at the back. There'll be a way in, though, I'm sure. A place like this would have an internal entrance for the hotel. Some kind of way for VIP guests to walk right from their rooms and into the park—"

Zoe cut herself off. She turned, craning her neck and frowning. In that beat of silence, Keira caught the sound that had made her friend pause.

A distant low rumbling.

It seemed to be coming from the direction of the town.

Keira pulled on the muscle that let her see the dead. They fluttered into sight; rows upon rows of them, their lifeless forms spilling out through the park, all facing toward her.

No, not all of them…

The most distant figures were beginning to turn. With small shuffling steps, they twisted around to face the open gates Keira, Mason, and Zoe had entered through.

Beyond that, she could see the foggy glow of the parking lot lights. And still farther past, something moving through the gloom. The rumbles grew louder until she could identify them: the distant purr of engines.

"Wait," she said. "What day is it today?"

"Thursday," Mason said before realization flashed over his face.

Every Monday and Thursday, trucks drive into the park…

The man they'd spoken to hadn't mentioned what time it happened. Keira hadn't expected it to be after dark. But if the site's owners were indeed doing something they didn't want seen by prying eyes, after nightfall was the best time to make their move.

Their shortwave radios all crackled. After a second, Harry's flat voice floated out of the tinny speakers. "Dead Man Walking here. I'm bored. Also, there are trucks."

Zoe clicked on her own radio. "Thanks for the advance warning," she said drily.

The radios fell to silence. Keira couldn't tear her eyes from the park's entrance. Even as she watched, one of the guards approached the old cord barrier she'd snuck past and lifted it out of the way.

It was there for effect, she realized with a jolt. *Deliberately aged cord and tarnished metal balustrades to make the place look abandoned. And it worked. When I passed it, I thought it must have been a relic from when the construction was canceled.*

There was a distant rattle of metal shifting; that would be the wire fences being moved aside. Keira knew she would be well hidden by the Ferris wheel's structure, but she still hunched down, making herself as small as possible, as the first truck came into view.

It was the size of a large van and a sleek glossy white. The modern lines were in stark contrast to the amusement park's aged architecture. These trucks were expensive, and they moved with purpose.

Three of them trailed into the park. They followed the sections of the road that had been paved, weaving easily through the abandoned buildings.

Their path led them close to the Ferris wheel. Headlights bloomed across the metal and broken glass. Keira inched down farther, her heart thundering, her friends squeezing in against her.

Mason's warm hand rested on her back, comforting. Zoe was pressed tightly in at her side, her breathing rapid.

They held perfectly still as the truck's engines moved closer. Wheels crunched over old concrete, and Keira began to understand why some of the paths had been so cracked. The headlights shimmered over the metal beams above her, then faded again, and the purring motors began to recede into the distance.

Slowly, cautiously, Keira raised her head. The trucks were continuing through the park. Aiming, like she'd guessed, for the back wall and the hotel behind it.

"We need to follow them," Keira whispered.

"Oh, no" was all Mason said.

She found his arm and squeezed it lightly. "We have to. If we're right and something belonging to Artec is hidden inside the hotel, it's going to be hard to get into. The trucks might be our only chance."

Already, the vehicles were merging into the mist, their engines growing faint.

Mason stared at them for a second, and then his face hardened. He gave her a quick nod. Zoe, on Keira's other side, echoed the gesture.

"Quickly," she whispered, and leaped out from their hiding place.

They ran single file, Keira leading. She moved at a crouch, keeping her head low and weaving behind the thin cover created by wild plants and unfinished buildings. It was impossible to be silent, so she didn't try. The trucks were making enough sound to mask their movements.

Large sections of the park were nothing but cobbled paths or bare earth, with very little to hide behind. She crossed those sections at a run before pressing in against the nearest concrete wall.

The trucks were faster than them. Even moving as quickly as Keira dared, they'd already vanished from sight. She could still hear them, though. The motors slowed. They'd arrived at the rear wall.

That area had been designed to house a water park. Slides and ladders cut their paths into the sky. Channels that should have carried log flumes or canoes were empty save for shallow, slimy puddles. A wide pool stretched ahead of them, the tiles cracked and jagged.

Keira skirted the area. There was a changing room at the water park's side, closest to the wall surrounding the area. She slipped behind it and pressed herself into the building's shadows as she watched the trucks.

They'd come to a halt ahead of the wall, lined up one behind the other. There was some kind of portcullis in the wall, looking almost exactly like a castle gate, sealing the road. In the same way that the trucks' sleek forms had been anachronistic to the park's dated design, the medieval gate was a jarring comparison to both of them.

"That would have been the miniature train ride," Zoe whispered. "It was going to be a feature of the park. Hop on and hop off to easily travel around. I bet it was planned to go up to the hotel as well, to make the route more fun for guests."

The trucks idled outside the gate. Keira could barely see the driver in the nearest one. He wore a deep blue cap low over his eyes, even though it was dark out, and stared ahead. He seemed bored.

Keira strained to get a better look at the gate. The structure could have been made to be purely decorative, but somehow, she doubted it. The metal looked genuine and thick; the bolts holding it together were large. The sharp tips pierced into reinforced slots in the ground, anchoring it in place.

It wasn't just a design choice. It was a barrier.

Which meant they might only have a limited opportunity to get past it.

She beckoned to her friends and then slipped out from behind the changing room. A hedge of wild plants clustered near the wall, and she slunk into a crouch behind them, Zoe and Mason pressing close to her back.

It was as near as she could get to the trucks without being entirely visible.

A small light embedded into a switch next to the gate flashed green. Keira froze, every muscle tense, as the portcullis began to grind upward, its heavy metal rattling with every shuddering inch.

This is it. If we can get in behind the final truck—run close to it, so that the driver can't see us in its mirrors—

The thought died before she could even finish it. The trucks stayed motionless as four men came out through the open gates.

They wore some kind of uniform, not unlike the guards outside. These figures carried extra tools, though. Metal detectors were swiped beneath the trucks. Then the rear doors were opened one at a time as a man climbed in and examined the contents. Keira strained and thought she caught a glimpse of pallets. The items on them were wrapped in plastic, and she couldn't identify what might be inside. Another metal detector was run over them, though, and the deepest reaches of the vans were searched.

They're scanning the contents, Keira realized, her heart sinking. *Checking all deliveries before letting them in.*

She didn't know if it was paranoia or not to imagine it might be connected to the van ferrying Zoe's mother to their facilities. If they'd guessed Keira had been involved with that, they might have recently tightened their security.

The four guards stepped out. The truck doors were closed again. Then two guards walked ahead, shepherding the trucks into the tunnel that led toward the hotel, with the final two guards bringing up the rear. One of the guards had an access card hanging from a lanyard, and he held it against the blinking lights of the panel. The portcullis ground closed again.

Keira slumped back. Her heart was running too fast and her tongue tasted bitter with fading adrenaline.

"We're no worse off than we were before the trucks arrived," Mason said gently. "We'll find another way through."

"I wish I could have seen what they were transporting if nothing else," Keira said.

Zoe's smile was wickedly wide. "I did."

They both turned to her, silently questioning.

"Those were near identical to the shipments we get at the general store. Long-life food, assorted drinks, and fresh food to start. I think I also saw toiletries and cleaning supplies." She chuckled. "A new delivery every Monday and Thursday isn't all that different to what Blighty's store gets. There are people living in there. And not a small number, either."

"Oh," Keira whispered, glancing back up at the stark hotel that towered over them. From their angle, the blinking light was no longer visible.

"Artec's staff, I'll bet," Mason said. He was crouched, his forearms braced on his knees. "We've been looking for their central office for weeks. Maybe, improbably, we just found it."

"I think you're right, but it's still hard to believe," Keira said. She could no longer hear the truck's engines and kept her voice quiet. "Why would Artec choose to put its base in an abandoned theme park of all places?"

"It's remote," Mason guessed. "Largely forgotten about.

Excluding the mostly abandoned houses we passed when we arrived, it's a long drive from any real habitation. Not many people could stumble on it by accident."

"And the park's history is enough of a distraction that no one would care too much about seeing trucks arrive," Zoe added. "If anyone *did* question them, I'm betting they could just claim that they're maintenance people, or assessors come to evaluate the park, or a routine inspection. They could easily spin off another rumor that the park might be sold or reopened, and it would work as a perfect deflection from what's really happening."

"I guess." She stared back up at the tower above them as a spit of cold rain hit her back. "I feel like we could get all the answers we'd want if we could just find our way in."

Zoe pursed her lips. "Well, we have one option, but I don't think you're going to like it."

Keira gave her a shrewd look. "Try me."

"We already established that we don't want to start many large fires." Zoe slung her backpack off her shoulder and unzipped it. She brought out a small plastic container not unlike a lunch box. "But how about a singular large explosion?"

Mason stared at the box in blank shock, then said, "No, no way, not a chance, never."

CHAPTER 21

"WHAT—" KEIRA STARED AT the plastic box Zoe held, blinking in shock. "Is that…?"

"A modest amount of C-4," Zoe said, nodding emphatically. "I was going to take it into an empty field and detonate it there for my birthday, you know, like the less legal version of fireworks, but I don't mind sacrificing it for the cause."

"Were we driving around with that in the *car*?" Mason sounded exhausted. He ran a hand over his face. "Zoe, no. I can't be a part of this."

"It'll be fine. I know the measurements to keep it safe." Zoe wiggled the box, a crooked smile lighting up her face. "We're not going to hurt anyone. We just need to make a small hole in that metal gate over there. That's all."

"And the noise will attract every single guard in a half-mile radius."

"Look, it's been a rotten few days. Just let me have this, okay?"

"*No.*"

"Hang on." Keira held up a hand, warily watching the box. "Can you detonate it remotely?"

"Well, yeah, it wouldn't be a good time for anyone if you had to set it off by hand."

"Huh." She turned a curious eye back toward the Ferris wheel. "I have an idea. One that doesn't involve drawing attention to us. But if we can time it right, we might be able to get our distraction."

"Explain," Mason said, still looking wary.

"Those cars hanging from the wheel are ancient, and the bolts are rusty. The roller coaster is already falling apart too. So I imagine it would be a shock to see one of the wheel's cars fall… but not entirely unexpected, right? You might go over to have a look at it, just out of curiosity."

"Yeah," Zoe said, her eyes bright.

"Well, the trucks are going to come back out of the hotel in a couple of hours, and when that happens, we need a distraction that doesn't immediately raise a red flag that there's an intruder in the park. I'm proposing we give one of the wheel's carts a nudge."

Zoe's nods became more emphatic the more Keira talked. Mason still looked grim, but he took a deep breath, held it, and let it out in a rush.

"Okay," he said. "That's not a bad plan. Minus the fact that we're working with actual explosives that should never have been brought in the first place. But it's going to be difficult to get it just right; too much of an explosion, and the smoke and flames will make it clear it's sabotage."

"And not enough and the car won't even fall," Zoe agreed. "Plus, I don't think the wheel's going to turn anymore. You'd actually need to get up there to plant the explosives."

"Leave that part to me," Keira said. She eyed the design and was fairly confident she could scale it. "Just give me the tools and tell me what I need to do when I get up there."

As a group, they skirted through the park and back to the wheel. As they stepped back into its shadow, it seemed enormous. Keira swallowed lungfuls of icy air as she stared up its fog-shrouded dark height.

The distraction wouldn't work if it wasn't loud and visible. It would have been easy enough to break one of the carts near the ground, but then it wouldn't be seen from the hotel's gates. Keira would need to reach one that was at least halfway up. Preferably more.

Rotating the wheel would be a simple option. The three of them lined up at the closest crossbar and pulled on it, at one point even hanging their collective weight off it, but the metal was fused into place.

"You were right," Zoe said, dropping off the bar and breathing heavily. "I think you're gonna need to scale it."

She could do that. She was good at climbing. The endless lines of glittering, broken metal drew her eyes upward, and Keira tried not to let the doubts creep in.

"I'm going to give you a conservative amount of this," Zoe

said. She'd crouched on the concrete, the plastic box open in front of her as she used a knife to shave off parts of a material that looked like putty. "As the killjoy said, we can't exactly afford a fireball. But it means you're going to have to find a connection that's already weak. Okay?"

"I can do that," Keira said. Several of the carts already hung lopsided, one of their two connections rusted away.

"Are you sure?" Mason asked. He had his arms folded against the chill as the rain began to come down in slow, thick drips. "This is dangerous, even for you. We can always find another way."

"I'm sure," Keira said. She gave him a tense smile. "Trust me."

His eyes softened a fraction. "I do." He shucked off his coat and offered it to her. "An extra layer to protect against the glass," he said.

Above, a thousand broken bulbs glittered menacingly. She was already wearing thick gloves, but Keira gratefully buttoned Mason's coat on over her own. It dwarfed her and hung heavy and warm from her shoulders.

Then, finally, Zoe gave her two parcels wrapped in scarves.

"Your C-4 is in this one," she said, pointing to the larger, lumpier shape. "It's like clay, so just squish it onto whatever connection you want to see disconnected. This other one is your detonator; don't worry, it won't go off until I make it. Just be sure you press it into the C-4 thoroughly."

"Got it," Keira said. Zoe said they were safe, and she trusted Zoe, but she still tucked the parcels into separate pockets.

Then she stepped back and gave her target one final look-over. She knew the basket she wanted to aim for. It was at the two-thirds mark and on the left-hand side. That would make it the most visible to anyone leaving the hotel.

But it was at least a hundred feet off the ground.

She fixed a smile on her face, inhaled deeply, and reached up.

Glass crackled as she pressed past a broken bulb to get her first grip. She'd need to climb up using the A-frame support structure until she was at the wheel's center, then use one of the crossbars to get to her chosen basket.

Even just the A-frame, already at a slope, was challenging. Handholds were few, and spaces she could balance safely even rarer. The surface was slick and growing slicker as the rain pinged over both her and the metal. Still, she climbed, her eyes fixed upward.

Yards of metal vanished under her. Keira's breathing was shallow and rapid, but her muscles hadn't failed her before, and they weren't failing her then. She moved lithely and quickly until she reached a crossbar where she could rest her weight.

She paused to gauge her progress. She was halfway through her climb. The ground seemed impossibly far below. Mason and Zoe waited there, their faces upturned to watch her, both pale and tense.

Her mind conjured images of what would happen if she slipped at that moment. How it would feel to fall that distance, her body ricocheting off the metal bars before slamming into the platform below.

Don't freeze now. She swallowed the bitter tang that had developed on her tongue. *We have to be back by the gate before the trucks leave. It's the one thing we can't miss, but we don't know how long we have until it happens.*

She reached up and began climbing again, her shoes skidding on the fixtures that held the lightbulbs.

"Take it carefully!" Mason called from below.

The broken bulbs crackled as she brushed over them, tearing tiny holes in the thick coat. She was nearly at the center point, the major crossbar where the entirety of the wheel balanced.

The wind made itself felt. The park had been almost unnaturally still, surrounded by its high walls, but up here, gusts of air buffeted her, sending her hair flurrying across her face and snatching her breath. Icy, spitting rain funneled across her back. The carts creaked around her, and the sounds were like deathly groans.

She hooked her leg around the bar just below the center point and felt broken glass press into her thigh. She grit her teeth and reached higher for the next hold.

The wind rippled around her again. The whole structure seemed to bow. Keira's foot, which had been braced on one of the rivets, slipped.

Her breath came out as a gasp as she fell. Her stomach rushed into her throat as her head turned light. She threw her arms forward. Her hands caught on the massive support bar and she pulled herself into it.

The impact jarred her whole body as she held on for her life. Multicolored bulbs burst as she crushed them. Jagged glass sliced into her. Suddenly, the cold rain was joined by the sensation of warm blood trickling down her arm.

Hold. Hold.

Tears stung her eyes as she wrapped her legs around the bar.

"Keira?" Mason called from below. His voice sounded shaky.

"Fine," she said, but she wasn't sure if he could even hear her. She could barely hear herself. A high-pitched whistling rushed through her ears as her limbs trembled.

She looked up. She'd only lost about six feet. The center—the place she fallen from—wasn't too far out of reach.

No time to stop. No time to reconsider the choices that brought you here. You have to get through that gate; you can't squander this chance.

She lifted her arm up and began climbing again, the rhythm falling back into place. Climb, breathe, climb, breathe.

The structure rocked as she reached the midpoint. Keira's fingers were numb as she dug them in to pin herself into place.

All around her, the Ferris wheel's arms stretched out like a massive spiderweb. It was harder to see the structure from her angle, and she had to lean back to find the carriage she was aiming for. Its arm stretched out to her left, angled upward, starting at her chest.

Slowly, tentatively, she extended herself onto it.

The metal groaned under her weight. The wheel was locked in place, though, too rusted and broken to spin the way it had been intended. Keira stayed on her chest, creeping forward an inch at a time toward the basket she wanted. It was only suspended by one bolt, and each of her movements caused it to sway precariously.

Keira grit her teeth, willing it to stay in place, willing it to not collapse before she could reach it. An inch at a time, over the bulbs, over the rusted metal, as the whole structure groaned like she was hurting it and the freezing rain got into her eyes and the wind pulled at her with invisible hands.

At last, she was at the connection. Half-blind and barely able to breathe through her aching chest, Keira drew out the package of C-4 Zoe had given her. It seemed like a very small amount. She smeared it onto the last remaining bolt, shoving it as deep into the seam as she could, then took out the detonative device from her other pocket. It was a tiny metal shape with two pins in it. Following Zoe's instructions, she mashed it into the puttylike explosive.

It looked like it would hold. She prayed it would be enough—that Zoe's calculations had been accurate, that the bolt was as precarious as it looked, that they could manage to get the timing right.

She didn't like how many factors could go wrong in that equation. But it was what they were working with.

She began to creep her way back along the metal rung.

CHAPTER 22

"OKAY," MASON SAID THE moment Keira touched back onto ground. "Okay, you're okay. Come here."

He began pulling the sleeve back from her arm. A trail of red ran over her fingers, slowly being washed away by the rain. Keira flinched as Mason pressed against the edge of the cut, and he muttered a tense apology. "I'm sorry. There's still glass in there. We need to get it cleaned out."

"Back by the gate," she said, and when he tried to argue, she fixed him with an insistent glare. "The only thing worse than getting stabbed in the arm would be getting stabbed in the arm for nothing. We can't miss this convoy when it leaves. You can de-glass me as much as you want, but only once we're back by the gate."

He sighed, then nodded. "Okay. That's fair. But lean on me."

Keira accepted his arm around her. She hadn't realized just

how sore she was from the slip until she tried to walk. Zoe came up on her other side, a fierce grin in place that Keira couldn't help but match as they retraced the looping, erratic roads through the park and back to their final hiding place.

Mason lowered her down against the wall, then took his medical kit out of his own backpack. He rummaged through it as Keira leaned her head back and let the drizzling rain cool her skin.

"This has to work, doesn't it?" Zoe asked. She unscrewed a bottle of water and offered it to Keira. "I don't know how we're going to get in if it doesn't."

She was right. It *had* to work. Because they didn't have the luxury of leaving and coming back again another day. Fish Face's distraction had gotten them in once; she didn't think their luck would hold for a second attempt.

Keira drank deeply before passing the water back. Mason, his lips a tight line, peeled wet clothes off her arm and used a pair of tweezers to pick at a sliver of glass that had become trapped. Keira pressed her eyes closed and did her best to ignore the pain as he worked.

Their wait stretched on, and on, and on. Once Keira was bandaged, the three of them huddled against the wall, doing their best to avoid the downpour. They were drenched through. Each of Keira's breaths came out as thin mist before vanishing into the atmosphere around her. She resisted the temptation to open her second sight and see the sentinel dead that she knew would be watching.

Mason kept checking his watch. "Eleven," he said, and Keira grimaced.

"What if that older guy was wrong?" Zoe asked. She was shivering as she clutched her jacket around her. "What if they stay in overnight? Maybe they don't want to drive through the rain."

"I think I'd actually start considering using the rest of the C-4 if that happened," Keira said, causing Mason to chuckle.

"Bet Harry's got to be hating this," Zoe added. "We invited him on an epic heist, then left him in the car."

"Do you think he'd rather be out in the rain?" Keira asked.

"Oh, hell yeah. He loves standing out in storms and looking mournful. It's like therapy for him or something."

Keira opened her mouth to say she'd had enough therapy for the night, then clamped her lips together. She raised her hand for silence, her eyes wide, as she listened.

There were engines again. Faint but there.

"They're coming," she whispered.

Zoe fumbled for her phone. She had an app open and gave Keira a quick, tense look. "Tell me when to activate it."

"We need to wait until they're outside." She chewed her lip. "But before they close the gate."

Depending on how quickly they were moving, that could be a very narrow window. The trucks had been searched on the way in. She didn't think they'd be searched again on the way out.

The engines were growing nearer. Keira crouched behind the bushes, facing the portcullis, waiting. She thought she could hear distant voices.

Then the light beside the gate flashed green. The metal shuddered as it began to rise.

Every nerve on Keira's body was on fire as she watched the metal creak upward. There was a low, heavy thud as the gate fully disappeared into the hatch. Then the first van emerged.

"Wait," Keira whispered, her palm held out toward Zoe as a signal. "Wait, wait..."

The white trucks grew slick with rain as they trailed out of the gate. The four guards marched alongside them, their flashlights panning over the muddy ground, looking irritable. If this was truly an extra precaution following the rescue in the mortuary's van, they weren't used to having to step out into the rain.

The second truck emerged. Then the third. The guards came to a halt beside the open gate, staring disinterestedly into the far distance.

"Now," Keira whispered.

For a second, nothing happened. Then two seconds. Then three. The trucks were moving away, along the concrete path. The first of the guards turned around to return to their fortress.

Then there was a distant snapping noise. Keira watched, her heart in her throat.

The Ferris wheel cart she'd sabotaged shuddered and plunged toward the ground. A puff of smoke swirled out of where the connection had once been, but it was quickly drawn away by the wind. The cart crunched heavily as it hit the ground.

The guards had swung toward the noise. The trucks ground to a halt. There was a beat of silence; then voices rose, full of shock.

All four guards left the tunnel as they moved up to speak to the van drivers. Keira flicked her hand, indicating they were going to move, and rose out of her crouch.

The distraction was working. But it wouldn't hold for long. Using the engine's continued rumbles to hide any noise she might make, she dashed toward the entrance.

It was a tunnel and longer than she'd expected. She could see grooves on the ground where the miniature train had been planned to run. Keira only glanced behind herself once, to make sure Zoe and Mason were keeping pace, then focused purely on the path ahead.

The tunnel had dull lights set into its ceiling at distant intervals, and they sent endless shadows of Keira racing alongside her. It felt like the passage was never going to end. Keira had expected the gate would let them into some kind of courtyard or garden—a place where they could hide and circle the hotel and build the next stage of their plan.

But they passed the thirty-feet mark. Then the forty-feet mark. And then she was forced to skid to a halt. The dim lights illuminated a flat concrete wall ahead, and in that wall was a set of sliding glass doors. They were motion activated and slid open, revealing a small air lock before a second set of doors. Those were tinted; she couldn't see what might be hidden beyond them.

"It's the hotel." Zoe was panting as she slowed at Keira's side. "The tunnel leads directly into the hotel."

Keira's stomach plunged. She turned. The only thing visible was the long straight passageway, cast in harsh light by the infrequent bulbs. And at its far end, the quiver of crisscrossing flashlight beams and the sounds of distant chatter.

The distraction hadn't held the guards for anywhere near as long as she'd been hoping. They were already coming back.

The passage gave them nowhere to hide. Nowhere to even pause for a second and collect their thoughts. The guards were closing in on them, and they only had one direction they could go.

Keira snagged Zoe's and Mason's arms and dragged them forward, through the first set of open doors. The space beyond was dark and small, furnished only with an old floormat.

The second set of doors clicked as they approached, then drew aside smoothly, granting them access directly into the heart of the hotel.

CHAPTER 23

KEIRA SHIVERED AS A rush of cold air passed over her wet skin. Lights, shocking after the dark night, felt blinding. She squinted against the sudden brightness, then forced her eyes open.

She didn't know what she'd expected, but somehow, an average hotel lobby left her feeling like she'd fallen into a twilight world.

There were no guards. An unmanned concierge desk stood ahead, computers and phones clustered over it. The carpet was a sweeping pattern of gray stripes, drawing her eyes toward the back wall, where a set of four elevators stood next to a stairwell.

An elaborate light fixture hung overhead. Its cubed shapes mirrored the decorations on the walls and the square armchairs spaced about. Open archways led deeper into the building, with signs directing guests toward a restaurant and a gym.

It was just like any other foyer in any other expensive hotel.

Except for one small thing: the logo. Artec's insignia, built in bronze, glittered at her from the concierge desk's front.

Keira felt like she was reeling. After everything she'd gone through to get inside the building, she hadn't expected the contents would be so...*normal.* It was almost like the hotel was on standby to welcome guests for a park that had never opened.

Mason nudged her arm and nodded toward the doors they'd just come through. The guards were only seconds away. There weren't many places in the foyer where three people could hide, and Keira made a snap decision: she crossed to the concierge desk.

It was a large structure, wide enough to seat at least four attendants, and would screen them from not just the door but the elevators and the dining room entrance as well. She ducked down behind it, Mason on one side and Zoe on the other.

The hotel's main doors sighed as they split open.

Keira held her breath. From her position, all she could see were the underside of the desk, the computer towers smattered with faintly glowing lights, and the tangled cables connecting them to the screens above.

She couldn't see the guards as they entered, but she could hear them. Low muffled conversations echoed through the foyer.

"It was bound to go eventually."

"Just wait till the whole thing topples."

"How long's that going to take? Another decade? Two?"

"I told you, I don't care. I just want to get dry."

The voices trailed across the space, passing by the concierge desk. There was a ping as an elevator opened its doors. The voices blended over one another, growing irritable, and then fell quiet as the doors closed over them and the elevator slipped away.

Keira slumped, finally letting herself breathe as deeply as she wanted to. Her heart was racing.

"Ugh." Zoe leaned forward to rest her head against one of the roller chairs, her eyes closed. "You've gotta warn me when your wild missions of justice involve prolonged running."

"Sorry." Keira used her sleeve to wipe lingering drops of rain off her face. "I'm planning the next one to happen entirely on a comfy couch."

Mason chuckled. Then, slowly and gingerly, he rose to survey the room.

"Good news," he said. "We're alone. For now. Bad news, I don't think we're getting back out without an access card."

Keira remembered the access pad next to the portcullis and how a guard had needed a card to activate it. She'd been so focused on getting *in*, she hadn't yet thought about how they were going to get back *out*.

"That's got to be our priority," she said. "It doesn't matter what kind of secrets we unearth here if we can't bring them back outside. We *have* to get a key card."

The reception desk was a mass of stacked papers. There were multiple monitor setups and three matching swivel chairs. The sight left nerves squirming through Keira's stomach. Just how many people worked in the tower? And how long until one of them needed to pass through the foyer?

Keira began leafing through the papers and tugging open drawers, looking for anything that resembled the key card the guard had used to activate the gate. Pens rattled as she pushed them aside. Mason crouched to search inside the cupboards. Then Keira accidentally bumped one of the mouses, and the computers came to life.

At the far side of the desk, four screens were stacked. As they lit up, she saw they were filled with security feeds from around the hotel.

"Well." Zoe grinned. "Looks like we've found the surveillance room."

"I guess it's given a low priority, considering how thoroughly forgotten the park is," Mason said. He leaned close, his eyes reflecting the grainy black-and-white footage as he scanned the images. Keira came up on his other side.

The four screens were divided into six camera views each. It was a phenomenal amount of coverage. She saw a lot of empty hallways. An empty dining hall. Two women sitting in a lounge area together, leaned toward one another as they seemed to be speaking. Then views of the outside and the gate they'd just emerged through.

The feeds were all very similar to what a regular hotel might look like at nearly midnight.

"There we are," Keira whispered. She pointed to a screen that displayed a view of the foyer and reception desk.

"There's a view of the park outside the gates," Mason said. "I bet that was the blinking light we saw earlier. Artec was able to disguise most of the office as an abandoned hotel, but they still needed one security camera to overlook the park."

"The cameras probably don't get watched much," Zoe said, staring at them intently. "I'm guessing they're only reviewed if something goes very wrong. Which, if we do our jobs right, is exactly what's going to happen tonight. Give me a second."

She pulled the swivel chair up to the desk and began tapping at the keyboard. Settings appeared, then vanished again before Keira could properly read them. Then a password prompt appeared.

"Yeah. Video editing is password protected." Zoe was already pulling a small black piece of hardware out of her backpack. "Time to bring out the decryptor. Assuming I can get past this, I should be able to erase the footage. Maybe even turn off the other cameras remotely."

"See what you can do," Keira said. She kept one eye on the elevators and one eye on the empty hallways. "But we can't afford to spend much time here."

"It depends on how complicated they've made the password." Zoe plugged her small black box into a USB slot on the computer. She was moving fast. "Or what level of encryption they're using. Sixty-four-bit should take less than ten minutes, but—"

"Um," Mason said. "Would this help?"

He looked almost embarrassed as he pointed to a Post-it Note stuck to the side of the monitor. It read **PASSWORD: ICECREAM32**

Zoe slumped, her eyebrows high and her lips pursed as a mix of incredulity and defeat washed over her.

"I'm going to be so mad if this works," she said, and typed *Icecream32* into the password prompt. The computer gave a happy little beep as it accepted it. More screens appeared.

"Ugh" was all Zoe said. She began clicking frantically. "Mason, keep looking for a key card. Keira, maybe take a look at that directory by the elevators and see if you can figure out where you want to go. I just need a moment with this computer here."

Keira glanced toward the elevators. A small bronze plaque was posted beside them, listing destinations. She gave Zoe a nod, then crossed the foyer, her feet light. She was hyperaware of the long empty hallways beside her as she began scanning the locations listed on the plaque.

A lot of the titles were meaningless to her: *Aspect Division, Mondal Division, Alternating Specs.* Some destinations were just letters and numbers: *3S, 15-IP*. It was like trying to read another language.

Panic began to grow. She hated how far she was from Zoe and Mason; the clicking keyboard and scrape of opening drawers sounded very, very distant. Worse, she hated how little she understood what she was looking at.

Did Old Keira understand any of this? She trailed down the listed destinations, feeling more and more out of her depth with each unfamiliar name. *Would Old Keira have known where she needed to go?*

Wait...

Near the bottom of the list was a single word: *Archives.* If she was going to find her answers anywhere, it would be there. She jogged back to the concierge.

Mason had abandoned searching the desk. He shook his head, his expression grim, in response to Keira's unasked question. No key cards.

"Any luck with the cameras?" she asked Zoe.

Zoe's eyes were mirror surfaces for the screens as her hands moved at an incredible speed. "Film from the last six hours is now deleted. I'm working on deactivating the recording function for the other cameras without turning them off entirely. I feel like missing recordings are going to take longer to be noticed than entirely blank screens."

"Good call." Keira bent close to the desk, her voice hushed. "But we can't spend much more time here. We're pushing our luck. And I know where I want to go."

"Yeah?"

"Archives. Basement level four."

Zoe finally looked up from the computers. "This place has a *basement*?" She made a face. "Basement archives are such a cliché. One of these days I want to see some archives on the penthouse level."

"I'm mostly just impressed they have basements to begin with," Mason said. "The building is already so tall. At what point did they decide they'd built it high enough and that they should start digging instead?"

"Okay, basement level four, huh..." Zoe hovered a hand over the screens as she scanned them. She found it within seconds. "Here. This has *got* to be the archives."

The camera was set high in the corner of a room. It showed rows upon rows of cabinets forming narrow twisting walkways.

"Looks like it's empty," Zoe said. "One of the perks of arriving at midnight. There's no guarantee it will *stay* empty, though, especially not if you need to spend some quality time down there."

Keira grimaced. "Yeah, *quality time* is one way to put it." She was searching for a metaphorical needle in an archival haystack, and she didn't even know what the needle looked like. Some key to bringing Artec down. Some way to release the spirits. *Something*. "I'm not sure we have many other options, though. We're just going to have to try it and hope our luck holds."

"Or..." An excited glimmer lit up Zoe's eyes as she pressed a button, rotating which security feeds were shown. "Make your own luck. I'm pretty sure I can watch the entire building from here. It had feeds for all of the elevators and the stairwells."

"I feel like you're about to suggest we split up," Mason said, his smile grim.

"It's the only option that feels anywhere close to safe." Zoe kept tapping, cycling through the images. "We still have our radios. I can warn you if anyone starts moving toward the archives. Or if I see anything that suggests we've been found."

Keira chewed on her lip so hard that she felt skin begin to tear. "Zoe..."

"I know, I know. *Don't split up.* But, seriously, if we stay together, we'll be searching this place completely blind. These cameras are an advantage we can't afford to pass up."

Keira glanced around the room: from the open hallway, to the doors, to the elevators. "You can get yourself somewhere safe if anyone comes into the foyer, can't you?"

"Absolutely. You *know* I'm not the reckless type." Zoe held up a finger. "Don't bring up the explosives."

"Wouldn't dream of it," Mason said drily.

Zoe pulled herself away from the computer just long enough to fix them with a steely glare. "Stay in contact. Work fast. I'll warn you if anyone's coming, but there's not much I can do to buy you extra time. You'll also need to look for key cards while you're down there."

"Thank you," Keira said, adjusting her backpack.

"Take the stairs. Less noise." Zoe's fingers flew over the keyboard as her focus returned to the screens. "Good luck."

Keira and Mason jogged toward the stairs. They were narrow and unadorned compared to the more lavish lobby. Obviously, with as many floors as the hotel held, most of the employees were expected to use the elevators.

They took the stairs down quickly, Keira leading. She counted off each level as they passed the small, neat signs by the doors. Basement One, Basement Two…

The radio clipped to her jeans hissed, and Zoe's voice came through. "Blackbird here. Keep going. Your path's clear."

Keira glanced up and saw a camera high up on the stairwell's wall. She gave it a thumbs-up as they turned the corner and descended lower.

The stairs ended in a hallway with a single narrow, wooden door. A small plaque was set in its front: *Archives.*

She'd been half-afraid that the room would be locked, but the handle turned at her touch. She looked to Mason to check if he was ready and got an affirmative nod.

This was it. They'd made it to Artec's heart, to where it stored its deepest secrets. Now she just needed to find out what those were.

Keira shoved on the door, forcing it open.

CHAPTER 24

THE SPACE WAS QUIET and cool. Even though she knew it was empty, she still rose onto her toes, fighting to see over the filing cabinets' tops.

She couldn't see anything moving, but that wasn't a guarantee. The room wasn't a rectangle; it twisted and turned, and the filing cabinets were pressed into any wall that could hold them. It was a maze, and the aisles were painfully narrow. They would need to move through it single file.

"Any thoughts on what we're looking for?" Mason asked. He kept his voice hushed, as though he could feel the weight of the place too.

"Anything labeled *Artec,* or anything that might be related to ghosts or the dead." Keira began moving into the room, her eyes darting over the tags stuck on the cabinets' fronts. "Call me if you find anything that looks promising."

Old metal runners squeaked as Mason pulled a drawer open. He rifled for a second, then shoved the door shut again.

He'd spent years in academia. He'd have a good eye for what information was likely to be relevant at a glance.

Keira worked on a different principle. She didn't try to open any drawers. She barely read the stickers on them as she drifted deeper into the maze.

There was a quiet longing in her chest, pulling her farther into the space. A sense that something was waiting for her there. Something important.

And she'd learned to never ignore that kind of instinct.

Behind, Mason pulled more drawers open in quick succession.

Richmond Files, AA–AF, one label read. *Arclight, 1985–1987*, said another. They meant nothing to her. But something did. Something close. She turned another corner.

A soft sound came from somewhere above. Keira raised her gaze toward the ceiling as she unclipped her radio and pressed the button to talk. "Zo?"

Her reply came immediately. "You already know I only answer to Blackbird."

"Right, Blackbird. I thought I heard something." Keira didn't take her eyes off the spot in the ceiling where she'd caught the sound. "Can you see anything on the screens?"

There were several awful seconds of silence interspersed by tapping on a keyboard, then Zoe said, "It looks clear from what I can see. But it's possible there are areas the screens don't cover. Be careful."

There was another crackle; then Harry's dull monotone came through the speakers. "It's getting late and I've eaten all the snacks. Fish Face went home *hours* ago."

Followed by Zoe again: "Dead Man Walking, I love your contributions, but I kinda need you to stay off the system right now."

He activated his radio one last time, purely to sigh into it.

Keira couldn't tear her eyes off the white plaster ceiling. No more sounds came from it. Her skin wouldn't stop crawling.

"I might have found something." Mason's voice sounded farther away than it should have. She craned and could barely see the top of his bronze hair over the walls of files. He spoke slowly and carefully as he turned pages. "There are death records here. Death records bundled with...readouts? Pages and pages of dates and numbers."

"Are there any patterns you can find?" She turned back to her path. The sense of purpose—of urgency—refused to fade. She took a step forward.

"*Grant Allen*," he read. "*Date of death: 11 May 1999. Cause of death: drowning. Age: twenty-eight.*"

Keira's mind flashed to the ghosts she'd seen through the development. All in their young adult years. All died during the same couple of decades. She had an awful sense that the Grant Allen that Mason had found could be seen somewhere outside.

Her wandering footsteps stopped. She'd walked to the archives' opposite side. There was a door there, set into the white-painted brick wall. A bronze doorknob, well worn, looked dull under the overhead lights. There was an access panel next to the door, but it was dead, its lights turned off.

The invisible thread leading her forward drew her toward that door.

"*Arclight Protocol*," Mason continued to read, and papers rustled. "And then dates, correlating with numbers. There are weeks of them. Hang on—"

Keira reached out for the bronze doorknob. It grated painfully as she turned it. The door hadn't been locked.

"It says, *measured in hertz,* at the top of the page. I think... maybe..."

The door drifted open. The air inside smelled stale and repulsive in a way that Keira hadn't experienced before. She turned her face aside even as she reached for the light switch.

"I think these are experiment results," Mason said. "I think they're measuring how much energy they can get from the ghosts using different methods."

The light clicked on. Keira found herself facing an office.

The room looked like it must belong to someone important. It was larger and more luxurious than the archival room. A feature wall filled the space's back, and in its center was a sleek, expensive wood desk covered in scattered piles of folders. On the left-hand wall were bookcases and filing cabinets—more modern and less dusty than the ones in the archival room—and the right-hand wall held a single elevator door. She had the distinct impression that this room couldn't be accessed by any of the elevators found in the foyer, though. This was a private, exclusive kind of place.

The office might have seemed commonplace to anyone else, but Keira's skin burned with latent electricity in the air. Her eyes drifted to the rear wall. There was a feature there: a screen, at least eight feet tall, which displayed nature scenes like an imitation of a window. It was recessed into the wall. A shelf jutted out below it, almost like a seat, except the cold steel surface looked anything but inviting.

Keira pulled open her second sight.

Four shades writhed.

Their smokelike forms emerged from the steel shelf beneath the feature wall. Spectral chains wrapped around them, pinning their arms to their sides and refusing to set them free. They twisted and bucked, their mouths stretched wide enough to break any living human's jaw. If Keira could have heard them, she knew they would be screaming.

Keira felt her skin turn clammy.

The shades been placed there, ahead of the feature image. And it had been a deliberate choice.

They'd been added as decorations.

The implications hit her like a derailed train and left her feeling sick. Those four shades, placed with impeccable care, meant that someone here—someone inside the building—could not only sense the dead but could see them, just like Keira.

She'd never encountered anyone with the same gift as her before, even though she'd been discreetly searching. Finding out that she wasn't alone should have been exciting; she'd hoped to meet someone who could help her, maybe explain how the whole thing worked and give her some advice.

But not like this.

Anyone who would stack wailing, writhing spirits up like a spectacle behind their desk was not someone Keira ever wanted to cross paths with.

There was nothing she could do to help the shades. Their chains vanished into the metal shelf, and she knew they'd be just as impenetrable as the chains in the Pleasant Grove graveyard had been. Keira let her second sight drop and turned aside, her mouth dry.

The presence of the dead confirmed one thing at least: this office was significant. She just needed to figure out why.

Moving quickly, she skirted along the massive bookcases, looking for clues in the volumes. The books were all nonfiction and didn't seem to follow any kind of theme. Volumes on philosophy and physics intermingled with literary criticism and essays. They were all hardcover and cloth bound and looked pristine. Keira guessed they were there as decoration, not for any kind of reference.

She turned to the desk instead. Files spilled over its surface. She read the names as she leafed through them. They looked to have been picked from the filing cabinets in the room behind her. Many of them were tagged with names and years, and when she opened them, she found echoes of Mason's discoveries in the main archives. There were reams and reams of printouts, rows of numbers that had been shrunk down to fit as many on the page as possible. Some had been highlighted, but Keira, working fast, couldn't find any pattern to them.

They're collecting data. On…the dead?

It seemed to make the most sense. She knew Artec was storing the dead for the electricity they produced. There would be electrical output variations depending on how their systems were set up, and they were likely trying to find the most efficient settings.

If she was right, it created an ugly explanation for the hollow specters that clustered the streets, and the stacks and stacks of cremated remains inside the park. They were the leftovers. The failed experiments. Old models that had been discarded once Artec no longer had use for them.

The bitter tang in her mouth intensified as she thought of how many files had to be crammed into the archival room behind her. Each file corresponding to a person. Each person sucked empty and left discarded in a development designed to hide what Artec was doing.

Keira chewed her lip, her movements becoming more urgent as she dug through the files. There had to be *something* here. Her instincts wouldn't lead her to this room without good reason.

But their time was running out. She could feel it in her bones and in her nerves. Each minute that trickled away from her was dragging them closer to discovery.

"Keira?" The radio on her hip crackled as Zoe spoke. "Are you still in the archives? I have eyes on Mason but not on you."

She kept flipping through the stacked folders with one hand as she pulled the radio up and pressed its button. "No, but I'm close. I found an office."

"…huh." Through the radio, keys clicked. "Okay, I can't find you. Which means we guessed right: there are rooms in this place that don't have video surveillance."

Mason's voice cut into the audio. "Be careful. Let me know if you want me to join you."

"I'm fine right now, but I'll stay in touch."

No surveillance. Keira clipped her radio back into place. *No one to see what happens in this room.*

Shivers crawled up the back of her neck and settled into the base of her head. She could feel the four shades' gazes on her, even though she could no longer see them.

The files were blending together and leaving her feeling scattered. She left them and instead tried pulling on the desk's drawers. They slid open smoothly, revealing containers of pens and reams of notepads. She found a locked box that rattled when she shook it but required a key card to be opened. And then...

One more folder. It was hidden in the lowest drawer on the desk's right-hand side, covered by blank notepads and a chart, almost as though it had been hidden there. Instead of the meticulously maintained dates and numbers on the other files, this one was tagged with a single word, written in bold strokes with a thick pen.

KEIRA.

CHAPTER 25

KEIRA FELT THE ROOM swim as she stared down at that single word.

They had a file. On her.

Why?

Her hands shook as she pulled the folder out. It was slim—compared to some of the others on the desk, some of which were thicker than her finger, this one seemed nearly weightless. It might have held a sheet of paper, maybe two.

Keira dropped into the chair behind the desk and felt it creak beneath her weight. She shoved the other folders out of her way and placed the file bearing her name in the center of the desk. Then she flipped it open.

A photo shimmered in the harsh office lights. Prickles ran up her neck again, and she knew the unseen shades behind her were howling.

It was a photo of a girl, probably around age five or six, sitting between two adults. They were on a patterned couch in what looked like a suburban living room. The man and child smiled for the camera, while the woman looked off to one side, seemingly answering a question she'd been asked.

The photo felt almost achingly mundane. This could have been any family, in any suburban home. Maybe there was a family gathering or some friends had gotten together for the afternoon, and someone had suggested snapping a photo to memorialize the day.

The image had been captured with a camera, not a phone, and had been printed out on proper photo stock. Based on that and the clothes, Keira guessed it was probably ten or fifteen years old. It would have been at home in any family photo album.

Keira picked it up to see it better, and a second photo fluttered out from beneath. This one was slightly smaller and more formal. It showed three people—two men and a woman—standing in a plain white hallway. They all wore white uniforms that Keira couldn't place but looked vaguely medical. They'd clearly been posed for the photo, their backs straight as they faced the camera. None of them smiled.

The woman, positioned to the left, and the man standing at the right were familiar. Keira only had to glance back at the first photo to confirm it: they were the couple sitting on the couch. A small *X* had been drawn next to each of them, along with four numbers.

The figure between them was older and had graying hair. And

as Keira stared into his pixelated eyes, a deep wrenching revulsion squirmed up from her stomach and threatened to choke her.

She hated this man. She didn't even know his name, but he left her feeling cold and sick and miserable.

Keira felt into her back pocket. When she'd arrived at Blighty, she'd had just two possessions with her: a small amount of money and a photograph.

She drew the photo out of her pocket and set it next to the formal hallway image. The result wasn't a surprise. It was the same man. Even the uniforms were identical. The only difference came from time—a few years, maybe—that had turned his hair grayer and added extra creases to his face in the final photo.

"Okay," Keira whispered, and laid the three photos out in front of her like they belonged to some kind of jigsaw puzzle and she just needed to find out how to slot them together. "Okay, so Mr. Creepy is friends with…"

Her gaze flicked back to the first photo, of the family gathered on the couch. They looked a lot more happy and relaxed than they did in the more formal shot. She'd only examined the image briefly before, but now her focus settled on the child between them.

Keira frowned and lifted the picture. She was used to seeing photos that had red-eye, where the iris and pupil were covered by a sheen of crimson from the camera's flash.

This was something slightly different. The girl's eyes were fully blacked out, the iris and pupil blending together into something so dark that the camera seemed to be struggling to capture it.

The woman had her head turned slightly as she spoke to someone outside the camera's view, but the man was facing forward, just like the girl. His eyes appeared normal: slightly glassy, with reflections from an overhead light glazing across brown irises.

Compared to him, the girl's eyes looked uncanny. Alarming.

And the more she looked at the picture, the more Keira realized she recognized little pieces of the girl. It was like trying to remember parts of a distant dream. The ears were familiar. The mousy brown hair too. And the shape of the nose.

"That's…" Keira lowered the photo back to the desk. The revelation felt like a stab to her stomach. "That's me."

She was the girl with the hollowed-out eyes. It was Keira's first time since her memory loss seeing herself as a child.

She tried to swallow, but it became stuck in her throat. If this was a picture of her, then the people sitting either side of her…

…they had to be her parents.

Her parents and her childhood home and at least two other people out of the camera's view, talking to her mother and taking the photo. People who knew her. Who might have possibly cared about her.

A sound echoed somewhere above. It was the same noise she'd heard before: like a heavy footstep pressing into an old floor. Keira barely glanced up. She couldn't tear herself away from the faces on the desk.

Her family.

She glanced at the photo next to it, depicting her parents

standing next to the unnamed man. He had to be connected to Artec; she didn't think she could fear him and loathe him so much if he wasn't. Keira's heart sank as she glanced across the three figures in the stark white hallway. In that photo, her parents were clearly employees of his company. They wore its uniform.

Did that mean they were involved in Artec as well?

An *X* had been drawn beside each of her parents in pencil, and below the *X*s were four numbers. Oddly, the numbers were nearly identical, and they were written unevenly.

It only took her a second to figure out what the numbers meant. They were dates, and dates that took place more than a decade before.

Death dates, Keira's mind whispered, and her whole body turned cold.

She knew she was right. Both of her parents had died, two days apart if she was reading the numbers correctly, and the person who owned the photos had noted those dates next to their likenesses.

Any dreams of meeting her family were doused before they'd even had a chance to form.

This meant, out of the three photos, only two of the recorded people were still alive.

Keira.

And the man she had to fear.

A floorboard creaked above her. Almost instantly, the radio crackled to life.

"Problem," Zoe said, sounding tense. "The cameras are gone."

Mason's voice cut through. "What do you mean?"

"The display on the screens—they've vanished. I just have three dozen blank boxes now."

Keira held the radio, but she still couldn't tear her eyes off the photos as she tried to absorb what they meant.

"Someone else has access to the cameras," Zoe said, her voice a husky whisper. "And I think they know we're here."

The floor above Keira creaked again. This time, it wasn't a stand-alone noise: there were footsteps moving with purpose. Before she could react, the door to the archives beeped. Keira was just in time to see lights appear on the access panel. It had been remotely powered on.

Keira spoke into the radio as she forced the photos into her pocket and rounded the desk. "Mason, get back to reception."

"Where are you? I'll come and meet you—"

"Not an option right now." She grabbed the door's handle. It twisted just a fraction before freezing up. Locked, like she'd feared. "I'll catch up as soon as I can. Go, quickly."

A soft *ding* echoed through the space. Keira turned. One of the walls held an elevator. She'd suspected it was a private shaft, one that the office's owner could use to access his room without having to walk through the archives. The light at its top indicated a carriage was coming.

Keira's mouth turned sour. She yanked on the door's handle again, then tried shoving her shoulder into it, but the lock held solid, and she doubted she'd be able to open it without a key card for the access panel.

Soft rumbling sounds came from behind the closed elevator doors as the carriage settled into place. Keira put her back to the wall, her heart thundering, as she watched the sleek metal doors.

They clicked and then slid apart. A very familiar figure emerged from between them—and smiled.

CHAPTER 26

"HELLO, KEIRA," HE SAID. "If you wanted to talk to me, you could have just knocked on the door."

The blood in Keira's veins turned to ice. He was older; the age lines had increased, and his carefully combed hair was now entirely steel gray. But the man emerging from the elevator was undoubtedly, unmistakably the figure from the photos.

The man who had known her parents. The man who had written their death dates next to their likenesses. The man who had placed those pictures into a folder and then tucked that folder into the bottom drawer of his desk.

As she stared into his face, his name floated up from somewhere in her subconscious. "Schaeffer."

His smile twitched a fraction. He wore a suit—expensive but understated—and his face gently rounded into his neck, making his jaw seem to vanish when he tilted his head at the right angle. His eyes seemed unnaturally bright.

Prickles raced along Keira's skin like crackles of electricity, and it took her a beat to realize it wasn't entirely because of Schaeffer. She opened her second sight and let the four shades in the recessed back wall become visible. They thrashed, their mouths stretching into inhumanly wide caverns as they shrieked voicelessly. They'd been struggling before, but at Schaeffer's appearance, their efforts redoubled into something frantic and utterly miserable.

"Magnificent, aren't they?" he asked, following her gaze.

Keira wasn't sure how much he knew about her. As far as she could tell, he wasn't aware that she'd lost her memories. And it seemed wise to keep it that way. But she still couldn't prevent the question from bubbling up: "You can see them, can't you?"

"Not as well as you do from what I understand." He tilted his head as he watched her. "To me, they're a smudge of smoke. But they grow a little clearer every year. If I may ask, how do they appear to you?"

The creatures writhed, miserable and bound. Empty eye sockets became impossibly deep pits of black. Their gaping mouths were lined with teeth. The sooty substance that made up their bodies billowed and twisted, like ribbons in the wind. They took on the vague form of humans—the slope of their shoulders, the narrowing of the legs—but with none of the detail of their mortal counterparts.

Keira kept that all to herself.

Schaeffer didn't seem deterred by her silence. He took a deep breath as he gazed at the recessed wall. "You know Marie Curie, the discoverer of radium, don't you? She died from exposure to the element she pioneered. Thomas Edison's assistant had both of his arms amputated before succumbing to skin cancer after extensively experimenting with X-rays. We already know that contact with the lifeless energy results in certain complications, but I...well, neither of us are likely to know the full consequences of our exposure for many decades yet. Such is the burden of creators."

Exposure...

Pieces were falling together. She couldn't see the dead because of some genetic fluke or happenstance: she'd been exposed...to *something*. And Schaeffer was gradually being exposed as well.

Her mind flashed back to the photo of her parents posing next to Schaeffer in the hostile white hallway. Had they offered her up as a test subject? Had she been dosed with something deliberately? She didn't want to believe her own parents would be capable of something like that.

Schaeffer crossed the room, and Keira felt every muscle in her body tense. He wasn't moving toward her, though, but to his desk. He slid into his seat and exhaled as he knit his hands together and rested them on the empty folder labeled *KEIRA*.

"I see you found your photos." A shallow smile twitched up, then dropped again. "You probably noticed how slim your file was. Please don't see it as a slight. It's been a challenge to keep knowledge of your abilities secret, but I've found the most effective method is to simply *not document it*. Papers can't be leaked if they never exist, now can they?"

The radio on Keira's hip crackled. She reached for it and

quickly turned the volume down to zero. The less Schaeffer knew about Zoe and Mason, the better.

Schaeffer barely reacted. He seemed wholly focused on Keira. His eyes glittered as he took her in, as though he were seeing something precious for the first time. It made her skin crawl.

"I'm glad we have this chance to meet formally, you and I," he said, and Keira had to be careful to keep the surprise off her face. Artec had been such an overwhelming presence in her life—and vice versa—that it felt impossible that they hadn't ever spoken before. "I'm sure you have plenty of questions."

She couldn't stop herself. "The spirits in the amusement park. What happened to them?"

A flicker of surprise lit up his expression, and Keira immediately regretted speaking. "Oh, can you see those as well? I can't. That's fascinating."

She bit her tongue and kept her back pressed to the wall as she watched him, silently challenging him to give her something more.

"As I'm sure you've already figured out, those were Mark Two of our experiments. The Faulkner Protocol."

Thoughts flickered through Keira's head, like whispers of memories that barely existed any longer.

Mark One: Harvesting energy from existing graveyards. Inefficient; too many of the graves no longer had spirits, so energy production was weak.

Mark Two…

"Artec established shell companies that offered refrigerated body transportation," Schaeffer continued. "Morgues would hire us. While the body was in our care, it would be removed from its coffin and diverted here, to our first attempt at large-scale harvesting."

He laughed, and he almost looked like a friendly uncle recounting the story of some old mishap except for how morbid the details were.

"What a disaster," he said. "We were intending to cremate the remains, store them in space-efficient boxes, and turn them into a battery grid beneath the amusement park and the town. And it seemed to be working for a little while. If you can see those spirits, I'm sure you'll be aware of how many there truly are. But their outputs were weak and only grew worse with time. Within two years of installation, the spirits stopped producing at all. I'm sure you already know why."

This time, Keira kept her mouth closed. Schaeffer only shrugged at her silence.

"We'd severed the souls during the installation process. The spirits we'd created were only a hollow shell—an echo of what should have existed. They could store energy, but they could no longer produce it."

She thought of the spirits she'd encountered: blankly staring, unresponsive. Unable to move from where they stood or answer her questions. They had no thread to be pulled, no soul. They were more like dolls than true ghosts.

"We realized we had to lay claim to the bodies closer to the point of death and mark them in such a way that the spirits could not vanish. True spirits were essential to productivity."

"Mark Three," she murmured.

"Yes, Mark Three was an improvement, but you've already seen that we didn't stop there." His fingertips drummed on the empty folder. "We focused on finding ways to increase output. We are now on the highly successful Mark Five, the Reyes Protocol. That was the point where we learned how to create shades."

Behind him, the four figures screamed.

"Mere ghosts produced energy slowly," Schaeffer continued. "We could line a graveyard with them and harvest what they created, but they were erratic and unreliable. Some spirits were strong producers; some were barely worth the space they occupied. And then we encountered a *new* type of residue. A type that exceeded previous production numbers exponentially. A type that never tired." One of his hands reached out to gesture toward the wall behind him. "Our marvelous shades."

Disgust built inside Keira's stomach. Any doubts about Artec's culpability vanished. Schaeffer not only knew what he was doing but had done it deliberately.

And it raised another question. One she wasn't sure she wanted to know the answers to.

How much had her parents been a part of?

Keira reached into her pocket and took out the photo taken in the stark white hallway. She held it out to face him, hoping that gesture alone would be enough to get him to speak.

"Ah, yes, of course, your parents." The wrinkles around his eyes deepened as he smiled. "Vivienne and Michael Collis. They were my partners. Until they chose to walk away from Artec."

His smile soured. He pulled open the drawer on his desk, drew out the locked box Keira had encountered earlier. He placed it into the center of her file and then stared down at it, his eyebrows slightly raised and the corners of his mouth twisted.

"It was company policy that certain individuals were not allowed near the experiment chambers—those with compromised immune systems, those who had recovered from cancer or had family histories of cancer, those who were pregnant. These experiments were new technology, and so we were rigid about those rules for our employees' safety."

He almost seemed to be trying to justify himself to Keira. She didn't move but kept the photo outstretched, waiting for him to continue.

"From what I later was able to gather, your mother hid her pregnancy for nearly five months while she was working in close contact with the experiments. We didn't know what the residue—the concentrated energy produced by shades—might do to a developing fetus. We didn't *want* to know. You were never supposed to exist."

Keira struggled to swallow around the lump in her throat. Her mother had known about the shades, then. She'd actively worked with them. And if she was understanding what Schaeffer was telling her, it was the reason Keira had been born with her second sight.

"Of course, your parents left the project without announcing the pregnancy." Schaeffer's mouth twisted again. "It wasn't until years later that we caught up with them...and learned about *you.*

It's very much a shame they'd hidden you away; you were never supposed to exist, but that aside, you could have been a great benefit to our program and to furthering our research. Instead, you have been nothing but a regrettable thorn in my side."

Keira placed the photo back into her pocket. She somehow doubted she would have enjoyed being *a great benefit* to Artec or the experiments she was certain that would involve.

"My parents are dead." She said it as a statement, but Schaeffer still nodded. Keira licked dry lips. She hoped she wasn't showing her hand too much, but she had to know. "You killed them, didn't you?"

"They were great scientists and great visionaries, the both of them," Schaeffer said. He reached into a pocket inside his jacket and drew out a key card, which he held over the locked box. The panel on its surface beeped and a light flashed green, but he didn't move to open it. "Before you, they'd dedicated their lives to Artec and to the future it promised. A world that offered limitless, clean, inexpensive electricity. No more blackouts. No more price hikes. No more fossil fuels. It's a utopia they strived for just as diligently as I always have."

A utopia of limitless energy…at the cost of tens of thousands of souls, trapped and in agony for eternity.

Keira tried to keep the disgust off her face even though she knew she couldn't fully hide it.

"And then you arrived, and they abandoned all of those dreams. As did the other two founding members. There were five of us in the beginning, you see—five innovators, five dreamers who stumbled onto something as close to magic as this mortal realm offers. They all fell away from the cause. All except for me."

Keira's breathing was fast and shallow. She hated the way Schaeffer was speaking—softly, almost affectionately, as though he was sharing the deepest secrets of his soul.

"Our knowledge was too precious to risk leaving in the hands of defectors." Carefully, Schaeffer opened the lid on the box. It was angled so that Keira couldn't see what was inside. "I did what I had to, although it was unpleasant. If it's any comfort, they all were able to contribute to Artec's research and our precious future, even in death."

Keira felt as though her heart had stopped. "No—"

"They are kept present and visible," Schaeffer said, turning his chair slowly and sweeping one arm toward the recessed wall and the four twisting shades inside. "To remind me of what this was all for."

The shades screamed, and screamed, and screamed.

Keira's eyes burned as she watched the figures. One of them was her mother. One was her father. They'd not only been denied rest after death, but they'd been turned into *entertainment*, a display for the man who had cost them their lives.

"As I said before, if we'd met earlier and under better circumstances—before your attempts to destroy our company's investments, as an example—I really do believe we could have worked together, and you could have been a valuable asset to Artec." Schaeffer reached into the box. "As it stands, the best course for the company is to have you join your parents."

Keira was still fixated on the smudged figures as Schaeffer's words flowed over her. She didn't notice what was happening until Schaeffer drew his hand back out of the box and she caught a shimmer of metal.

He aimed his pistol at her face.

CHAPTER 27

KEIRA FELT LIKE A fool. If she'd been even a bit more focused—a bit less desperate for answers—she would have realized what Schaeffer was doing.

His slow winding words had distracted her. The more he'd talked, the more her focus had bled away. And he'd been more than happy to feed her whatever information she wanted as long as it kept her occupied while he worked his way over to his desk and unlocked the box that held his gun.

Now Keira had no time left. No time to react. No time to defend herself. No time to even bark a warning to Zoe and Mason.

Schaeffer pulled the trigger.

There was a split second where Keira was certain she was dead.

And in that split second, something she couldn't fully understand happened. A small black shape appeared above the table. It twirled as it fell. And in the exact same split second as Schaeffer pulled the trigger, he saw it and flinched.

Three sounds came so close together that it was a challenge to tell them apart: The deafening bang of the pistol being fired. The snap of the bullet hitting home. And the thud of the small black shape landing on the desk.

Keira dropped into a crouch, one arm over her head. Flecks of plaster trailed past her. The bullet had hit the wall just above her head; when she looked up, she saw the hole it had made, barely an inch from where she'd stood.

Schaeffer had reeled back in his chair. He still held the gun, but it was now limp in his hand and angled away.

Between them, on the desk, was a small black cat. It arched its back as it saw Schaeffer, and its fur sprung up to stand on end. A furious, wild little hiss escaped.

Schaeffer's mouth twitched open a fraction, but no sound came out. He only stared, stunned, at the cat. It skittered backward on the desk, its bushed tail curled defensively.

Keira felt her breath leave her in a rush. She didn't know how the cat had gotten into the room. Or how it had seemingly dropped from nowhere to land on the desk. But she *did* know what she was looking at.

"Daisy," she whispered, quietly shocked.

There was no explanation for it. She'd left Daisy in Blighty—five hours away. And yet, she was there, unmistakable and undeniably solid as she hissed at the man opposite her.

Schaeffer's shock morphed to disgust. He raised the gun again. This time, it was aimed at Daisy.

"No!" Keira lunged forward. The desk was between them, but

she threw herself over it, reaching for Schaeffer and the weapon. Folders scattered everywhere, papers flying free and cascading around them.

Daisy darted away, leaping off the desk and landing on the wooden floor.

Keira managed to get a grip on Schaeffer's wrist. She twisted it, forcing the gun to face the ceiling. They were close. She could smell the mouthwash he used and see the individual curling gray hairs in his eyebrows. His face contracted, hard and furious, as he used his other arm to shove against her, trying to force her back.

Daisy shot in again, sprinting between Schaeffer's legs and landing a sharp bite on the way past. He swore and kicked a foot out but missed the dexterous black cat.

It was the slim advantage Keira needed. She lurched forward, sending more folders spinning, and managed to tip Schaeffer's chair backward.

They landed hard on the floor, Keira still holding on to Schaeffer's wrist as his spare hand grappled at her—tugging at her collar, at her hair, trying to scratch her face. She didn't give him so much as an inch of space. Instead, she strained, twisting his arm farther back, and finally his hand spasmed hard enough to let go of the pistol. It skidded away from them and came to rest not far from the small bristled cat in the room's corner.

Schaeffer hissed between his teeth. His knee came up and hit Keira's sternum. She gasped as air was forced out of her lungs, and lost her grip on him. They came to rest two feet apart, crouched on the floor, both of them panting.

Keira's eyes landed on the piles of scattered papers between them. In among the printed notes was Schaeffer's key card from when he'd unlocked the box.

Schaeffer turned and lunged for his gun. Keira snatched up the key card as she followed him.

Daisy's jaws opened into a hissing, spitting yowl as Schaeffer reached for his weapon. She swiped forward, claws bared, and Schaffer snatched his hand back.

Keira darted past him. The papers slipped under her feet, threatening to topple her, and she was a second too slow to see Schaeffer's hand snake out. He grabbed her ankle and pulled, sending her to the floor. She gasped as her shoulder hit first and sent sparks of pain along the limb.

But she'd landed next to her wailing cat…and next to the gun.

She grabbed the weapon. There was no time to aim it, though. No time to do anything. Schaefer was dragging himself up her body, his grip painfully strong, as he reached for the pistol.

He didn't fear her. He knew she wasn't going to use it on him.

She did the only thing she could think of. She pointed it toward the ceiling and squeezed the trigger six times, emptying it.

Six bangs deafened them. Schaeffer recoiled, his eyes squinted closed. Keira squeezed the trigger three more times, making sure it was empty, then threw it.

The gun sailed past Schaeffer, skidding to land in the corner next to the recessed wall and the four shades. Their movements became faster. Excited, almost.

Schaeffer watched the gun land, then turned back toward her.

She was ready for him and drove the heel of her palm into the center of his face.

She not only heard but *felt* his nose break. He lurched back, letting Keira go, and pressed one hand across the space where a burst of vivid blood had already started to seep.

Keira scrambled back, putting some space between them. Daisy had curled herself into a defensively tight ball, the fur along the ridge of her back standing on end. Ghosts had never rattled the cat before. But there was something about Schaeffer that Daisy absolutely hated.

Same, Daze, same.

She had the key card clasped in her left hand. The door was close by. She just needed to get around Schaeffer first. And she needed to do it fast. The gun might be empty, but she didn't doubt he'd have replacement bullets in the locked box.

Seemingly thinking along the same lines, Schaeffer dropped his hand from his face and began to crawl toward the gun.

This might be her only chance. Keira reached for Daisy. The cat released a low throaty growl as Keira's hands slipped around her, but she let Keira lift her. She clutched Daisy to her chest and circled around the desk.

Schaeffer reached the empty gun and picked it up. With his other hand he pulled a handkerchief from his pocket and pressed it into his still bleeding nose.

His eyes were cold and unblinking as he watched her move, but he didn't try to stop her. Without a loaded weapon, they both knew Keira had the upper hand. She edged around the desk and closer to the door.

Daisy twisted in her arms, claws digging into Keira. She desperately tried to shush her cat, to beg her to hold still for just a moment, but every movement seemed to make Daisy more frantic. Terrified of losing her cat, Keira squeezed tighter. And then…Daisy simply slipped away.

One second she was a warm writhing ball of fur in Keira's arms. The next, she sank *through* Keira, *into* her, and Keira sucked in a pained breath as ice and fire burst like fireworks through her body.

She dropped to her knees, her eyes watering and her limbs shaking. She felt like raw electricity had been poured into her. Into her *mind.*

I remember…

It was like plugging power back into a long-dead machine. Images emerged from darkness. Memories rising out of nothing. Multiplying. Populating her mind so fast that she couldn't keep up with them.

"Oh," Keira groaned, fighting against nausea, and shook her head as the emotions and sensations threatened to drown her under their sheer weight. "*Oh.*"

She was faintly aware of Schaeffer moving behind her as he crept back toward the locked box. Keira blinked, but her vision swam as long-dormant images flowed across it.

She had to move. She knew that much. If she stayed kneeling in the office for much longer, Schaeffer would kill her.

And not just her, but…

Zoe. Mason.

She hadn't heard from them since she turned her radio off. But she needed to get back to them. Get them *out*.

She no longer had Daisy, but she still had the key card. She fumbled with it as she crawled to the door and pressed the card into the faintly glowing panel.

There was no satisfying click as it unlocked. No give to the handle when she pulled on it. Keira blinked, fighting to get her vision to focus. The panel held a number pad.

Slow insidious chuckles rose from behind her. "You thought the key card would be enough?" Schaeffer's voice was thickened and distorted by his broken nose. "You thought I would take that kind of risk with *you*?"

She heard the rattle of metal as he plucked replacement bullets out of their box. Waves of electricity poured off the shades in the back wall as they became frenzied, but there was nothing they could do to prevent Schaeffer from reloading the gun.

Her mind was clearing. It was growing easier to see through the fog of lost memories that had been dropped into her all at once. And in among them…

Knowledge. Skills.

And a rune to unlock doors.

Her thumb hadn't gotten much of a chance to heal since she'd cut it in the back of the transport van. She lifted it to her mouth and bit into it as hard as she could.

Already sore nerves screamed. Hot blood burst across her teeth. Keira raised her thumb to the panel and drew across it: *arrow, arrow, circle, spikes, arrow.*

Her blood glittered under the cold lights. The lock held for barely a second, then clicked as it unfastened.

At the same time, the prickles of electricity at the room's back redoubled. Keira sent a desperate glance over her shoulder. Schaeffer stood behind his desk. Blood ran down his jaw and dripped onto his expensive suit. He clicked the pistol's barrel back into place and raised the weapon.

Keira wrenched the door open and threw herself through.

CHAPTER 28

THE BULLET HIT THE wall beside Keira. She kicked the door closed behind herself, hoping it would slow Schaeffer down by at least a few seconds, and raced the hallway back to the archive room.

The dizziness threatened to topple her, and the space's dull lights made it feel like a maze. She ducked and wove as she pressed through narrow aisles. She only paused briefly—to drag open some of the drawers, effectively blocking the route for Schaeffer to follow.

There was no sign of Mason, and she hoped he'd gotten back to reception like he'd said he would.

There was another kind of movement, though.

A small black cat flitted out of the gloom and ran beside Keira. She stared at it without breaking pace; then a small grateful smile formed.

"Hey, Daze, welcome back."

Her cat's amber eyes seemed to glow as she frisked and wove, her tail thrashing.

A filing cabinet drawer banged closed behind them as Schaeffer followed, but they were already at the door that led to the stairs. Keira snatched up her cat and held her over one shoulder as she jogged, her breath coming hard and ragged, up the twisting stairwell.

The stairs vanished under her. Small plaques flashed past with each level. Keira didn't stop until she saw the one that said *Reception.* She burst through the door, still cradling Daisy, and came skidding to a halt.

The reception had been quiet and empty save for Zoe when she'd last seen it.

It was far from empty now.

Twelve guards, all wearing body armor that resembled riot gear, stood with weapons raised. They'd backed Zoe and Mason up against the far wall. Their gear—the backpacks and weapons they'd brought—was piled on the floor next to the reception desk. Keira's two friends stood, hands raised above their heads, faces pale.

Keira hadn't been subtle with her entrance. Four of the guards swung toward her, firearms aimed at her face.

"Away from the door!" the leader barked, his voice husky and furious. "Step forward, away from the door!"

She didn't have much of a choice. Daisy hissed as Keira slowly, cautiously progressed into the room. She caught a glimpse of Zoe and Mason over the guards' headgear. Zoe's teeth were clenched with frustration; Mason mouthed, *I'm so sorry.*

"Hands up," the guard yelled. "Above your head!"

"Okay, but I've got to put my cat down first." Moving incrementally slowly, Keira let Daisy drop back to the floor. The she raised her hands as the guards corralled her toward her companions.

"Are you okay?" Zoe whispered as soon as Keira was close enough. "You stopped answering the radio—and is that *Daisy*? How—"

"No talking," the guard snarled. He nodded to one of his companions, who stepped forward and felt around Keira's clothes. He took her backpack and her radio, and tossed them toward the reception desk. He missed the key card, which Keira had hidden in her jacket pocket along with the photos.

"Hold that position," the guard said as they stepped back. "Keep your arms up."

"Sure," Keira said. Her heart was running fast and her mouth was dry, but not from fear.

She had her memories back. And she was pretty sure the guards were underestimating exactly what she could do.

When they'd backed her against the wall, she'd deliberately put herself between Mason and Zoe. They were close enough for their raised arms to brush. And now she reached her hands out, just a little, to press her pinkie fingertips against her friends'.

They both glanced at her, and she knew they'd felt the prickle of energy passing between them, just like when she'd borrowed their energy to banish the shade back in Blighty.

She didn't have enough power on her own for what she planned to do. But if she could get just a little more…

Both Mason and Zoe pressed their arms back against her, offering her their energy. Daisy, who had attracted some confused stares but was otherwise going unnoticed, wove around her legs. She passed Keira once, twice, and on the third time she slipped around Keira's ankle, she vanished, lending Keira the power she had stored.

Which was good. She'd need everything she could get.

Welcome home, Old Keira. Let's see what we can do.

She took a deep breath, focusing, concentrating everything she had. Winding it into a small tight ball inside of her. A burning little elastic band of energy, almost painful in its intensity.

And then she let go.

Energy rushed out of her like a shockwave. It rippled the air as it billowed across the foyer. And she saw the exact second it impacted the ring of guards around her.

She'd feared it wouldn't be enough, but if anything, she'd made it too strong. As the ring of energy slammed into their chests, it was enough to throw the guards backward. Their feet rose into the air and their rifles fell from spasming hands. They hit the ground, scattered wide.

One of them pulled their headgear off to be sick on the floor. More groaned as they rolled over. She hoped she hadn't broken too many of their bones.

"Quickly," Keira said, grabbing her friends' hands and pulling on them.

She'd used a lot of energy, and not just her own. All three of them were exhausted. She didn't know how long she could get her friends to run for or whether they had any hope of making it out of the park before the guards recovered. But this narrow window would only last a few seconds, and they couldn't lose it.

They snatched up their confiscated gear on the way past the reception desk, then ran for the automatic doors. As the glass panes slid open for them, Keira threw one final look back at the room.

A few of the guards were struggling onto their hands and knees, though most were still down.

They were no longer alone, though. Schaeffer stood in the foyer's back, near the stairs, shrouded in shadows. Blood was smeared over the lower half of his face. His eyes looked like pinpricks of light in the gloom as he stared at them.

Then Keira was through the glass doors and into the tunnel that would lead to their freedom.

The tunnel was long. Both Zoe and Mason gasped for air, and Keira's legs shook even as she led the way. The portcullis appeared through the dim lights ahead, its access panel glowing a faint green next to it.

She pulled Schaeffer's card out of her pocket and held it up to the screen. The lights flashed red, then turned green again, and the metal bars shuddered before they began to rise.

She'd feared Schaeffer would try to disable the keypad, but

just like he hadn't tried to stop her from leaving the foyer, he didn't try to bar the exit now.

It's because he thinks I won't get through the amusement park's gates, she realized. *And he's very likely right.*

They wouldn't be able to creep through a carefully cut hole in the wire mesh this time. And she doubted either of her gasping companions would be able to scale the park's twelve-foot wall, not after how much of their energy she'd spent.

They ducked to get under the portcullis and spilled into the abandoned amusement park. Rain poured around them—no longer the heavy downpour of earlier, but a sad, moody drizzle. The wind was bitterly cold, but it felt good on her too-hot skin.

"Are you okay?" Mason bent over, hands braced on his knees as the gates slowly closed behind them. "What happened?"

"Too much to tell you now." Keira squinted at the derelict buildings around her. "I'm so sorry, but we need to keep moving. We can try to hide, but I'm pretty sure they'll sweep the park. So…"

"Got to get outside the fence," Mason said, nodding.

"We'll skirt around the edge, where the plants grow the thickest. We'll be harder to spot that way." Keira swallowed thickly. "It might buy us some time."

"I'm going to ask the question that he's too polite to," Zoe said, one hand pressed to a stitch in her side as they set off at a jog. "And that question is, specifically, *What the hell*?"

"Yeah, that's valid," Keira said, head craned as she watched for any signs that they were being followed. "Sorry, everything's kind of overwhelming right now."

"What was that zoom-y force-field thing? I didn't know you could do that."

"I didn't. I got an upgrade, I guess. Or…a downgrade? Reset to factory settings?"

Mason shot her a sharp glance. "Your memories…?"

"They're all a bit muddy right now." Keira led them behind a concrete shell that might have been intended to sell concessions. "But they exist."

His smile was like the sun breaking through clouds. "Then this was all worth it."

The park's concrete walls loomed ahead of them. Keira felt her heart sink as she took note of just how immense they were. "Let's hope so."

Picking through her old memories was like sorting through a pile of laundry that had been dumped on the floor. The patterns and fabrics blended together until it was impossible to tell a skirt apart from a blouse or a scarf. But Keira dug in, throwing metaphorical jeans and jackets aside as she looked for anything that might help them.

Anything to get them over the wall. Or under. She wasn't picky. Some latent teleporting abilities would have been welcomed, or possibly the ability to fly.

She had none of that. Just a mental catalog of runes that ran the gamut of *mildly useful* to *why do I even have this*? She somehow doubted a rune for making weeds grow slightly faster was going to save them at that moment.

She chewed her lower lip as she turned in a semicircle. The

wall was only their first barrier. Beyond that was the chain-link fence and its floodlights, effectively creating a moat with nowhere to hide.

Behind them, Keira heard the unmistakable rattle of the portcullis reopening. The guards were already in pursuit. She led her friends behind one of the buildings, where they'd at least be shielded from sight.

Out of nowhere, static crackled through the air. Keira flinched. "Hello." A muffled voice spoke, distorted and echoing as it came from two of their radios. "Dead Man Walking here. I know you told me not to use the radios but I'm bored."

They all exchanged a glance. *Harry.* They'd all but forgotten about him over the past hours.

Mason had thrown the radios into his backpack when they were escaping the hotel. Now he rummaged for them and lowered the volume so that Harry's voice wouldn't risk drawing so much attention.

"I hear you, Dead Man Walking," Zoe said into her set. "Blackbird here. We're trying to reach you, but we're trapped."

"Hi, Harry," Keira said, leaning over to speak into Zoe's radio as well.

"Trapped?" he sounded vaguely disinterested, nothing more. "Inside the park?"

"Yeah," Keira said. "We're trying to find a way around the guards."

"I'll pick you up."

The three of them exchanged a glance.

"No," Mason said quickly, reaching over to activate the *talk* button. "Harry, absolutely not. Stay where you are."

Anemic trees rattled in the icy air. Metal creaked as the ancient constructions around them flexed. The radio stayed silent.

"He can't possibly plan to…" Mason's eyebrows drew tighter together. "Does he?"

Keira reached for the radio. "Harry, you have to stay with the car. Can you hear me?" There was no answer. She grimaced and tried again. "*Dead Man Walking*. Respond."

"Yes," he said, his voice flat and mellow. "I hear you. I'm still with the car."

There was a sudden bang, followed by the sharp screech of breaking metal. Keira realized, with a wash of horror, that it sounded very much like a car being driven through a wire chain-link fence.

A motor roared. Headlights washed through the entrance to the park.

Zoe stared at them with wide shining eyes. "What have we unleashed?" she whispered.

"Damn it!" Keira grabbed their arms. "We have to get to him."

Her limbs shook as she ran. Zoe staggered, then caught herself. Keira blinked against the drizzling rain as she watched Mason's car skate through the park's entrance, dragging the old balustrades and ropes in its wake. The car fishtailed, its trunk knocking against one of the buildings before it careened down the main path.

Guards ran through the entrance behind it, yelling into their radios. Keira didn't know whether to laugh hysterically or break into sobs as the car rocketed closer.

They leaped onto the main road, waving their arms to catch Harry's attention. Tires screeched as he braked hard, and the whole car rocked violently as it stopped just feet from them.

"In," Keira hissed, hyperaware that guards were closing in from both the tower and the park's entrance. "In, in, *in*."

Mason ended up in the front passenger seat, while Keira threw herself into the rear, closely followed by Zoe. Harry, blank-faced and seeming bored, didn't even wait for them to close the doors before he leaned on the accelerator. The car rattled as it rose up onto a curb, then slammed back down again.

"You're safe to drive, right?" Mason asked, trying to pull his seat belt free. "Zoe said you'd had lessons."

"Two of them," Harry said calmly. "That should be sufficient."

Mason's struggle with the seat belt redoubled.

"I've never been so happy to see anyone in my life," Zoe said. "Get us out of here, Dead Man Walking."

"Heard, Blackbird."

The car screeched as it scraped against a building, leaving a trail of paint on the concrete wall, but Harry had managed to get the car pointed back toward the park's entrance. Four guards blocked their way.

That didn't seem to deter Harry. His face remained flat and disinterested, his fringe covering one eye, as he pointed the car at them and pressed on the accelerator. The motor roared. The closest two guards set their stance and raised their guns.

"Duck!" Keira yelled, dragging Zoe down beside her.

There was a snap of fracturing glass as a bullet passed through the windshield. Harry didn't so much as flinch, and he didn't let the car slow. Its engine roared as it devoured the road and barreled straight at the guards.

They leaped away at the last second. Keira actually felt the car clip one of them, and she had a split second to wonder if Harry would have driven over them if they hadn't moved, but then the second row of guards were firing at them even as the car sped out through the park's enormous sun-themed opening.

Keira dared to lift her head. Zoe was panting but also grinning wildly. Mason, sunk low in his seat, had one hand braced on the dashboard as horror set his face in rigid lines.

Harry, calm as always, accelerated through the gap he'd already carved in the chain-link fence. The car bounced as it coasted over the fallen metal walls. One guard fired a token shot after them, but they were moving fast and already past being easy targets.

Then their headlights were pointed toward the distant town and the trees beyond, and as Keira felt her heart thunder against her ribs, she realized they were free.

CHAPTER 29

"WE DID IT," ZOE said, and she sounded like she didn't fully believe herself. "We got out."

"Hooray," Harry said very unenthusiastically.

"You wrecked my car," Mason said dully. Then he squeezed his eyes closed and shook his head. "No. I take that back. We're alive. You got us out alive. A car's a small price to pay for that."

Harry hadn't let their wild trajectory slow. They careened across the hills surrounding the amusement park, the tires kicking up mud behind them.

"Aim for the wooded area," Mason said, twisting to look through the rear window. "Once we're under cover, we'll switch out and I'll drive."

"But I'm so good at it," Harry said, right as one of the windshield wipers came loose and clattered away.

He got them under the shade of the dense trees with only two additional scrapes. Mason looked unspeakably relieved as he slid into the driver's seat and forced Harry back in the passenger side.

"Okay," he said, squeezing the wheel with white knuckles and easing the car forward with significantly more skill than Harry. "Do we know our next move?"

Keira glanced behind them. Between the branches, she could still see the lights surrounding the park's barrier. "They're going to try to follow us. We have a head start, but we'll need to be careful as we get out of here. Follow quieter roads, stay out of sight."

"Got it." Mason turned the headlights off. They were on a narrow trail leading through the trees; between the rain and the darkness, it was nearly impossible to see where they were going, but Keira understood they'd be easy targets if they didn't dim the lights.

She leaned back in her seat, breathing deeply. It was the first time she'd had a moment free to actually process what had happened to her.

She had her memories back.

It was a bizarre sensation. The version of herself that she'd been calling New Keira—the Keira that had woken up outside Blighty and had been forced to rediscover her gifts—still felt distinct to Old Keira. It was like two versions of herself lived inside her mind, and they were battling over space. A low headache throbbed at the back of her skull.

Zoe had been sitting quietly next to Keira, her jacket clutched around herself to ward off some of the cold. She suddenly sat up straight, a pained gasp choking in her throat.

"What?" Keira reached for her, alarmed. "What happened?"

"We forgot the cat." Zoe's eyes were enormous and shimmering as she turned to Keira in the dark. "Daisy was in the hotel—we left her—"

"Oh." Keira slumped back, laughing weakly. "No, don't worry, that's fine. She's still here."

She placed one hand on the center of her chest. Then she moved the hand forward, pulling lightly. The small black cat spilled out of her, all whiskers and flicking tail, and landed heavily in Keira's lap.

Zoe screamed.

Mason screamed.

Harry, apparently not wanting to miss out, took a deep breath and then released a noise that sounded something like, "Aaaaauugh."

"That's good," Keira said, cradling her cat to protect it from the way the car swerved abruptly. "Get it out of your systems."

"The hell," Zoe managed. She was pressed hard against the door, gripping both the seat she was in and the headrest ahead of her. A look of understanding flashed through her expression. "Magic cat. You've been saying it all along."

Mason had managed to steer the car to a halt. He turned in his seat, staring first at Keira, then at Daisy, with a look of wonder and faint admiration. "How does it work? Can she just…disappear back into you? Is this how she managed to escape from my house when I was supposed to be looking after her?"

"Don't know, yes, and I'm pretty sure, yeah." Keira scratched under Daisy's chin. She was calmer now that they were out of Artec, and her bright amber eyes closed contentedly. "I'm pretty sure I can explain, but you've got to give me a minute. All the memories are getting jumbled in my mind."

She blinked and saw the small cat slinking between concrete pillars late at night. She remembered herself, hungry and cold and desperate. Trying to…trying to…

Tears burned Keira's eyes. She squeezed them closed, breathing deeply. An ache had started in her heart, and she wasn't sure it would ever go away. "Okay, I know we're all eager to go home…"

"I'm not," Harry said, blinking slowly. "This has finally gotten interesting."

"Minus Harry, we're all eager to get home. But can we stop by somewhere first? There's something I need to do."

Mason glanced at Zoe, and when she nodded, he said, "Of course. We're with you to the end. Tell me where to go."

"Get us through the trees. There should be a road on their other side. Turn left on it, and follow it until it passes through a tunnel." Keira watched as Daisy curled around in her lap, tucking her tail in neatly before lying down. She didn't seem bothered by the car's motions. "I'll explain everything on the way."

It wasn't an easy story to tell. Keira was still trying to untangle the threads of who she was and how her new memories meshed together. She began haltingly by explaining how her abilities were an unintended side effect of Artec's experiments. How her parents, knowing what Artec and its founder, Schaeffer, were likely to do with her if they knew of her existence, had hidden her for most of her early life. How, when Keira was twelve, Schaeffer finally caught up with them.

Keira's father had stayed at their family home to act as a distraction, and he'd died first. But it only took Schaeffer two days to catch up to Keira's mother.

Two days had been just enough time, though. Enough time to hide Keira with Mina, a great-aunt who had lived in the mountains. Her parents had sacrificed everything to give Keira a second chance at life.

Mina had been a good, if absent-minded caretaker. Keira had spent her days outdoors, climbing trees and chasing after wild birds. To keep her safe, Keira was never enrolled in school or allowed to talk about her past life.

There had been very few ghosts in the mountains around where Mina lived. Keira saw some when they traveled into town but never got much chance to use her gift.

That changed after Mina passed. Keira stayed long enough for the funeral and to make sure Mina's spirit hadn't lingered, and then she'd left the town. Since she'd never formally been registered as living with Mina or as a next of kin, she wasn't able to keep the house but had taken an envelope of savings that Mina had put aside for her.

The next few years had held a series of new homes, new towns, new faces. Keira, all too aware that Artec was still watching for her, never let herself stay in one place for more than a few months. She lived in motels, hostels, and shared apartments when the owners didn't want a background check.

There had been plenty of ghosts on those travels. Keira had been able to help some of them, but not all.

She'd hoped, one day, she could start to live a more mundane life. She'd dreamed of finding a place to settle down, of being able to make—and keep—friends.

But it hadn't been possible. The more she'd researched Artec and the more she realized what they were doing, the more her urgency to stop them grew.

She started attacking their graveyards. Just small stabs at first—breaking cables, cutting off power where she could. But it was never enough. Artec, having perfected their scheme with the discovery of how to create shades, was expanding fast. For every grave she managed to free, a hundred new coffins were interred.

So she'd turned to something more central. The power stations.

Artec had several and traditionally placed them only a short distance from the cemeteries. Unlike traditional power stations, which manufactured electricity, Artec's were more like converters. They took in the power generated by the shades and transformed it into an electrical current that could be supplied to power grids. The buildings were large and full of machinery, but most of that was smoke and mirrors to pass the inspections. They only needed the plants to look legitimate enough that no one would be suspicious about where the enormous quantities of current were coming from.

Zoe cut across the story then. "So like money laundering but for electricity?"

"Yeah, that's not a bad analogy." Keira ran her hands across Daisy's rumpled fur. "Artec can't tell anyone where the electricity is *actually* coming from, firstly because no one would believe them and secondly because no one would go along with it if they actually did manage to convince the world. So...fake power plants. Actual, real power storage. I realized, if I was going to do anything to stop them, it would need to be there."

"Cool," Zoe said. "Keep going. This story was supposed to be about the cat, but I don't want to stop you when you're on a roll."

"We're getting to Daisy," Keira said, grinning. "Be patient."

Zoe just gestured for her to continue.

"I broke into one of their plants. And I found a way to overload the system. If it worked, it would not only break the plant, but the overflowing energy should have been enough to free the shades in the graveyard attached to it as well. But..." She frowned, fighting with the memories. "Something went wrong. There was a stray cat in among the transformers."

"A*ha*," Zoe said, then pressed a finger to her lips and lowered her voice. "Sorry, didn't mean to break your flow."

"It's fine." Keira gazed down at Daisy, who, despite the bumpy drive, was fully asleep. The cat was drooping off either side of her lap, and Keira had to keep a hand on her to make sure she didn't fall off entirely.

"It wasn't Daisy's fault. She was just hungry and frightened. But I was most of the way through the process before I realized she was there. I lost my concentration. And..."

Blinding pain. Currents, harsher than she'd ever experienced before, coursing along her nerves. She'd been certain she was going to die.

"The cat was gone," Keira said. "I could barely move, but Artec's guards had heard me and were coming for me. I ran. And ran. And ran. Into a forest. And I collapsed into a hollow, and..."

Old Keira's memories ceased. New Keira's began.

"I woke up in the woods outside of Blighty, sore, injured, and with no idea how I'd gotten there. People were chasing me. But a friendly pastor let me hide in his house until they were gone." She took a deep breath, then exhaled it. With the timeline in place, the memories didn't feel quite so discordant any longer.

Mason glanced at her in the rearview mirror. They were on the main road and far enough from the amusement park that he'd switched his headlights back on. They still had a good few hours of driving to go, though. "I remember you telling me that Daisy arrived outside your cottage door the same night you turned up in Blighty," he said.

"Yeah." Back then, it had seemed like a coincidence. She now knew that it wasn't, not at all. "Because she's a part of me now. I think...I think the spectral electricity would have killed us both if we hadn't found one another."

"I'm not sure I get that," Zoe said.

"I'm not sure I do either." The cat's tongue was beginning to poke out from between her tiny teeth. "I think a piece of me was stored in her. She had all of my old memories. All of this time I thought they were inside me, and I just needed to fight hard enough to get them back. But they weren't. They were in Daisy. When she first merged back into me—back in the office—that was when I started to remember."

"You said she's helped you too," Mason noted.

"Exactly. Leading me to safety when I was lost, creating the rune under my bed to help me regain energy. And back in Artec's tower, she appeared out of nowhere right when I needed her. Because...I don't think she's entirely a living cat any longer."

"You mean..." Zoe squinted. "She's dead?"

"Not quite. But she's not fully alive either." The whites of Daisy's eyes were showing as she drifted deeper. "She's still a real cat. But she's also...a part of me. Like an extension of who I am."

"A fursona," Harry said, nodding knowingly.

"Um."

"Zombie magical cat fursona," Zoe added. "That makes sense."

"I feel like it shouldn't." Keira sighed.

"Can you control her?" Mason asked.

"I mean, she's a cat, so no." Keira smiled at her own joke, then let the expression fall. She knew what Mason was really asking: Could she direct Daisy or alter her behavior? And Keira genuinely didn't know. She didn't *feel* like she could, but then, the cat had always seemed to know what to do to help Keira. And...

"Oh," Keira whispered.

She suddenly understood why the memories had felt so chaotic and difficult. Earlier, she'd thought it was like there were two versions of herself fighting for space inside her mind. Now, she realized there were *three*. Old Keira, New Keira, and Daisy.

"I can see Daisy's memories," she said, faintly shocked. It was like opening a different drawer in a filing cabinet, but once she did, the images flowed over her. Daisy, chasing bugs through the long grass of Blighty's cemetery. Daisy, full of fury and fear, biting Schaeffer's ankle as she darted past him. And Daisy, being cradled by Mason as he scratched her chin. She felt herself smile.

"You're in control," Mason said, breaking through the pleasant memory. "What's our last stop for tonight?"

"Just a piece of unfinished business," Keira said, gazing out of the car's window at the countryside flashing past. "I'm going to topple a power station."

CHAPTER 30

THE FOUR FRIENDS WERE quiet for most of the drive. According to the clock on the car's dash, dawn would be arriving in a couple of hours. They were all dead exhausted but too jittery to actually rest.

Mason seemed to be dwelling on something. He was always cheerful, but Keira had begun to notice the little signs he developed when his smiling face didn't match the mood inside.

Keira wasn't the only one to notice. Zoe, slumped in the back seat, used her foot to nudge Mason's elbow. "What kind of bee do you have in your bonnet?" she asked.

"I'm bee free today."

"Liar."

He chuckled. "Okay. I meant what I said earlier. About how our lives are more important than a car."

"But..." she prompted.

"My parents left me with their much-loved sedan in pristine condition, and I'm going to return them a crumpled wreck that's pockmarked with bullet holes. I have a feeling I'm about to be demoted from the role of Favorite Child. And to be clear, I'm their *only* child."

"It's healthy to disappoint people every now and then," Zoe said. "I've spent my whole life disappointing as many people as possible and it's worked out great."

"Thanks," Mason said, looking grim.

Zoe just shrugged. "I mean it. You're a chronic people pleaser. And that's fine. But you'll never truly get what *you* want unless you make it your priority. Stop being a minor character in everyone else's story and be the main character in your own."

For a moment, Mason only gazed out at the rolling hills through the windscreen. Then he said, very softly, "Huh."

"Yeah, I've been reading a lot of self-help books lately. But only the ones that get, like, two-star review averages. That's where you get the *real* juicy advice."

"Huh," Mason said again, this time with more doubt.

"I know you don't want to hear this…" Keira glanced behind them to check that the road was still empty. "But it might be wisest to abandon the car entirely. Someone back there could have recorded the license plate. Even if they didn't, they know what your car looks like now, and it's pretty memorable in its current condition."

Mason grimaced. "That's a good point. We'll have to leave it somewhere far from home too—maybe in a mine shaft or somewhere it won't be easily found. I'm just glad it's registered to an address in a different town."

"Sorry," Keira said, offering an apologetic smile. "I know you liked this car."

"Well, like I said...lives over possessions. I can't exactly buy a replacement for any of you lot. Ah—is this our turn?"

Keira craned to see the signpost in the headlights. "Yeah, this is it. We're close."

The prior version of herself had memorized the power plants that Artec ran, their addresses, and which cemeteries they fed from. There were only three at the time she'd lost her memories, but two more had been under construction. She wondered if they were finished yet.

This one was special, though. And she hadn't known how much until she'd met Schaeffer in Artec's tower. This power plant connected to a nearby graveyard for a new residential development...and it also connected to Five Suns Amazement Park.

Old Keira hadn't known what truly became of her parents. She'd feared that Schaeffer might have tried to keep their spirits like some kind of morbid trophy. She'd hoped, maybe foolishly, that he would be too empathetic for that. But she'd never been able to guess where they'd been stored...until tonight.

Overloading the grid would, theoretically, not only break the system but force the spectral energy back along the cords and into the graveyard. It would be like a power surge frying electronics but on a much larger scale. If she did it right, she could break the entire graveyard as well as the Five Suns development, and free every shade and spirit trapped in them.

Including her parents.

If she never made it past this night, she wanted to at least know that they were no longer suffering. No longer sealed in the office of the man who had killed them. No longer forced to participate in an experiment they'd denounced.

She'd been young when her parents had died, but they'd tried to explain what they'd done—and why Keira had her gifts—as gently as they could to a child. And they'd made one thing incredibly clear.

They'd been involved in the earliest experiments with spirits, when all that remained after their conversion was the hollow shell of a ghost. No spirit, no memory, no emotions. No suffering. Those spirits were more akin to a photograph of their past selves than a true ghost.

But those graves—Mark One—hadn't been profitable. Without a conscious spirit inside, they hadn't been able to pull energy from the ether like from a true ghost.

And so Artec, and Schaeffer, had pushed for innovation.

And Keira's parents had gone along with it. Up until Keira's mother had learned she was pregnant. She told Keira about how she'd lain awake at night, dreaming about how her child might one day end up in Artec's graveyards, a miserable, screaming husk of a ghost.

And fully aware of the risks—knowing that Schaeffer did not take lightly to betrayals and knowing that he would kill to protect the knowledge they had—both of her parents had walked away from Artec.

Keira's eyes stung with tears she fought to blink back. They'd been involved in Artec and all of its ugliness. But they'd also wrestled out of it when it became too obvious that what they were doing was wrong. She was proud of them for that.

Heavy gray buildings rose out of the gloom ahead. Keira recognized them. Every one of Artec's power plants followed the same design, barring a few cosmetic changes.

A ring of multistory buildings held a mix of machines that were just complex enough to look convincing to the employees who worked there and to any inspectors who might pay an unexpected visit.

But Keira was more interested in what was kept in the internal courtyard.

A mesh of metal towers, connected by humming cables, made up the power grid. One set of cables ran into it, ferrying in the power produced by the graveyard connected to it. Another set of cables ran out, supplying the power to its buyers. In between were the transformers that converted the spectral electricity into something more compatible with the average home.

It was one of the only weaknesses in Artec's designs: a necessary flaw that gave Keira access to the cables in an unprecedented way.

It was what she'd been attempting to destroy during her final night as Old Keira. It was what she had to destroy now.

As they coasted into sight of the fences surrounding the power plant, Keira ran through a mental inventory of what she'd need. It wasn't a large list. "Zo, I'll need to borrow some pens. And a small knife, if you have one."

"You've got it." Zoe began digging through her backpack. "What else do you need? You can take some of my energy. I have a bit extra I can spare."

"Thanks, but not right now." Keira's strength was still depleted after her stunt at Artec's headquarters, but ironically, that was the way she wanted to keep it. It gave her a few inches of leeway if she came in contact with the ultra-charged cables. "Speaking of, though—hold still a second."

She used one of Zoe's markers to draw a rune on both Zoe's and Mason's shoulders.

"That'll help you recharge," she said, frowning as she added the final details to Mason's. "Not quickly, mind, but it will be better than waiting for it to happen naturally."

"Neat," Zoe said, twisting to see hers. "So, what's the plan? How're we getting in? What do we need to do once we're there?"

Keira managed a tight smile. "*I'm* going in. You're all staying in the car. Park it somewhere it won't be easily seen from the station or the road."

"I'm going to sound like an echo of myself, but we shouldn't split up," Mason said. He'd turned sideways in his seat to see her better, and concern and tiredness mingled together to line his eyes with creases. "Zoe and I promised we'd be with you to the end, remember?"

Images danced in the back of Keira's mind—the arcs of

electricity racing overhead, the crackle of raw power discharging through the air. "I know. And I can't tell you how much I appreciate it. But it's not an option today. Having too many bodies near the power source increases the risk; the only way this is going to work is if I do it alone."

"Ah." Mason frowned, rubbing at the back of his neck. "Okay. But is there anything else we can do? I don't like the thought of you going in there alone."

Harry, his pallid face lit uncomfortably by the car's internal lights, slowly rotated to fix her with his unblinking stare. "I can light several large fires."

Keira opened her mouth, then closed it again. She worked her jaw and let her eyebrows rise. "You know what? Yeah. That...that might be good. Several large fires could help."

Zoe and Mason exchanged a glance.

"For real?" Zoe asked.

"There will be guards." There had been on Keira's first attempt too, but they'd been lax and asleep. It had been easy to slip in without being seen. Now, though? After she'd partially damaged one power station and had just slipped out of Artec's grips at its headquarters? "A distraction could actually help."

"I have some gas in the back of the car," Zoe said, her smile gathering enthusiasm.

Mason looked incredulous. "Just how many flammable things did you *bring*?"

"Just those! I would have gotten a flamethrower but they're wickedly expensive."

Mason sighed. "Sure. You know what? We've already broken so many laws tonight—trespassing, vandalism, battery, illegal explosives—may as well add arson to the list."

"Hooray team," Harry said.

"We'll start some fires," Mason said. "If we can get them big enough, it should be enough to draw the guards. At least for a little while."

"That's exactly what I need. Keep yourselves hidden. We'll meet back at the car once we're done." Keira nudged the sleeping cat in her lap, and Daisy vanished into her, like a shadow flitting away under light. She could feel her companion's presence inside of her, like a very small warm heat in the center of her chest.

"I'm never going to get used to that," Zoe said, watching in amazement.

"Be safe, okay?" Mason gave her a tight-lipped smile and a nod, but she could read the worry in his eyes.

She'd spent the last five years of her life knowing that, as long as she was fighting Artec, she could never settle down. Never grow comfortable. Never have relationships that went deeper than acquaintances.

And that belief had been so deeply baked into her that remnants of it had remained, even when her memories were torn away.

She'd loved Blighty, but she'd been ready to leave it at a moment's notice. And she loved her friends, but something small in the back of her mind was always prepared to lose them. To step away from them to keep them safe.

Maybe that was the wrong choice.

She looked between the other occupants of the car: Zoe, fierce and protective and smarter than she let on. Mason, full of compassion and steadfastness, giving her more loyalty than she thought she deserved. Even Harry, the dark horse who'd, knowingly or not, risked everything to get them out of the amusement park.

Old Keira had thought it would be safest to work alone.

But Old Keira had stepped aside to make room for New Keira, and New Keira was starting to understand that the only reason she'd survived this long—the only reason she had any chance to make it through to dawn—was because she let herself trust.

Mason was still watching her, and she felt her stomach twist. She felt something for him, horribly, intensely, more than she'd wanted to admit to herself, but every time he'd given her a chance to get closer, she'd pushed him away.

Because she was too desperately afraid of losing him.

You don't know what's going to happen tonight. You don't know if you'll get another chance to make things right.

"Hey," she said. "I don't think you should go back to medical school."

"Hell yeah!" Zoe turned in her seat, a fist raised in victory. "Reject institutional education! Stay ignorant!"

Keira kept her focus on Mason. "Or you could. But it'd mean a lot of traveling for the both of us. Because I'd miss you too much to let you disappear across the country for months at a time."

"Okay, slightly less agreement on that point," Zoe said.

Do it, you fool. Do it now, or you'll never get up the nerve again.

"We should go out for dinner sometime," she said, feeling heat rise up through her stomach as she forced the words out. "It doesn't have to be dinner. It could be a walk. Or anything else. Just as long as it's a date."

Mason blinked rapidly. He looked faintly stunned as a shocked, pleased smile began to form. "Really?"

"Yeah, really."

"Yes. Okay. I'd like that."

"Great. You have my number. Or…or we can just make plans in person, like we normally do. I've got to go destroy some expensive stuff now. I'll be back in an hour." Keira barreled out of the car before the embarrassment could suffocate her.

As she closed the door behind herself, she heard Zoe ask, "How many wheels does this car have again? Because I think I'm the spare."

Followed by Harry's morose: "Love is a pit of endless misery, you know. I'd avoid it if I were you."

Mason didn't answer either of them. As Keira jogged down the narrow path that would lead her to the power plant, she sent one final glance over her shoulder.

The lights were still on inside the car, and she could see Mason, leaned back in his seat. He had one hand pressed across his mouth, but it didn't completely hide the smile.

Keira felt herself grin as she turned back to her mission.

CHAPTER 31

THE POWER PLANT LOOMED out of the darkness. Its massive buildings were illuminated with lights that never went off, but Keira knew there would only be a skeleton crew stationed there overnight.

The fence surrounding it was both more modern and more rigid than the one around the Five Suns Amazement Park. Thick vertical bars reminded Keira of a prison. They ran high overhead, decorated periodically with metal signs warning about high voltages and danger.

Keira knew of a way in, though. They all followed the same designs, and they all had the same weakness, hidden near the compound's back: a small drainage ditch, just large enough for her to squeeze through.

As she followed the fence's perimeter, she thought she heard a distant sound. Keira froze, her nerves turned tight, as she listened. The night was quiet save for the low chirrups of a cricket.

She could have sworn she'd heard something, though. It had sounded like the rumble of a car's motor suddenly falling still.

Mason, moving the car to somewhere less visible? She wanted to believe that was all it was, but memories tugged at the back of her mind: the mysterious figure she'd seen in the distance near her cottage. The feeling of eyes on her at the pub. She waited another minute, but no noises came. Keira breathed out and watched the warm air from her lungs turn to condensation. Then she kept moving.

She hated how paranoid small sounds made her, but her margin for error was so slim it nearly didn't exist. Any mistake—even a small one—could mean disaster.

The drain was little more than a concrete slot running underneath the fence. It would be tight, but Keira already knew she'd fit. She'd managed to get under a very similar one at the first power plant she'd targeted.

Cold water seeped through Keira's clothes as she dropped onto her back and shimmied under the bars.

She was nearly through the other side when the distant crackle of leaves reached her. She froze, the metal pressing into her chest with every tight breath. The sound didn't repeat. Teeth clenched, Keira dragged herself through the rest of the way and stood.

The patchy bushes outside the fence were nothing but a crisscrossing wall of shadows and thin moonlight.

It could have been an animal. Or it might have been nothing.

Keira had a flashlight, but she didn't dare use it—not when it was so vital that her presence went undetected.

If she'd had more time, she might have pulled back to reassess. But that wasn't an option; dawn would arrive in less than an hour, and she had to be far away from the plant when it did.

In the distance, someone yelled. Keira flattened herself, her heart in her throat. The voice continued shouting, but it wasn't growing closer; it was moving away. On the horizon, past the power plant's fence, were flickering golden lights. They were small but growing rapidly as they caught on dead bushes. Plumes of smoke rose from them, stretching like fingers into the starry sky.

Several large fires. Her friends had come through.

Keira rose from her crouch and jogged toward the stark brightly lit buildings.

They were a mess of brutal concrete blocks and fake smokestacks. Keira kept herself small and fast as she darted across the empty lawn of mostly dead grass and pressed herself into the shadows at the foot of the nearest structure.

Already, she could feel the thrumming energy. It was the same painful, uneasy prickle that had infected her at the Pleasant Grove graveyard. The same ache that had radiated off the four shades in Schaeffer's office. The crackle of energy drawn out of shades.

There were no spirits at this site, though. Just their power, brought in from a nearby graveyard and from Five Suns, to be converted and released as a traditional electrical current.

Voices led away from her as the guards employed by the site

left to check on the fires. Lights were on in most of the windows, but she knew she was unlikely to be seen. In fact, she was banking on that. She moved again, her footfalls light as they carried her around a corner and into a narrow passageway that led to the central area of the power plant.

It was nearly the size of a football field and filled with rows of transformers and truck-sized battery compartments. Cables ran both underground and overhead. It was a mesh of metal: spiky, cold, unforgiving. The electricity was so condensed that she could hear its hum.

No grass was allowed in this central compound. The floor was concrete. Keira shivered with each step as the power rose out of the ground and threatened to drown her.

Focus...focus...

She had no idea how many souls might be serving this one power plant. But it would be considerable.

Floodlights were positioned high overhead, leaving no shadowy areas for Keira to work. She'd have to be fast and just hope that none of the guards thought to search the compound. Keira pulled her pen out of her pocket.

Starting at the outside of the transformers, Keira began forming runes. On their own, they were relatively weak. If she meshed together several hundred, they would be capable of significantly more.

The first set of runes contained the energy. When she reversed the connections, she needed the power to flow back down the cables, not dissipate into the air. She pointed the runes inward, directing everything back into the center of the system. She covered as much space as she could, drawing them both on the floor and as high up the walls as she could reach.

Her wrist was starting to ache. She shook it to loosen it, then kept moving, gradually narrowing the rings of images to point to one central location.

A metal hatch, no larger than a book, was discreetly tucked into the center of the complex. Four screws in its corners kept it in place.

To Artec, it was a simple access panel to measure voltages.

For Keira, though, it was something much more powerful. She'd needed months of research and trial and error to learn that *this* was the one weak spot she could reach.

Keira knelt next to the metal plate and drew her pocketknife out. She used the blade's tip to carefully unscrew the panel, then held her breath as she lifted it aside.

Lines and lines of cables twisted beneath that access hatch. The power coming off them was enough to turn Keira's blood to fire and set her nerves sparking. She'd been weak and tired after spending her energy at Artec's tower. Now, being so close to the cables, she felt the charge building up inside of herself again.

This was the most dangerous part. And the part that had nearly killed her the last time she'd attempted it.

Keira took her pen out once more. She drew a series of runes in a loop around herself as she crouched next to the box. Those runes were for protection from the surge.

She'd used them before, on her first attempt at rediverting

the power plant's energy, but it hadn't been enough. Especially not when she'd seen the small black cat creeping between her messages and realized what was about to happen to it. She'd panicked and reached toward the cat, trying to scare it away before it was killed. And she'd paid dearly for it.

She was going to be more careful this time. The runes ran in a tight circle around her, warding her. She'd put down nearly forty of them, five times the number of her first attempt. She hoped that would be enough.

Keira took a deep breath to brace herself. This was it. The entire concrete area was covered in ink, but she only had one more mark to place.

She drew the final rune directly onto the largest cable. Energy sparked out of it, surging through the pen and burning its way up her arm. For the first time she'd attempted this, she'd used gloves. Now, though, she could feel it pulling at her skin. She grit her teeth and pushed the pain to the back of her mind.

This was not something she could afford to rush. She drew carefully, getting the final rune exact and layering it in bold lines.

A rune to reverse the flow of energy.

Then she slid back into a crouch, capping the pen, and made sure she was perfectly inside her circle of protection.

The rune took a moment to work. She could feel it, though, fighting against the flow of power. Slowing it. Trying to push it back into itself. It was going to work.

And then a sound echoed across the space, and Keira's heart missed a beat.

"You're all alone, little mouse," a cool calculated voice said.

Keira's gaze snapped up. A figure stepped out from between the transformers. His blond hair might have once been neatly combed but now hung in strands across his forehead. His thin lips curled up into a snarling smile.

Somehow, improbably, against all odds, Gavin Kelsey had found her.

CHAPTER 32

GAVIN'S SMILE TWITCHED AS he gazed down at her.

"What?" was all Keira could manage. She felt strained to her limits. Of all the problems she'd anticipated—of all the people she'd feared would step out of the shadows to confront her—Gavin had to be the most unpredicted.

She'd been ready for Artec's guards to reappear. For Schaeffer to emerge to gloat over her. Even a low-level employee at the power plant could cause serious problems if he stumbled on her.

But...*Gavin*?

She felt like the universe was laughing at her.

And that didn't mean Gavin was a laughing matter. He was sociopathic. He was a killer.

But she thought she might have been less shocked if Polly Kennard herself had leaped out from between the towers.

Gavin wore a dark turtleneck sweater, and a smear of grimy

dampness running along one side told her he must have followed her through the drainage ditch. Which meant he was the thing that had disturbed the trees. The unaccounted-for engine in the dark.

It still didn't explain how he'd found her out here, hours from Blighty, when Keira had been watching the roads around them and hadn't seen any cars at all that night.

He paced closer, rounding the farthest transformer, and Keira felt her heart seize up. She could see the edge of the barrier she'd drawn, only a few feet from where Gavin now stood.

Energy crackled in the cables. It was working. Building. Her ring of wards was keeping her safe, but she didn't want to think about what would happen to anyone who stepped into the field without protections. Especially when the station overloaded.

"You're probably wondering why I'm here," Gavin said. He was slightly younger than Keira, and his Adam's apple bobbed thickly.

"I mean..." She waved a hand. "To kill me. I'm not winning any prizes for guessing the obvious. I want to know *how* you're here."

His smirk faltered. He didn't like being made to look foolish. His right hand shifted forward, and she saw a familiar shimmer of metal.

His father's gun. The same gun Keira had owned for a very brief and confusing stretch of time. She'd hidden it in her wardrobe and vowed not to touch it again. She couldn't believe she'd forgotten to check it was still there after she realized that someone had been in her cottage.

"Okay, one mystery down. You broke into my home and

rifled through my clothes. Gross. But I still want to know how you found me."

She knew she shouldn't antagonize him, but she was finding it hard to moderate her words. Only half of her attention was on Gavin. The other half was on the crackling, building power beneath her hands.

"You left your phone on your shack's bench," Gavin said. He tilted his head, and the loose strands of hair threw spiderlike shadows over his face. "It took less than a minute to install a GPS tracker on it."

My phone. It had been a gift from Mason, upgrading her into the modern world.

Only a few people had her number, so Keira almost never checked it. She could have gone weeks without noticing a foreign app had been installed. She'd gotten in the habit of keeping the phone in her pocket, though, just in case.

Amazingly, and not for the first time, Zoe had been in the right: Keira would have been safer with a brick of a phone that didn't have internet capabilities.

At least that solved another mystery for her.

"*You* were the person I kept seeing in the distance," Keira said. "The weird ominous figure that stood between the trees and stared at me. That was *you*, following me."

Which meant he'd been trailing her for days. His clothes were rumpled, she realized, and dark circles lined beneath his hooded eyes.

Why? He's hateful and petty, but this isn't his style. He goes for easy targets. And nothing about this would have been easy. So why...?

It clicked into place. He wasn't following her for revenge. He was following her out of desperation.

His father had approached Keira several weeks before and challenged her, threatening her in an attempt to force her out of the town. During the encounter, she'd let slip that she knew about Gavin's crimes. And Dr. Kelsey, the overbearing, controlling father, had no doubt confronted his son about it. She'd seen them arguing in the town shortly after her house was broken into. It wouldn't have been the first fight they'd had about her, she was sure.

Gavin had realized Keira would not let the truth stay buried.

That knowledge would have terrified him. He must have spent every day between then and now in fear that his past was about to snap closed around him like a bear trap.

In his mind, killing her was the only way to be free from that perpetual dread. The only way to ensure his safety.

"I knew I just had to wait long enough," Gavin said, and his hands trembled as he spoke. "Your little buddy group couldn't hang around you forever. I knew I just needed to give it a bit of time and I'd find you alone. But this...this is more perfect than I could have imagined. Far away from Blighty. In a restricted area. In a power plant of all places. You could die here, and people might even think it was an accident."

His smile grew wider as he spoke, until it looked painful. He took another step forward.

The energy beneath Keira was boiling. And it was about to burst. She crouched, hands pressed firmly into the concrete inside her circle.

Gavin was right. Either of them could die here, and the circumstances would be so strange that law enforcement might rule it as an accidental death. Like a teenager, trespassing somewhere they shouldn't, at just the wrong moment.

You could do it, the little voice in her head said. *Let him come closer. Let him reap what he's sown. He's a killer, and this might be the only chance you have to get justice for his victims. Just let it happen.*

Her mouth was dry. Her nerves were on fire as the power beneath her surged.

She feared and hated how easily that voice had whispered into her mind. How simple and obvious the suggestion had seemed.

Once, long before, she'd thought of killing Gavin when she'd had the chance. And it had haunted her. It had made her doubt who she'd once been and what she might have been capable of.

Now, though, she knew the answer. She knew Old Keira. The girl raised by parents who had sacrificed everything to turn their backs on a corrupt business. The girl who adored her aunt—an aunt who was generous and kind to a fault. The girl who had spent her life trying to stop Artec because it was the right thing to do.

She wasn't a killer. The thought had come easily. But she just as easily dismissed it.

Trying to save him was objectively a terrible decision, and Keira knew it. Gavin had a gun and he was going to use it if she gave him the chance. But she couldn't, *wouldn't* be the kind of person who let a man walk to his death.

"You've got to step back," Keira yelled. "The electrical field will kill you if you get any closer. Move back!"

A manic light shone in Gavin's eyes. "You think you can scare me? You're right in the middle of it, and you're fine."

Keira grit her teeth. There was no time to explain the runes to him, or the reversing power, or how she knew they were just seconds from the whole system overloading. "I'm not joking! This isn't a gamble you want to take, Gavin. You'll die!" He kept walking.

She scrambled for something—anything—to force some distance. "Just—just one minute, okay? Move back for one minute, then we can talk!"

"You're out of time to buy," Gavin said, and he took a step closer. The edges of his sneaker grazed the circle Keira had drawn. He lifted the pistol and gripped both hands around the barrel as he aimed. His other shoe rose from the ground as he took his final step. "Goodbye, little mouse."

The energy beneath Keira hit its zenith. She opened her mouth to yell, begging him to move back as she reached a hand toward him, but there was nothing she could do. Light exploded out of the hole in the concrete. She hunched down and threw her hands over her head as the power billowed outward like an explosion.

The lights were everywhere. She closed her eyes and pressed her palms against them, but she could still see the streaks of shockingly bright white searing across her retinas.

The electricity burned across her skin. It got into her lungs and seared them. It sent every hair standing starkly on end. It threatened to melt her, to absorb her, to annihilate her.

And then, it was over.

Keira collapsed sideways. It took a beat for her lungs to

remember how to breathe; then she was sucking in lungful after lungful of bitingly cold air.

The dark sky swirled into sight first. Keira blinked, trying to fight through the aftereffects of the light, only to realize that what she was seeing wasn't her imagination.

Arcs of white light spun outward, rippling across the sky.

She sat up, even as every muscle and bone in her body ached like it had been disassembled and put back together haphazardly.

The transformers were melted wrecks. The ground was scorched an angry, sooty shade. The lights in the power plant—both inside and the floodlights keeping the outside lit—had gone out, leaving Keira to be bathed only by moonlight.

The energy must have surged out like a shockwave, Keira realized, as the ripples of light faded into the distance. She looked down at the power cord she'd written her rune onto. It was melted and trails of smoke drifted up from its surface. Gingerly, she reached out to touch it.

The metal was still hot, but there were no prickles coming from it. No energy arriving and no energy leaving.

She wouldn't be certain until she saw it with her own eyes, but she was fairly sure the nearby graveyard would now be empty.

And, she hoped, so would the graveyard of hollowed-out ghosts surrounding the Five Suns Amazement Park…and the shades inside.

Keira let her smile drop before it even had a chance to form. Almost against her will, her gaze drifted over toward the space where Gavin had been.

Something dark lay curled on the concrete. Keira bit her lip, afraid to move as she watched it.

Her heart froze as she thought she saw it twitch only to realize she'd seen a mirage. Smoke was rising from the blackened shape.

Her legs threatened to rebel as she tried to stand. She staggered and leaned against a melted alternator as she waited for the shakes to pass.

"Gavin?" she whispered.

There was no reply. No movement. Keira swallowed thickly as she inched toward the crumpled figure. Nausea rose as she saw blackened flesh and exposed bone, and she turned away before she could be sick.

There wasn't much of Gavin left. The surge had been worse than she'd anticipated. The only mercy to be found was that Gavin would have already been gone before he had a chance to realize what was happening.

She glanced back. The circle of protective runes was the only unscorched part of the courtyard. And even they had barely been strong enough to save her.

"I'm sorry," she said to the pile of melted clothes and charred remains. "Not even *you* deserved this."

The whir of a motor starting made her flinch. Lights were flickering back on inside the power plant. Someone had activated the backup generator. Which meant she couldn't stay any longer.

She turned back to Gavin's remains. There was one final thing she needed to do before she left.

She opened her second sight.

CHAPTER 33

A THIN, WISPY SPIRIT emerged from the smoke and the gloom. He glowed faintly, but he wasn't a strong ghost. Barely a whisper of one.

Keira knew he would likely dissipate on his own, given a few hours. She didn't think Gavin had enough unfinished business, or enough force of will to hold himself to earth. But she still didn't want to leave it to chance.

"Hold still," she said, reaching toward him.

Gavin's spirit reeled back. His stringy hair floated about his face as he stared at her, his expression a blend of fear and confusion, his eyes empty pits.

He didn't understand what was happening. He likely didn't even realize he was dead.

Keira swallowed. "I'm not coming back here. I need to send you over, and it needs to happen now."

The wariness in his face didn't change.

Keira closed her eyes for a second. She did her best to forget everything she knew about Gavin. The snideness, the cruelty, the bitter, simmering anger. Everything he'd done to her and her friends. Wilson, the lonely traveler, and Evan, the student, killed by his hands. Those memories bubbled through her as simmering fury, but she pushed them aside.

Right here, right now, he was a spirit that needed help. And that was Keira's job.

"It won't hurt," she said, and she forced her voice to be gentle. "Let me set you free."

His face softened a fraction. This time, when Keira reached for him, he didn't try to pull away.

Her fingertips disappeared into the center of his chest. It was achingly cold. A sizzle of electricity drew her toward the knotted thread that existed in every spirit's chest. She found one end of the string, felt the electricity cutting into her like broken glass, and pulled.

The thread unraveled. Gavin was there for one final second, his eyes large and frightened; then his form bled away, melting into the cold night air.

Keira sighed deeply as she let her second sight drop. Gavin's body still remained, but that was beyond her ability to fix. His gun, partially melted, lay a few inches from his hand. She left that as well. She was done with guns.

Keira turned toward the passageway that led outside. In the distance, dawn was seeping into the edges of the horizon. The distant bonfires had burned out, and all that was left of them was straggling, wispy smoke.

She could sense a flurry of activity inside the power plant. Soon, the employees would be swarming outside. Keira jogged the field of dead grass to reach the fence and wormed her way back under the same drainage ditch she'd entered through.

She hadn't had the time to properly clean the area. There could be traces of her fingerprints on the metal hatch and on the alternators. But she didn't think that would matter. Artec wouldn't need any evidence to figure out who was responsible.

And they had something larger to worry about now: the body on their premises. They would likely want to sweep Gavin's death aside as quickly and as quietly as they could. A murder investigation would be dangerous for them, especially if investigators started asking too many questions about how the power plant worked.

Outside the massive metal fence, Keira let her pace slow to a walk as she retraced her steps to the patchy trees. She was dead tired. The energy from the power surge still crackled through her, but that didn't override the desire to crash into a bed and not emerge for three years.

Mason must have seen her coming because he opened the car's door before she'd even reached it.

"Thank goodness," he whispered as she slid inside. "We saw the power surge. We were arguing over how long to wait before we went looking for you." His eyes dropped to her arm, and immediately he switched into doctor mode. "You're hurt."

"Oh." There hadn't been enough light to see in the courtyard, but ugly bruise-like marks spread across Keira's right hand and arm. She flexed her fingers experimentally, but they still worked. "I reached toward Gavin right as it overloaded. I guess that was a mistake."

There was a beat of silence, then Zoe, half laughing, said, "Sorry, I thought you said *Gavin*. My ears must be playing tricks on me."

"Yeah, no, they're not." She let her burned hand drop back into her lap. "Gavin's here. *Was* here. He's dead now."

Zoe said something that might have been a swear word or might have just been the mangled noise of disbelief.

Mason had already gotten his first aid kit out from under one of the seats. He opened it, then hesitated. "Should I check? Is there any chance that...?"

"Sorry, none. He's..." She cast around for a less morbid word but couldn't find one, so she grimaced as she finished with, "*Crispy*."

"Should I commiserate?" Harry asked dully from his place in the front seat. "That's what people normally do when there's a death, correct?"

"Thanks, Harry, but you can skip it this time," Zoe said.

Mason began sifting through his kit for equipment, but Keira shook her head. "I want to get out of here first," she said. "Maybe find somewhere to rest for a bit."

"It will only take a moment—"

"Please," she said, and he nodded as he closed the kit.

They drove back the direction they'd come. It was risky to go back to Artec's headquarters, but Keira needed to be sure. Mason kept their car on the smaller roads for as long as he could, and then, finally, turned down the narrow road that led to the Five Suns development.

The sun had fully risen by the time they crested the hill to the valley. Keira didn't speak as they coasted down toward the empty grid of roads. She held her second sight open, even though she'd known the answer the moment they crossed the ridge.

There were no uneasy prickles. No sinking feeling in her stomach. She could no longer see the haze of white forms trailing into the distance.

The town would never feel pleasant, not while it existed as a shell of what had been promised, but the hollow spirits had vanished.

Which meant the beings in the tower would be gone too.

Tears stung her eyes, and she blinked furiously to push them back. She'd never had a chance to speak to her parents. To tell them she was grateful. To say goodbye.

She just hoped they'd understood when they felt their spectral chains melting.

"We can go," she said, and Mason turned the car back around midstreet.

The few built houses clustered off at the edge of her sight. Despite the early hour, Keira swore she could see Gina standing on her front lawn, staring toward the car.

She hoped things would be better for the residents now. Even just a little.

They drove for another hour before Keira felt like they were far enough from Artec to not be easily found. The streets were growing busy with commuters by the time Mason pulled into a small hotel nestled in a town whose name Keira hadn't caught.

They parked the car in the sheltered back corner of the lot, where the damage to it was least likely to be noticed, and covered the bullet hole in the windshield with an old and crumpled sun protector they found in the trunk.

Mason sweet-talked the concierge into letting them book a room at eight in the morning. Then the four of them trailed up the stairs and tumbled into a warm and relatively modern space. Mason had picked a nice hotel. He hadn't needed to. Keira thought she could have slept in the middle of the road.

"They said the couch will have a pull-out bed," Mason said to Harry as he closed the curtains. "Get some rest."

Keira was already crashing into the queen bed, Zoe at her side. Zoe's spiky black hair poked in every direction as she sank back into the pillows. She groaned.

"Ditto," Keira mumbled, and she was asleep before she could think anything else.

The room was still dark when Keira woke. She blinked, her vision hazy, as she struggled to remember where she was and what had happened.

Her hand felt sore but nothing like the burning static she'd experienced the night before. She held it above her head and saw bandages swaddled the fingers and ran up as far as her elbow. A faintly greasy sensation and antiseptic odor told her Mason must have covered it in some kind of cream.

Zoe slept next to her, tangled in the sheets and with her limbs thrown out wide. Harry was on the couch, lying flat on his back with his hands crossed over his chest, a perfect mimic of a corpse in a casket. Only his smudged eyeliner and patchy foundation showed that he'd gotten any real rest.

Mason wasn't there. Keira felt a small sting of panic. She lurched out of bed only to see a note has been left on the side table. It read, in Mason's impeccable script, *Left to run errands. Will be back by 3 p.m.*

"Phone," Keira mumbled, searching for it. She found it in her back pocket; she hadn't even removed it before falling asleep. The time showed as two thirty.

Keira sank back onto the edge of the bed, careful not to disturb her resting companions. She swiped through the phone's preset apps until she saw one she didn't recognize.

Gavin really had used it to track her. She grimaced as she uninstalled the app. It would probably be wise to let Zoe take a deeper look at her phone later, just in case.

As she sat, her phone clasped in her hands, memories from the previous night returned. Gavin, alive and speaking to her. And then Gavin, dead. Less than a minute apart.

It was starting to sink in, and she didn't know what to make of the emotions that came with it.

Dr. Kelsey had lost his only son. He'd never struck Keira as an emotional kind of person, but there was no way this news wouldn't hurt.

The hotel door rattled. Keira instinctively stood, but then Mason whispered, "It's just me," as he stepped inside.

He must have showered while Keira was asleep. His clothes were still rumpled, but his hair was clean and slightly damp. He lowered bags of takeout food onto the table. "I brought us some lunch. Or breakfast. Depending on how you look at it."

Zoe and Harry were stirring. Zoe pressed the heels of her hands into her eyes as she tried to rub the bleariness out of them. "Eugh. Okay."

"I'll make some coffee," Mason said, smiling apologetically.

The hotel had plates in its kitchenette, and Keira went about setting the table while Mason made drinks.

"You didn't need to go out just for food," Keira said, pulling cardboard boxes out of the bags. "Not that I'm complaining. But you need rest too."

He shrugged. "I had plenty of practice pulling all-nighters at university. Besides, this wasn't just for food. I couldn't stop thinking about what you'd said about my car being too memorable now. It didn't seem safe to leave it parked outside the hotel. So I took care of it."

"*Took care of it* is such an ominous phrase," Zoe said, blinking wearily as she sank into a chair at the table. "What did you do to the poor thing?"

"Eh." He grimaced. "There's a lake about an hour's walk from here. And it now has a new ecological feature."

"Wow, no half measures," Zoe said. "RIP car, you were a good piece of metal. I hope you'll now be an equally good home to the fish."

Keira laughed, but she couldn't help but feel a small sting at how the car's loss had earned more grief than Gavin, the human.

He was a horrible human, undoubtedly. But still a human. One who had always been fighting to compensate for how small he felt and how he never managed to live up to anyone's expectations.

She'd meant what she'd said to him. No one, not even Gavin, deserved to end up like that, a melted pile of char to be scraped off the concrete.

Mason must have sensed her thoughts because he reached across the table and took her hand. Keira felt a twinge—*Pull back; don't let him get too close*—but she ignored it until it passed. And then she let their fingers fold together, all warmth and tenderness, and he smiled at her.

"Ugh," Zoe said, stabbing a fork into her salad. "You guys are going to be *so* gross now, aren't you?"

"The worst," Mason confirmed. "PDA central. Brace yourself."

CHAPTER 34

THEY CHECKED OUT OF the hotel after four, with Mason showering apologies and thanks on the tired-looking assistant. Keira was sore and still foggy from sleep as she pulled her backpack over aching shoulders. A welcome sight greeted them in the parking lot: a small familiar sky-blue car parked close to the door.

"Hello, all," Adage called, stepping out of the driver's seat.

Mason had called the pastor while the rest of them slept. With Mason's car now devoted to the lake, their options for getting home had been limited, and they were so far from Blighty that a taxi would have bankrupted them. They'd been lucky that Adage had agreed to pick them up, no questions asked.

His bushy eyebrows rose as he took in their disheveled clothes and the way Harry's makeup was bleeding across his face. "I take it you've had something of a dramatic day."

"We could start a theater company with all the drama we've

gathered," Keira confirmed. She lowered her backpack into the trunk Adage had opened for them. "Thanks for coming all this way. It must have been a long trip."

"But not an unwelcome one," Adage said, smiling gently. "The church committee was meeting to discuss the long-planned hedge for the church's driveway. We've been talking about it for actual years now, but no one can agree on the *kind* of hedge. The committee is firmly divided into two camps, and neither side is willing to give ground. It was getting ugly. I was glad for an excuse to get out of there."

"I can't believe the hedge thing is still happening," Mason said, a hint of fondness entering his voice as he slid into the car's back seat with Keira and Zoe. "Hawthorn or laurel. Someone actually taped leaflets around the town last spring in an attempt to get support for the laurel option."

"As pastor, I'm an unbiased mediator," Adage said, turning the key to start the engine and gently maneuvering out of the parking lot. "But if Team Hawthorn doesn't win, I fear I may never emotionally recover."

Harry, sitting in the passenger seat, gave Adage a very intense, unyielding stare. "Hedges are dumb. You should have rows of open graves either side of the drive. It would help remind people of their impending mortality."

"I can't say that's an idea we've discussed yet," Adage said placidly. "But I do appreciate the suggestion."

They chatted gently on the drive home, with Adage sharing news from the community. After everything that had happened over the previous days, it felt surreal to Keira. Almost like she'd briefly stepped out into a strange and alarming world, only to slip back to the one she knew so well.

But that wasn't what had really happened. There was no threshold she could dance over and come back from. She'd stepped out of her old life, and now there was no way to return.

The phrase *Gavin is dead* lingered on her tongue, but she didn't dare speak it. Telling Adage would just shift the guilt onto him. He'd have to find out like everyone else: when Gavin's body was identified and his family was given the news.

Guilt squirmed, and she knew that was something she would need to learn to live with.

It was night again by the time they made it back to Blighty. Adage asked if they wanted to be dropped off at their houses. Zoe and Mason exchanged a glance.

"Harry needs to get home," Mason said. "I'm sure his mother misses him, and I know for a fact he's supposed to be watching the shop tomorrow morning."

Harry's sigh sounded like the moan of a wounded animal.

"Zoe and I will stick with Keira, though," Mason said, meeting her eyes and earning a nod in return. "I feel like that might be safest for everyone."

Adage's glance was quick. "*Safest?* Is anyone in danger?"

"Those flowers will be in danger if I'm left in charge of them for even one more day," Harry muttered.

Both Zoe and Mason looked to Keira, waiting for her read on how to respond. She licked her lips and chose a half truth.

"Remember those people who were looking for me on the night I arrived here? We had another brush with them."

Adage's bushy eyebrows furrowed. "Is there anything I can do?"

"Thanks, but I can handle it." Keira hesitated. "But if anyone asks after me, maybe keep my presence in Blighty quiet. At least for now."

"I've never met you before in my life," Adage confirmed. He glanced at her in the rearview mirror, then sighed. "You say you're safe, and I'll take your word for it. But remember I'm just down the lane if you ever need help. I may only be a pastor, but even shepherds will fight a wolf if it comes near their flock."

They left a despondent Harry outside the floristry, then Adage drove them back to the church and graveyard. Keira got him to park outside his parsonage, instead of closer to her cottage.

"My legs need a stretch," she explained as they piled out of the car.

"Remember, you can always call me if there's trouble," Adage said, helping lift their bags out of the trunk. As they approached the dirt path leading into the cemetery, he raised one hand in farewell and disappeared into his parsonage.

Keira waited until she heard the distant strains of jazz as Adage turned on his ancient record player, then she made a beckoning motion in front of her chest. Daisy spilled outward and landed neatly on the dirt path.

"She's been wanting to be free for a while," Keira said, watching the cat immediately launch itself after crickets hidden in the grass. "But the car was crowded enough with the five of us in it. Plus I didn't want to accidentally terrorize Adage."

"He'd probably take the magical cat part in stride," Mason said. "But, yeah, an advance warning would definitely help."

The graveyard was alive that night. Keira could feel it in her bones and in her heart, even before she opened her second sight. Ethereal forms stood like pillars among the thickening mist. Their empty eyes tracked her as she passed over the boundary and stepped between the graves.

She'd been gone a long time. They'd worried. Mist-white fingers reached out to graze her arm, leaving trails of gooseflesh in their wake.

I'm sorry, she mouthed. *I'm back now.*

Daisy leaped between the graves, her amber eyes seeming to glow in the dark as she whipped her tail behind her. Keira could feel it every time her paw touched the bare earth, could almost taste every inhale into her tiny lungs.

There was a lot she still had to discover about herself and to remember about herself. Not even Old Keira had owned all of the answers. But her memories were providing her with an arsenal of tools she hadn't even known she could wield, and her hands flexed in anticipation of relearning them.

Then they were at her cottage, and some of the tenseness drained out of her as she led the way through the door.

"Good to be home?" Mason asked, sensing the shift in her mood.

She grinned as she shut the door behind them and switched on the lights. "Very much."

It was more than just *good*. Home was something she'd never allowed herself to have before, not since her aunt's passing. It was a danger, yes; having a fixed home made her vulnerable. But it also filled a gap in her soul she hadn't known existed. There was a feeling of groundedness that she'd never managed to scrape from any of the cheap motels or shelters.

Mason drew the curtains; then they made dinner together, using whatever was in Keira's cupboards. Zoe played music through her phone's tinny speaker.

Daisy scratched at the door to be let in just as they were plating dinner and contentedly made her way to the bed, where she spent a few minutes kneading the blankets before curling up. Keira briefly wondered how many insects she'd eaten to make her that happy, then decided she didn't want to know.

For the first part of dinner, the friends talked about anything and everything as long as it wasn't truly important. They formed little threads of conversation that faded into nothing. It was Zoe who finally voiced the question hanging over them.

"So. What's next?"

Keira's smile felt more like a grimace. "Yeah. I'm wondering the same."

She'd taken down one of Artec's power grids and, in that one movement, freed a deluge of spirits that Artec had painstakingly collected and tethered.

She was more than a distant concern to them now. More than a loose thread to be tied off. She'd cost them, and cost them dearly, and both sides knew it would happen again if they didn't act fast.

And this time, she'd left a trail for them to follow.

Gavin.

His identity would be uncovered, either by Artec or by the

inevitable police investigation. And when it was, his address would lead them to Blighty.

"They're going to find me," Keira said. At Mason's and Zoe's expressions, she raised a hand. "It's inevitable. Even with Mason's car gone, and even though we cleaned up behind ourselves as well as we could, they're going to find me. It's just a question of *when*."

"Don't think you're leaving Blighty," Zoe said. "If you try to skip town on us, I swear I'll write the angstiest blog post you've ever seen."

Keira chuckled. They knew her too well. Or more accurately, they knew *Old* Keira too well. "No. I'm not leaving." She was past the point of running. Wherever she went, Artec would find her. Now was the time to make a stand. To go on the offensive. "I'll need to stay hidden for a few days—to build a plan and to get the tools I need. Then I'm going to challenge Artec head-on. And hope it's enough to topple them."

She felt very small in that moment. One girl against an entire organization—an organization that had been developing its strategies for decades, led by a man whose ruthlessness terrified her.

Mason leaned forward, his arms folded on the table ahead of himself and his face set and firm. "Anything you need, I'll get it for you. My parents left me savings for when they're away, and it's not a fortune, but it's yours. Whatever you need."

"And I have my network," Zoe said, the angle of her eyebrows sharp. "You've already met Fish Face, so you know what they're capable of. They trust me. If I call to them, they'll answer."

As Keira looked between her two friends, the sense of smallness vanished. She was one girl but no longer alone.

She reached out, and they each took one of her hands, forming a circle around the table.

"Whatever it takes," Mason said. "We're with you to the end."

"Thank you." She could barely breathe. "I'll need a few days first. To work out a plan. To prepare."

"Prepare..." The word slipped out of Zoe as a whisper. She swallowed. "Yeah. We're going to need to wrap up our unfinished business while we still have a chance because we don't know what's coming next, do we?" She swallowed again. "I should do that, and quickly."

She was talking about the funeral for her mother. Something she'd already been pulled away from as Keira chased Artec across the country. A stab of guilt passed through her.

It wasn't fair that Zoe's rawest moments of mourning were being stolen. Or that the growing urgency over Artec was superseding her grief. Keira opened her mouth, only for Zoe to raise a hand to silence her.

"No, don't apologize." Zoe's smile was lopsided. "This is fine."

"I'm sorry," Keira said anyway.

Zoe just shook her head. "I think I needed a push. I can't put her funeral off forever, even though I kind of tried. I'll set the date for as soon as possible. The siblings can either make it or not, their choice. With Artec out for blood, we don't have much of a window to tie up loose ends. To get closure on the stuff that's important to us. So I'm going to take a moment to do that now, while I still can."

Keira squeezed her hand. Zoe squeezed back, her eyes damp and her smile fierce.

They cleared up from dinner in silence. As she dried one of the dishes, Keira drifted toward the window that overlooked the cemetery. Mason had pulled the curtains when they arrived, making sure none of their light was visible from the town, and Keira twitched the cloth back to see outside.

In the far distance, Blighty's lights blinked through the trees. Slightly closer was Adage's parsonage, half-hidden behind the overgrown shrubs.

Her cottage was remote. Nestled against the edge of the forest, it was hard to find unless you knew where to look. She felt certain that Adage wouldn't give away her location, and she could trust Zoe and Mason to do the same. Other people in town knew she lived here, but not many, and she hoped they wouldn't talk about her presence too loudly.

All she needed was a few days, maybe a week. The memories and forgotten knowledge were like a tangle of yarn inside her head, and she needed to work the threads out into something she could use.

She hoped they would be enough, though. Enough to save the people she cared about. Enough to save the souls Artec had collected.

A chill ran over her exposed skin. Keira instinctively reached for her second sight.

The specters flooded into view, a ribbon of glowing mist tracing through her cemetery. Some stared toward her. Some watched the path winding past the church and toward town.

Keira had the sense that they knew something had changed. They seemed more alert than usual. Almost like sentries, keeping guard for her.

She was far from alone.

CHAPTER 35

KIMBERLEY ELIZABETH TURNER'S FUNERAL was held three days later at Blighty's church. It felt as though the entire town had come to attend. They squeezed in through the doors, crowding the corners and spilling into the aisles.

Keira dressed in the most respectful clothes she owned, which was slim pickings, considering her wardrobe had come from a donation bin. The Santa Claus cross-stitch sweaters and neon-pink dress shirts were thrown aside in favor of a dark purple knit top and gray scarf. They weren't the traditional black, but they were the best she could manage.

When she arrived at the church, Keira discovered she probably shouldn't have worried so much. Zoe waited outside the doors in a riot of color. She wore a sweater that was a size too large for her, made up of at least twenty colors in alternating lines, and covered in tiny balls of yarn that bounced each time she moved.

"Mum knitted it for me," she said by way of explanation as Keira joined her. She fidgeted at the hem, which was only partially finished. "She always worried I'd get cold in winter and kept knitting me tops that I never wore. This is the last one she made, and I wanted to wear it today. So that she'll know I'm warm."

Keira pulled her into a hug and felt hot tears hit her neck.

Mason arrived a moment later, and they split apart—Zoe to the front of the church, in the pew designated for family. Keira and Mason stayed at the building's back, standing, so that Kim's friends could take the closer seats.

"Looks like they all made it," Mason whispered. In the aisle next to Zoe were three other figures, each sharing the same shade of black hair. They wore expensive black suits and dresses, looking entirely at odds next to the colorful Zoe, but they stood in solidarity.

Kim Turner's coffin stood at the front of the church. It had a wreath on the top, which Zoe had said was donated by Polly Kennard floristry. As people moved through the church, they left their own tokens: flowers, both bought and picked from gardens. The mound on the casket grew until it threatened to spill over, nearly as colorful as Zoe's sweater.

Adage gave a talk. He spoke about love. About a life that had been well spent. And as Keira stood in a church so packed that the air grew humid and bodies jostled against her shoulders with every shift, she thought Adage was right. All of the people in that room had been brought there by their love for a woman Keira had only briefly known.

The service ended. The pallbearers raised the casket and carried it through the crammed aisle, and then the mourners spilled outside to follow it to its grave.

Keira had watched the hole being dug that morning. It was in the section closest to town. She liked that; it would make it easy for Kim's friends to visit. Keira would be one of them, watching over the grave site and clearing away weeds, even though there was no ghost lingering to see the effort.

As the casket was lowered into its grave, Keira and Mason hung behind the group, half-hidden behind a cluster of trees. There had been no word of strangers searching the town yet, but Keira was still being as careful as she could. She didn't allow herself to go into town or to walk the back roads, and even when she left her cottage to tend to the graveyard, she was always conscious of who might be out there, watching.

Her moment of peace was about to end, she knew. Adage had visited her early that morning to tell her about Gavin's death. The police had visited Gavin's father, Dr. Kelsey, to share the news. There had been so little of Gavin left that they'd relied on dental records to ID him.

As Adage told Keira what he knew, he'd watched her closely. Keira knew he must have put the pieces together. But he never asked, and she never volunteered, and he'd squeezed her shoulder briefly before leaving to prepare for Kim's funeral.

Zoe and her siblings each threw a handful of dirt into the grave, then stepped back. One by one, the guests did the same, pausing to speak with Kim's family before slowly disbanding to journey back to town in a trickle of twos and threes, possibly to attend the reception.

As the crowd thinned, Zoe was pulled into a group with her brothers and sister. They formed a circle, their heads bowed as they spoke. Zoe faced away from them, so Keira couldn't read her expression, and they were too far away to hear any words.

The group only lasted for a few moments; then Zoe stepped away. Keira felt herself relax. Zoe's face was damp with tears, but she was smiling. She jogged to reach Keira and Mason at the edge of the graveyard.

"You okay?" Keira asked. "They're not being jerks, are they?"

"Not today." Zoe used her palm to wipe moisture off her cheeks. "Sorry. I know I said I wanted to have lunch with you both after the funeral, but they're asking if we can spend some time together catching up. I don't think any of us realized how much we missed one another."

"Yeah," Keira said, nodding. "Of course you should."

"Thanks. I'll text you later." Zoe made to turn away, then caught herself. "Ah—I was going to share this over lunch but might as well now. Since we're trying to wrap up loose threads and everything."

She wore a bag over one shoulder and pulled it open then. Inside was a book, which she held out toward Keira. "Remember that woman whose daughter married the poet? Well, Fish Face is a bit of a poetry buff, so I asked him about it. And he came through for us." She held up the book so that Keira could see it. The title read, *The Yates Family Legacy.*

Keira drew a sharp breath. She'd almost completely forgotten. "My ghost. Henrietta Yates."

"Exactly. There are plenty of books on the poet Cora married, Wentworth, but relatively little about Cora herself, or her family. Not even Fish Face knew about them, but he did some digging and mailed this to me, under strict instructions that I wasn't to ask where he got it from. I can't imagine what kind of dark-web backroom deals he must have—oh." Zoe had turned the book over. "There's a sticker from a secondhand bookstore. Okay then."

"You're amazing, Zoe."

"No need to state the obvious." She stuck out her tongue to show she was joking. "Anyway, I think this has our answer. I stayed up late last night reading it."

Keira glanced toward the church, resplendent with light, and then toward the open grave and the last mourners around it. Guilt squeezed at her. "I'm so sorry—"

Zoe narrowed her eyes. "You've gotta stop apologizing for things you didn't even do. I wasn't sleeping last night no matter what. At least this gave me a distraction."

"Oh."

Zoe waved the book, sending the pages flapping. "You can read this later if you want, but I can give you the abridged version now. Henrietta Yates loved her daughter, Cora, more than anything. Even when Cora was an adult, they were near inseparable. That was something Cora's father didn't like. When the poet Wentworth put in an offer of marriage, Yates agreed to it against his wife's—and his daughter's—wishes. Supposedly, he thought Wentworth's fame would help boost the family's reputation, but it wasn't the comfortable life Cora should have had. Wentworth squandered any money he had on drinking and gambling."

"It wasn't a case of star-crossed lovers, then," Keira said.

"Sadly, no. There are letters in here. Cora and Henrietta stayed in touch, which was made difficult by how frequently and erratically Wentworth moved towns. Repeatedly, Henrietta promises her daughter that she'll find a way to save her from her husband and bring her back into the Yates family."

"Ah." Keira felt her heart sink. "But Cora Wentworth passed away during a cholera outbreak."

"In a hospital for the poor." Zoe held the book out, and Keira took it. "You're the ghost expert, but it seems to me like that's Henrietta Yates's unfinished business. Here, one more thing."

Zoe passed her a cloth bag with two heavy items in it. They gave a metallic clink as they shifted against one another.

"Open it later, when no one can see," Zoe said. "You'll know what to do."

Then she turned, hurrying back to her family, the little knit balls on her sweater bouncing with each step. The black-clad siblings parted to let her join them; then all four of them turned toward town, close enough for their shoulders to brush.

Keira took a deep breath, then let it out. The book and the bag were both heavy in her arms as she pulled them against her chest.

"I know you normally work alone," Mason said, tilting his head toward her, "but I'm always a willing assistant."

Keira smiled. She'd barely seen Mason over the previous days. While she'd been secluded in her cottage, Mason had been keeping an eye out for strange activity in the town and helping Zoe with the funeral preparations. "I'd like that."

They walked close together. Keira shifted the gifts into one hand so she could let the other hang at her side. It brushed against Mason's. He leaned into the touch, and their fingers twined together.

Keira glanced up at him and saw he was already watching her, his eyes tender and his smile seeming almost nervous. Keira bit her lip, her own smile growing as warmth rose across her face, making the skin burn in defiance of the cold morning.

They didn't let go until they reached the grave nestled in the far corner of the clearing. Keira placed the book and the bag on the ground near the gravestone, then held her second sight open and faced Henrietta Yates.

"I think I understand," she said to the gaunt woman who stared back at her. "You promised Cora you would bring her home. But there wasn't enough time to save her."

Henrietta's fingers shook as she clasped them in front of her chest.

"Cora's gone. You understand that, don't you?" Keira gazed down at the grave beside them. The words, old and slowly fading as the decades washed over them, marked a grave with no occupant. "Cora has moved over to the next life."

Henrietta nodded, her empty eyes beseeching.

"But you can't." Keira took a deep breath. "Not until you finish your last wish. To return Cora to the family. If we change the tombstone—if we give her marker the name *Cora Yates*—will that be enough?"

There was a second of hesitance, and then Henrietta nodded emphatically. There was no way to fulfill her promise to her daughter. But the name change, although symbolic, would give Henrietta the closure she needed.

"Adage said the church could provide a new grave marker if the old one was vandalized," Keira said, crouching and opening the bag Zoe had passed her. She thought she knew what was hidden inside. "I couldn't justify it before, but now?"

She tipped out two items: a chisel and a mallet.

Mason lowered himself to his knees beside her. "My budding résumé as an unrepentant criminal continues to grow. And I really don't mind as much as I thought I would."

Keira picked up the chisel, then tilted her head as she regarded the gravestone. "What should we do? Just lines across it? Adage said the vandalism needed to be severe."

"Maybe we should write something," Mason suggested.

Keira glanced toward the book Zoe had given her. The wind had blown its cover open, and as she stared at what was written on the first page, she felt herself smile. "Yeah. I think I have it."

They worked together, trading the chisel and the mallet every few minutes, until their inscription was deep and clear. Then Keira sat back, her fingers gritty with dust as she smiled at their handiwork.

No amount of scrubbing would remove the message. There was no way to hide it. When she brought it to Adage's attention, she knew he would have no choice but to request an entirely new gravestone be made. And she didn't think anyone in town would notice that the replacement marker, hidden so far near the back of the cemetery and belonging to a long-gone family, now held a different surname.

"It'll probably take a few weeks to get the replacement," Keira said to Henrietta's ghost. "But I guess you've already waited so long, you'll probably want to see it through to the end."

Henrietta stared at the gravestone, then turned to stare at Keira, her mouth hanging open and her features aghast.

"Sorry," Keira said.

Carved deep into the stone, right across Cora Wentworth's name, was a message:

FISH FACE WAS HERE

"We promised we'd build him a monument," Keira said, glancing down at the book ahead of them. Fish Face had left a scrawled note on the first page: *Build me a monument!* "I'm sure it's not the towering structure he imagined, but we owe him *something*, and this is the best I can do on a gravekeeper's salary."

Henrietta pressed one hand over her eyes as she turned away, as though blocking it from sight would make it stop existing.

"Hey," Keira said to her. "This is just to get the replacement tombstone, remember?"

The look Henrietta threw them over her shoulder was grudging and sour. Keira chuckled.

"She's not impressed, huh?" Mason guessed.

"Extremely not."

He sat next to Keira, his long legs stretched out on the grass between the graves. A smudge of tombstone dust had somehow gotten smeared across his chin. Keira couldn't help herself. She reached up and brushed it free.

Mason's eyes turned tender. "You said you wanted to go out somewhere with me. To dinner. Or on a walk. Or anything. Do you think this counts as anything?"

Keira's heart fluttered in a way that felt strange and foreign and not completely bad. A first date spent vandalizing a grave wasn't in any way conventional, but somehow, it felt right. "Yeah. I think this can count as anything."

She leaned up. He came to meet her halfway. Their noses brushed, a gentle touch. Keira tilted her head, and his arms moved around her, and then their lips were together, and Keira felt like she was going to melt.

His breath was hot on her cheek as they came apart, both smiling hopelessly. Henrietta Yates rained her scorn down on them, and Artec's net was going to close soon, and Keira still needed a plan, but in that moment…

Mason kissed her again, and in that moment, everything was good.

ABOUT THE AUTHOR

Darcy Coates is the *USA Today* bestselling author of *Hunted*, *The Haunting of Ashburn House*, *Craven Manor*, and more than a dozen other horror and suspense titles.

She lives on the Central Coast of Australia with her family, cats, and a garden full of herbs and vegetables.

Darcy loves forests, especially old-growth forests, where the trees dwarf anyone who steps between them. Wherever she lives, she tries to have a mountain range close by.